LeeAnn Roberts lives in Glasgow Scotland UK where she was born.
She did not always live there though; she spent many years as a dancer and model
in Spain.

15

Daniel Dischino who generously gave me his wonderful poetry for free. Thank you so much Mr talented wordsmith.

Keithy wolf who is always there with his wise advice and real care. Team Awesome

LeeAnn Roberts

IMMORTAL MAGIC BOOK ONE

AUSTIN MACAULEY PUBLISHERS™

LONDON * CAMBRIDGE * NEW YORK * SHARJAH

A CIP catalogue record for this title is available from the British Library.

ISBN 9781398477131 (Paperback)
ISBN 9781398477148 (ePub e-book)

www.austinmacauley.com

First Published 2022
Austin Macauley Publishers Ltd®
1 Canada Square
Canary Wharf
London
E14 5AA

My amazing parents Margaret and George who always gave me the freedom to follow my dreams and were always there to pick me up to try again. I've been lucky enough to have the best mum and dad ever. Thank you for always believing in me no matter what I undertook.

To James who is great at word changes minus a thesaurus. I love you millions.

To Tricia my best friend who is always there good and bad. My cheerleader and rock to cling to. Love you Chica.

Immortal flows the blood of innocent youth
Who set off to conquer a world for the taking
Till that blood flows on the ground and street
And stains of the hands of competing passion
And calls to venomous foes for miles around
With the scent of life
and the crimson glow of power
Beware words that charm form faces of beauty
And beware of glowing eyes
that pierce through the night
For the allure of the immortality thief
is a s dangerous as any knife to the heart
And will draw as much blood

The shadow of the darkness in the alleyway concealed the creature, except a strange subtle colour that came through from where its head would be.

It was ripping humans apart, limb from limb dropping them as they went.

As though it were nothing.

It was vicious, frenzied, and yet, somehow completely controlled in how it was executed.

The reason it was so ruthless, fast, and inhumanly strong was protection of someone loved from afar, someone it would never let harm.

The dark hidden shadow was every bit as frightening as who was within it. Maybe more so…

Slowly, very slowly, in an almost deliberate showing, the shadow came into focus… Starting from the feet as it stepped forward, then the legs which were clearly masculine, and up to a very male torso.

Finally, his face. He stepped forward into the light…

He stood there in an expensive suit. Gorgeous, powerful and completely immaculate. Despite the slaughter he had just indulged in, there was *not* a mark on him. He looked perfection personified.

The only sign he had partaken in this slaughter was when he very causally and slowly licked the blood from his elegant white fingers.

Then, he disappeared faster than the eye could see, leaving behind the pile of limbs of the dead bodies behind him.

Completely unrepentant.

Despite the horror that occurred her.

The utter protection of one you loved was absolute.

Being a prescient being *he knew* what they were planning for her, as he could read auras perfectly, and had to intervene in this human girl's fate.

Death Cannot Kill That Which
Is Not Measured by Time.

Do you believe in fate, destiny, something so meant to be that nothing can stop it?

My name is Angelica Phoenix (everyone calls me Angel).

I come from Scotland, and I am a magical witch. My family are the most elite family of witches, and our magic is old and revered. I have been prophesied as 'the key' or 'the chosen one', but no one can ever seem to tell me exactly what that means, all I know is there are many dark forces who wish to destroy me.

My entire life has been about fighting evil and sacrificing many normal things because my destiny dictates 'the greater good must always come first'. I complied (sometimes with reluctance or downright bitterness) whilst everything in my life took second place to my magic, that is, until I met Michael De Marco.

Soul mates is one of the most overused words in the English language, people throw it around so often it diminishes the true meaning, but soul mates are what Michael and I are. We have a seminal link so unique and so deep there are no known words to really explain it or do it justice.

Chapter One

Practice Magic

Since I'm supposed be this mysterious 'prophecy, or the key', I figured I best stop being so lazy and relying on just my powerful telekinesis, blasting ability and destruction balls.

I'm supposed to possess active and passive powers from both side of my family tree and it's been bugging me lately that I can't do half those things, especially if something big is coming and my sorry arse isn't prepared.

My mum and dad are always on at me to practice and become as good as I am supposed to be with the three fun powers I do rely on too much, they say I have to be ready for anything and the more I can do the more chance of winning or connecting with this so-called key to win.

Problem was I found it incredibly boring doing all this practice for no exciting stuff. I could self-heal, go invisible, through up invisibility shields, throw lightning bolts and say spells.

I *needed* to work on mind reading, psychic abilities, and controlling the elements (controlling the elements does sound fun to be fair): fire, air, earth, water, light, darkness, and best of all, spirit. If I can master spirit, I will be able to call it to me to protect me, and those around me and make me more powerful.

I will have to practice on a chalk drawing of a pentagram with candles representing each colour of the points on the attic floor. But the plan is eventually to be able to just call them to me at any time.

I drew a wiccan pentagram on the floor placed red for fire, blue for air, aqua for water, black for dark, white for light and brown for earth. I sat in the middle, cross-legged amongst runes holding a purple candle for spirit.

"Fire come forth,"… nothing…"fire come forth to me."

This wasn't going to be as easy as I imagined. I'm going to have to check some wicca books on controlling the elements.

I looked out the many wiccan books we had, and went through the ones I think fit, and found one on calling the elements, luckily it was for beginners.

It told me drawing the ancient runes within the pentagram would not work, I needed the real and appropriate runes, damn it, now I'm going to have to go through centuries of wiccan tools passed down form each generation.

Oh well, nothing else for it, I swiped my had across a wall and revealed the hidden room, only visible to phoenix witches, I entered the room where all the extremely and old powerful artifacts were kept. Artifacts we didn't even know just how powerful for each witch, or all witches. Who knew?

Luckily, my mother had a thing about keeping things in alphabetical order and ridiculously organised by items.

I went through the rune box, carefully picking out the ones the book said to. Then closed the hidden door behind me.

I rubbed the pentagram out, including the rune drawings and started again. Placing each candle and lighting it, then following the book on exactly where the runes need to be placed for calling the elements. I was excited about learning a new power, and a powerful one.

I closed my eyes, lifted my hands palms up and as per the book instructions and said, "Fire come to me."

The fire candle lit up. I was ecstatic, it worked.

I called each element in turn and the candles all lit one by one as I asked them to.

Finally, the one I was most compelled to was spirit, when I asked spirit to come to me the purple candle lit straight away with a huge flame, and I felt an exhilarating surge of power shoot through me it almost knocked me over.

For some reason spirt appeared to be my element.

I would practice this constantly as the book advised, until I could call the elements minus candles and a pentagram, unless I needed the extra power.

I practiced for so long, I was surprised when I noticed eight hours had passed.

The next day and day after I practiced again for hours, and the flames came faster and higher each time. The elements book said when that happens to do it minus the paraphernalia.

It read some witches will always need the pentagram, runes and candles except the most gifted of the wiccan kind.

I decided to practice outside as I didn't want to start a fire, flood or hurricane or something if I was a powerful at this as I thought I was now.

Here we go…

"Fire come to me." Flames came shooting across the ground all around me, protecting me, but I knew from the book I could use it as a weapon.

"Air come to me." High winds appeared awaiting instruction.

"Water come to me." Water flooded everywhere, and a torrential downpour happened.

"Earth come to me." The ground lifted knocking everything in its path.

"Darkness some to me." The sky darkened to jet black, yet I could see, but I knew others would not.

"Light come to me." Everything went incredibly light, blinding anyone who I happened to use it against.

"Spirit come to me." I was used to, by now, the power surge, but this was much stronger, I felt complete power, almost invincible. It was amazing. And it dried me from the water element.

As the book instructed when you were finished with each power thank it and release it. Which I had done after the elements.

That is power I thought, so much potential in fighting enemies.

OK, now to move on to mind reading. I knew vampires could do mind control, known as the razzle dazzle.

I would work on my mind reading ability first so back to the attic for me, and back to the books and practicing.

Back into the hidden room for me in case there's any equipment that can speed this mind reading thing up.

As I was searching, I came across a painting behind a whole load of old boxes, like it wasn't meant to be found.

It was of the knights of the round table. Having always wondered if King Arthur had been real, I picked the photo from the wall. As I did, spikes shot out from within, what?

I got the torch on my phone and there was a gold sword inside with a black and silver handle inscribed with something.

It couldn't be, could it?

Was that Excalibur?

Knowing my ancestors, I wouldn't be that shocked, but if that was Excalibur then King Arthur had been real. I was amazed and happy, but not surprised given the magical things I'd seen.

Now how to get the sword out without losing a hand… who knew how many more spikes or worse might come out in there?

I either heard a voice or had a feeling that it wouldn't hurt me, so I reached in and navigated the sword out. I held it up and it was the most beautiful thing I had ever seen. I could feel power radiating from within it in my hands.

I examined the inscription in Latin around the handle, it read 'Comparari cum ulla hostilli', translated to 'unmatched by any foe'.

I looked in and there was a leather harness for keeping the sword at your back reaching to you neck. I put Excalibur into its harness, and it felt like it belonged there somehow becoming part of my skin and mind, like part of me somehow. I couldn't explain it.

Excalibur spoke to me in my head, if that's what it was, and opened my senses, showing me, someone knew I had discovered the sword. It showed me it was my mother, creeping on the attic stairs invisible cloak on. Why not just show herself, tell me what she knew, why the sword was hiding and protected?

I wondered what else Excalibur could do. Obviously apart from being the most powerful sword in folklore.

I hit the real book for this one, searching for Excalibur, King Arthur, the knights of the round table… Anything. I found one page saying King Arthur existed before time began around 977, but how powerful Excalibur was supposed to be was unknown, undocumented.

Wonderful.

Guess it'll have to figure it out myself.

Turns out I didn't need to figure out any more powers or what else Excalibur could do, the sword didn't speak directly to me, but to my mind. It was the most bizarre experience, and that was coming from me!

I somehow knew Excalibur would make me almost invisible, there was just one piece missing for that to become a reality.

The energy flowing through me was almost interstellar between Excalibur and myself. Not of this world, from somewhere in unknown time and space waiting patiently for me to discover it.

Suddenly I had it, the missing element was spirit, I felt the same kind of feelings from when spirit entered my body.

I had cracked it; between the unbelievably beautiful Excalibur and the beautiful element of spirit I was invincible like a vampire. Well, best not get carried away with invincibility but once I called spirit, I would have the driving force I needed to be the prophesised most powerful.

Chapter Two

Meeting Michael

"Angel, have you finished the potion?" my mother shouted from downstairs.

"Yes, Mum, just bottling it now," I answered. Where in the hell were Kennedy and Dylan anyway, I mumbled, I don't even need a potion for this elimination. I could take this demon out without even breaking a sweat.

My father (who gets visions) saw the demon attacking tonight in the living room, so they decided to stay home with me. There goes my quiet movie night. I had planned a horror movie fest since no one would be home. They all hate what they term 'slasher flicks'. With the evil we deal with on a weekly basis, I guess I couldn't really blame them. It's not exactly an escape from reality, well not our reality anyway.

I grabbed a couple of potion bottles and went downstairs to find my parents. I gave my father the bottles because his powers are non-lethal, he needs potions more than the rest of us.

Right on cue, the demon appeared, and he had brought a couple of friends along to die with him; how thoughtful.

My mother took out one demon with a light bolt, my father threw a potion at another, and I blew up the last one. It was all over in less than three minutes thanks to my dad's vision. He doesn't always get forewarning, so sometimes we are caught off guard with attacks. Tonight, we just had to be in the spot they were going to appear, but when it is unexpected, we must wing it and it does not always go as smoothly as this one.

Fortunately, some demons really are not that bright. In fact, some of them are just downright stupid to the point of suicide.

"So, when are you seeing Jason again?" my mum asked me in a forced casual tone as she washed up the breakfast dishes the next morning.

"Stop forcing him on me, Mum, it's not exactly loves young dream." I sighed, instantly irritated. This was getting on my nerves. Jason was nice enough but there was no heat, no romance, nothing that got my brain saying therefore life is worth it. He didn't make my heartbeat faster or send shivers up my spine. In fact, he didn't make me feel any of the things I should feel for the person I was to fall in love with.

I was beginning to think maybe that was all crap anyway and if it weren't then, would it ever happen to me? There was no guy I had ever met that I could say was even a maybe in that department, and my prospects for meeting one wasn't the best. I mean where was I going to meet somebody, I could be myself around? Sixteenth-century Salem? On the other hand, I didn't want to be with someone just for the sake of it. I wanted true love, I wanted somebody who would make my heart stop, set me on fire of burning desire, make me die without his touch, and I didn't think I should have to compromise on that. Goddess knows I had compromised on everything else I had ever wanted so true love was non-negotiable. For me it was all or nothing.

"We don't all have to marry another witch, Mum." I snapped hoping she would sense my tone and drop it. She didn't.

"All of our ancestors have married magical beings Angel, it is what has made us so powerful, and generations of witches being born from these unions have been more powerful than the last." She had that preaching voice on that she gets when telling my siblings and me how important it is to marry a fellow Wiccan. We had all heard it a thousand times.

"Well, maybe I'll be the exception to that rule, Mum, because I do not love Jason; in fact there is nothing between us that would even suggest a sliver of a feeling that may one day slightly resemble, love. I tried, we went on four dates, and every one of them was a disaster." I turned away knowing I was wasting my breath. "Can we just drop it please? I've got to go to uni." I grabbed my bag and darted quickly outside because I knew that once the Jason conversation began it was best to leave; otherwise, the same stuff was boringly repeated.

It was exhausting. Jason was my friend; if you could even call him that not my boyfriend, although sometimes he forgot that fact and I couldn't get rid of him.

I knew he had feelings for me, but I had told him time and again that nothing romantic was ever going to happen. I didn't even let him so much as hold my hand on any of the dates. I had only gone out with him to get my mother off my back. He had taken to dropping by to see what we were doing, as if we had made plans or something. It was infuriating and I had had enough; I was going to have to hurt him now since telling him I wasn't interested in him romantically was obviously just too vague.

As I pulled up to a parking space on campus, I realised I was late. My mother and her bloody Jason talk had made me late.

To make matters worse it was ready to rain, and I didn't have an umbrella. This was just a wonderful start to my day. In my haste to get away from my mum I never even had my morning cup of coffee to give me a boost, and of course everyone walking past me had hot steaming cups. Obviously. There are just some days I shouldn't get out of bed.

"Damn." I dropped my bag. My books and other crap I kept in there went scattering across the ground. I bent to pick everything up with an irritated sigh.

"Need a hand?" asked a cool silky voice.

I looked up and into the most beautiful eyes I had ever seen, they were a vivid lilac in colour; I had never seen anything like it. The nearest I could think to describe their colour was the gem stone amethyst. He was utterly staggering; his flawless face was pale and luminous. I had never seen anyone quite so beautiful anywhere, not in real life, witch life, or in the movies. My eyes were wide and unblinking, I actually felt myself slipping backwards, and he reached out a pale hand – so fast I barley saw it move – and steadied me.

"Thanks," I said, embarrassed by the effect he was having on me. His hair was so black it was almost blue and I had to fight the urge to run my hands through it, it was the kind of hair that could be shaken up with hands, or the wind could blow it around and it would still look like he was on the cover of a magazine.

He was truly breath-taking and I could not look away from his face. He looked deep into my eyes and the world stopped… just for a second, then he spoke to me, "My name is Michael De Marco." His voice was smooth as melting chocolate.

"Hi," I said, still unable to look away from his gaze. "I'm Angel Phoenix. Pleasure to meet you." Boy was it a pleasure. He broke the look as he let me go, and I felt dazed. I watched as he collected the stuff from the ground, and put it back in my bag.

"Thanks." I took the bag from him still staring at him, mesmerised by his unreal beauty.

"No problem, Angel," he replied with a slight smile and I noticed his lips were perfect, full, and red and his teeth were a lovely white, with slightly elongated canines. Was there no end to his beauty? The way he said my name was like a caress, and I never wanted anyone other than him to say my name again.

I was beginning to think I had inhaled too many potion fumes and I was actually just hallucinating this godlike creature's existence, but no way; not Even my wildest imagination could I have ever thought up someone so blinding, so flawless, and so utterly dazzling. It was like he had been carved by angels of the perfect man.

"Are you going to a lecture?" I asked, feeling a bit winded as if I couldn't quite catch my breath, my heart was pounding. I didn't want him to leave.

"No, I'm off to the library now." He tilted his lovely head, almost as if he was listening for something, and then he looked at me with the strangest expression. "I should go now; it was very nice to meet you, Angel. Maybe I'll see you around." With that he was off, he was halfway across the court before I felt I could breathe again.

I hurried to my lecture thinking it was a bit strange he left so abruptly. Maybe he didn't like me, although that didn't make sense, he doesn't even know me. Something spooked him though; most likely my open-mouthed gawping at him. He may have thought I wasn't quite right in the head.

I spent the entire lecture thinking about him and the next two lectures. In fact, I took in nothing anyone said and my notepad was blank.

If I were any good at drawing, I would probably have sat drawing pictures of him in my notebook, although I was certain not even Michelangelo would be able to capture just how amazing his looks were in real life.

I continued to see his face, his eyes when he said his name to me. He was strange. But then I suppose I was too. I couldn't have many real friends because I wasn't allowed to tell anyone I was a witch.

Even if I could, what the hell would I say? Hi, I'm a powerful witch who fights evil creatures and have a magical destiny to fulfil with my powerful magical family.

I could see how that conversation would end. With me in a psychiatric ward or worse, a government lab being studied.

I went to the nearest café for lunch with a few of my classmates. I got a chicken salad and water and sat down wholly distracted.

Everyone was talking about the fancy dress party in the union on Friday and what they were going to dress up as.

I wasn't paying much attention to them and I just sat pushing my food around the plate.

"Angel, there's a guy looking at you and he is gorgeous and I *mean* gorgeous," my nosy gossiping classmate Sally said with excitement.

"That's Michael De Marco," Liam said. "He's in my American literature tutorial." His voice was disapproving, and he didn't look so happy about him staring at me. Yes, Liam fancied me too. Beauty was a curse.

"Do you know him?" asked Sally wide eyed.

"Not really. I met him this morning He helped me pick my books up when I dropped them." I forced my voice to be neutral. I didn't need any of this lot knowing I had a crush on someone I could never get.

"Well, you must have made an impression girl cos he's staring. He is seriously hot. Why don't I ever drop books in front of someone who looks like him?" Sally sighed. I secretly thought even if she did no one would pick them up for her for fear of interrogation about their whole lives that she could then spread around.

I looked up at him because I figured I had better since no one was exactly being subtle about telling me he was looking over. My breath caught as his unbelievable beauty hit me all over again. I smiled and waved, my cheeks burning, feeling like a little girl with her first crush.

He got up and walked towards me, the fluid way he moved made my head reel and I took in his body for the first time. He was tall and broad shouldered, and muscled without being bulky. Elegant.

Oh no, was he coming to sit with me? My heart was racing so fast I thought it would burst through my chest. I have nothing to say to him. Well, nothing that would resemble an actual conversation as I would most likely just stutter and stammer.

He got to the table and looked down at me with those smouldering eyes. "Hello, Angel."

I could feel my hands shake a little and that breathless feeling sweep over me again.

"So did you make your lecture this morning?" His lips lifted slightly at the corners, and his tone seemed amused. He was looking only at me and ignoring everyone staring at him.

"Yeah, although I was a bit late and a tad disorganised." I had actually managed to get a sentence out and felt myself getting cocky about it so I went on with what I hoped was a casual tone. "Do you want to sit down?" I had to fight the urge to not bite his chiselled jaw.

"Thanks, but I can't, I'm meeting someone," he said quietly.

Of course he was meeting someone, how stupid could I be.

Just at that my fragile illusion of cocky confidence came crashing down around me as a beautiful girl appeared next to him. She looked at me for a few seconds, curiosity crossing her lovely face then looked at him with confusion. I was devastated… totally irrationally devastated that he had a girlfriend. He didn't look at her but kept his eyes on me.

This was ridiculous I could not possibly be this upset over a guy I didn't know. What the hell was wrong with me? I looked around the busy café for a quick escape route, and really started to wonder about the inhalation of potion fumes.

I really had to get a grip. "Well, it was nice seeing you again and thanks again for helping me this morning," I said as I stood up to leave. I hadn't eaten my lunch and I didn't care. I just had to get out of there.

I picked up my plate and threw it in the bin next to the table and turned to go. "Bye everyone, see you later," I said hurriedly over my shoulder.

I forced myself to not sprint out of there but walk calmly. The last thing I needed was to knock over everyone I passed in my haste to escape this madness.

I got outside and decided to skip studying in the library and just go home; I didn't want to chance bumping into him again, I had made enough of a clown of myself for one day.

I fished my keys out of my bag as I headed to the car park, thinking that, if I were away from here the crazy fog would lift. Sanity was imminent as I spotted my electric blue Alfa Romeo Spider about ten feet away from me.

"Angel."

I did not have to turn around to know it was him; no one else had a voice like that. This was the third time today he had said my name, and every time it made my knees go weak. The very fact I was keeping count of the amount of tines he said my name was an indication of how mental I was becoming.

What was going on now? Couldn't I just slink off home and nurse my humiliation alone.

I stopped and he was next to me in a flash, I looked up at all 6"3' of him. "Hey," I said, "was there something you needed?"

"I just wanted to ask you to have lunch with me tomorrow, I absolutely should not, but I cannot seem to help myself." His cool voice was quiet and he had the same strange expression on his gorgeous face as he tipped his head slightly to the side as if he was listening for something. The exact same way he had this morning.

"What?" I was utterly confused. This was so weird. "If you shouldn't be asking me, then why are you?" I was getting irritated.

"It's… complicated but I do want to talk to you Angel." His expression was unsure. Not even the way his tongue glided over the letters of my name placated me now.

"Well, let me un-complicate it for you, Michael, and say no. I've got to go and I'm sure your girlfriend is waiting on you." My tone was a bit icier than I was going for given that I was trying to dial back the crazy.

We were at my car now so I opened the door and got in. I started the engine and drove off totally baffled.

I looked in my rear-view mirror and saw him standing in the same spot watching me drive away.

Why was he watching me? What was that all about? Maybe I should have said yes just to find out what he wanted to say to me.

No, it was better to stay away from him. The whole situation was ridiculous and I had a better chance of forgetting my silly crush if I did not go lunching with hunky mystery man.

I put my foot down on the accelerator and cranked the stereo.

Chapter Three

What Now

I turned up our mile long driveway still singing along to music.

We lived in a huge white house set on three levels, miles away from anywhere on the outskirts of Glasgow. It was surrounded by thick trees and acres of land where fences covered the entire perimeter to stop random trespassers.

Not that we got many people passing through here, and we certainly did not encourage many non-magical visitors.

My mother's family bought it generations ago, so we can fight evil here and no one will accidently stumble upon it getting hurt or worse, discovering our secret.

I loved this house it was beautiful, spacious and my haven.

I loved the giant white pillars that jutted out from the front door and the pond with tropical fish we had in the middle of the circular driveway.

It makes no sense considering how evil always finds us here, but I always felt safe and protected in my home, as if nothing bad could ever happen to any of us as long as we were within these grounds.

I pulled my car into our massive garage and got out. I entered the house through the connecting door and heard a ruckus.

Glass was smashing upstairs so instead of wasting time running up, I transported myself there. Transportation was a gift all my family had, and believe me it came in handy, we could be anywhere in the time it takes to blink an eye. It was useful to escape danger, and to help each other or innocents. It was also useful for times you couldn't be arsed travelling somewhere via car, plane, etc. but I did try to keep that to a minimum.

I arrived to chaos. The loft was today's battlefield and there were ten demons attacking my father and sister.

My dad had only two potion bottles, which he was throwing as I arrived, and my sister was throwing light bolts. I quickly held out both my hands, halted their movements using telekinesis, and asked if either my dad or sister knew what they were after. They didn't so I told my sister to take the remaining ones out while I held them in place, and to leave one to interrogate.

I waved my hand and our magical book came towards me, our book is called Niveus Veneficus and it is the most powerful of all magical tones; we just refer to it as the book.

It has everything in it spells, potions, weaponry, demons and other creatures of the underworld as well as magical beings of good. If it's magical then it will be in our book and if it needs to be destroyed, the book tells us how to do that.

My dad took it and started to look for the demon species in it.

"One move and you go kaboom. Understand?" I said calmly to the creature. "Why are you here?"

"I'll tell you nothing, witches," he answered viciously, he was either full of bravado or extremely stupid.

"I'll ask again. Why are you here? What is you were foolish enough to think you could get?"

"You're going to have to kill me, witch, 'cause I'm telling you nothing." He had a disgusting voice like polystyrene being grated.

"Do you think killing you is the worst I can do, demon? How about torturing you instead?" My tone was amused. "You are going to tell me what I want to know; it's just a question of how much it's going to hurt."

With that I blasted off his left arm. Amidst his cry of pain, he said, "Let me go, witch, so I can kill you."

I was enjoying myself now. "You really think you can kill me? You are even more stupid than I thought. Now WHY ARE YOU HERE?"

Silence…

I blasted off his right arm and his left leg before he gave up with cries of pain. "We were here for your book. It holds the key. There are others in our clan who will come after it." Something about all this book obtaining from demons. The book protects itself I felt like it was really something else they were after, besides killing me of course. I just couldn't think what it could possibly be.

"Really? Well, I'm guessing when none of you make it back, they'll think twice about taking us on." With that I blew the rest of him up.

"Here they are. Sakki demons. A powerful clan of demons looking to move up the food chain by destroying good witches. They have the power to outnumber and trap their victims and kill them with heated hands. Their hands heat thousands of degrees and they incinerate their targets within seconds of touching them," my father said reading from the book.

"Nice," said my sister Kennedy. "So if they don't get to touch you, they are more or less useless?"

"Looks that way," Dad said, "although they do seem to be very adept at laying traps to catch their victims in order to touch them."

"That's just creepy," I said. "Someone fill in Mum and Dylan when they get home, just in case their buddy's do want to have a go as well." I waved my hands a few times and the room began to tidy itself up.

I loved my power of telekinesis; I could make anything move with my mind, or by waving a hand at it or simply just staring at it. In some ways it was my favourite power. Even though my blasting ability was the most lethal in a Demon fight.

My father's side of the family all had non-lethal powers; They could heal, transport, read minds (though not our minds), use mind control, see the future, block physical attacks with a shield, and they also had the power of invisibility.

It was my mother's side of the family that had the serious firepower. They had telekinesis, blasting ability, throw destruction balls, shoot electrical bolts (sort of like a currant) from their hands, start fires with their mind, and move the elements.

I could do most of it; I was the only one that had most of the gifts. It was just I was better at some powers than others. Mind reading, mind control, moving elements, and seeing the future. I pretty much sucked at all of them, so I wasn't sure I actually had those gifts at all.

Everyone else in my family only had a few each; this was why I was prophesised to be the most powerful.

It was silly really because I couldn't possibly use all these gifts at the one time during an attack and would need another family member with me to maximise the use of our powers. That being said; there is still no underworld figure able to defeat me.

With one exception… Vampires.

We didn't actually cross paths with Vampires though because they weren't pests of the underworld looking to move up the food chain by killing witches.

In fact, they were so powerful, they could take over and rule the underworld if they wanted to.

They don't… thankfully, because they are quite literally indestructible.

According to our magical book, only a vampire can kill a vampire. Besides one dagger passed from father to son for generations designed to kill the lead vampire, it has to be blessed with the strongest magical blood, which would be, I guess.

Instead, they choose to live above ground and have lives among humans. They have houses, cars, and jobs and are governed by a higher body of vampires who punish those that break the rules.

In all honesty they were the only creatures who scared the crap out of me, and I hoped I would never have to deal with one.

There was a lot I hadn't read about them in the book, and I hoped I would never need to. I'm not Van Helsing, nor do I want to be.

I went up to my bedroom and put on some very loud music.

I was in serious need of chilling out so I ran a nice hot bath with music.

I scolded myself for being dumb; I had obviously imagined the moment simply because I couldn't take my eyes off of him.

Despite trying not to, I was still thinking about him when I went to bed. I switched my light off and could not erase the image of those smouldering good looks, and piercing amethyst eyes that were going to haunt me if I did not catch a grip of myself.

That was the first night of many to come that I had a restless sleep because of him.

I woke up sweating and aching, not physically aching, but an ache where it seemed there was a void. A void called Michael De Marco. As much as that makes no rational sense whatsoever. I was an idiot, plain and simple. Idiot.

I wished I could force these feelings for Jason but he only made my bloody head ache.

I showered and got ready taking extra care of how I looked today. As I straightened my hair, I toyed with the idea of having it a different colour from black to bright red or something equally startling. I sighed and brushed it until it shone knowing I would never have the nerve to do it. I applied careful make-up that accentuated my green eyes without making it look like I had tried too hard.

My mum had made delicious eggs and pancakes, my favourite. Yet when she put my plate in front of me, I couldn't seem to eat anything. Great! I was off my food now, what bloody next?

I realised I hadn't eaten a thing since breakfast yesterday.

"Not hungry, Angel? It isn't like you to pass up pancakes and eggs," my mother observed staring me down. "I hope you're not coming down with something. You look a little flushed too. Maybe you should go see the doctor."

"I don't need to see the doctor, Mum. I'm not getting sick."

"Well, there are only three reasons I know to be off food; One is illness, the other is being on drugs and the third is falling in love." She eyed me shrewdly, sizing me up so she could judge my response. Damn.

"Oh, Mum, will you stop fussing; I am fine, I am not sick, nor am I speeding and I do not have a new boyfriend." I was pleased with my clever wording.

"I've got to go. I'm meeting sally in the library to research our essay." And with that I was up and out of there before she could question me further. What was it with mothers and their uncanny ability to see right through us? To sniff out the truth and know what is going on just by looking at us closely? I had to get a handle on this crush before she sussed me out.

Michael wasn't in uni or if he was, I didn't see him, I didn't see him the next day either or the day after that.

The rain poured down every day making Michael's absence even bleaker.

I was confused at what the hell was going on, my potion fumes theory was really starting to make sense and I had in fact just hallucinated him. My eyes constantly scanned my surroundings in the hope of catching a glimpse of him.

Perhaps he was avoiding me due to my over the top reaction to his having a girlfriend, I couldn't blame him if he was, it was completely ridiculous.

Even though I was very aware, it would be better for me not to see him, I still couldn't help being more than a little disappointed he wasn't around. At least if he were here, albeit not talking to me, I could still look at his beautiful face with some sort of excruciating pleasure/pain.

I was a masochist for wanting someone so unattainable but I couldn't seem to help myself.

Sally was grilling me about what was going on but I had no answer for her because I wasn't sure myself; not that I would tell her anyway, with her gossiping ways half the campus would know about my insanity by lunchtime.

She had decided to ask around about him after the cafe and filled me in on what little she knew. I was quite pleased she had actually, since I was on the verge of stalking him, it saved me from doing some non-magical detective work. I laughed aloud at the absurdity of me stalking anyone and Sally eyed me with annoyance as she rambled on; she detested interruptions when imparting information. Nonetheless, I listened avidly to her gossip for once.

She heard he had one brother and two sisters, one of whom goes to this university. His family were supposedly very wealthy although no one knew what they did for a living; and they apparently lived in an old castle about an hour drive out of the city.

She said they seemed very mysterious because they didn't interact with people; so no one knew anything about them and she couldn't find anyone who knew who he had ever went out with.

She also told me his car was a black Lamborghini Elemento.

I remembered seeing and admiring – OK drooling over – a sexy black Lambo with blacked out windows in the car park. It was a dream machine. I couldn't remember exactly when I had first noticed it, but it stood out because it was an exclusive supercar. I believe there were only ever three made and this guy had one. Wow.

I had more or less resigned myself to not being wonderfully tortured with his presence by the time I was driving into the car park on Friday.

I parked my car and got out carefully, looking to see if Michael's Lamborghini was anywhere around, it wasn't. OK, good… or bad, depending on which part of the day you asked me.

I went to the library and Sally wasn't there yet it was cold out so I text her and said I was going inside and to meet me on the third floor.

I had just taken off my jacket when he appeared out of nowhere. I was doubly surprised because I hadn't seen his car outside. Damn I hated being caught so off guard.

His smooth voice caressed me and I shivered despite trying not to. "Hello, Angel, if you have a few minutes I would like to talk to you if I may?"

"Regarding what?" I asked. I honestly couldn't think what this ravishing guy had to talk to me about.

"Monday," he replied. "I would like to clear up the matter of Ava."

"Listen, Michael, you don't have to explain anything to me. I mean we hardly know each other and I really don't care anyway." I realised my tone was a tad snappish but I couldn't seem to stop.

His eyes were penetrating as he looked carefully at me; I felt like he could see straight into my soul and knew I was lying through my teeth; because I did care… I cared very much indeed, more than was rational.

He started to speak just as Sally came through the door; she half skipped over, all bubbly and amused to see me again with this godlike creature.

"Hey, Angel. What's up?" She was full on grinning now.

"Hey," I replied, relieved to be interrupted. "I've got to go, Sal, I just remembered I have a dentist appointment."

I had no such appointment, but I figured it sounded like a good reason why I had to leave so abruptly that did not make me look like a psycho, I just hoped no one would question why I turned up at all if I had the dentist.

With that, I turned quickly and walked away, desperate to escape.

On my way to the lift, I was trying to figure out why I didn't want to hear what he had to say.

I knew why actually; I didn't want to hear about his girlfriend and have him look at me with pity, because he knows I have a pathetic crush on him when he was just trying to be nice to me.

I also knew that I didn't want to hear it because once he spoke the words out loud, it became all too real and I would have to then deal with, and get over, my fantasies of this gorgeous mysterious stranger.

I got into the lift annoyed at myself and hit the ground button a little harder than was called for.

Just as the doors were about to close, an elegant white hand reached in and stopped them, and he entered the lift looking at me like some god of all things lust.

Oh crap. I knew there was no way I could avoid the conversation now.

He had just walked over beside me when a huge jolt went through the lift and it began to shudder.

I stumbled as the force of it knocked me sideways until I felt a pair of strong arms go around me and he lifted me upright. The lift came to a complete stop and the lights were flickering on and off, but as I looked up into his face, I could clearly see the staggering beauty of his intense amethyst eyes boring into me with concern.

"Are you alright, Angel?" he asked quickly. "You look a bit freaked out."

"I don't like small, enclosed spaces I can't get out of. I'm a bit claustrophobic so I'm freaking out at being stuck in a lift," I answered him tightly.

His arms were still around my waist and I could feel his hands on my back as he pressed my body tightly against his and held me there like a vice. Suddenly it wasn't the stuck lift that was making me feel unsteady. The scent of him was intoxicating and my hands were on his chest where I could feel the hard contours of his muscles beneath my fingers. I was having trouble making them not move, this was embarrassing enough without him having to deal with me groping him.

I reluctantly pushed my hands against his chest, freeing myself from his arms and moved away to the far wall.

Once out of his grasp, I could think clearly again and began to panic about being stuck in a lift where I couldn't just transport out. It was just my luck to be stuck in a lift with a human. I knew I would have to calm down and endure it because there was no way I could use my powers to disappear and blow my family secret all because I was having trouble with a little claustrophobia.

I could feel myself begin to sweat as the thought of being stuck in here for hours was slowly taking over my brain.

How much could I take before I had a panic attack? I had to chill out, I was stuck for however long it took to fix the lift and using my magic was not an option.

I realised I had the biggest distraction possible standing three feet away from me. "Michael, distract me please so I don't panic," I asked him.

He looked over at me and said in a calm voice, "It'll be OK, Angel, we won't be in here long." He pressed the bell and someone came on and said they were working on rebooting the lift computer.

My mouth was very dry and I had a complete flash of panic when I realised I had no water; I began to think I couldn't swallow and thought my throat was constricting.

He seen the expression on my face and came towards me. "Hey, you're OK, I promise I won't let anything happen to you." He pulled me towards him and somehow I believed him. In that moment I felt like my soul recognised his and connected somehow out of known time or space. It was the most bizarre feeling and completely unexplainable.

My head was against his hard chest and the scent of him was making me dizzy; but suddenly, I felt safe, like home and I felt the panic subside as he tightened his arms around my shoulders.

It was strange and made no sense to me but I somehow had the thought that he would always keep me safe.

"Who's your favourite band?" he asked.

I told him Bon Jovi and he nodded approvingly.

"OK, let's sing something of theirs to keep you distracted." He smiled at me.

I thought that was a very cool idea and really nice of him to offer and it definitely couldn't hurt.

He began to sing in a beautiful voice, not as strong as a rock stars voice but very pleasant to listen to all the same.

He started singing one of my favourite ballads, *Bed of Roses*. I couldn't believe it.

I just listened to him sing, staring at his exquisite face and his wistful expression in wonder as he sang. He didn't take his eyes or his hands off of me. I joined in with him at the chorus.

Wow, this was incredible and I knew I was cooked. Having already been utterly drawn in by his mystery, and mesmerised by his looks, he was now he was singing one of my favourite love songs to me. Kill me now.

The lift jerked and began to move. I barely noticed.

Neither one of us moved away from the other until the doors opened and reality came spilling in with Sally standing there. "Oh my god, are you alright?" How she knew the lift had been stuck with me in it I had no idea. She possessed some form of gossiping superpower.

"Yes," I said as I reluctantly moved from his arms and tore my eyes from his.

I turned to walk out the lift when I felt his hand take mine and I stopped dead, not turning around, not even breathing as he moved against my back. He reached up with his other hand and brushed my hair away from my ear.

His breath sent shivers all up and down my spine as he whispered gently, "Ava isn't my girlfriend, she's my sister." He let go of my hand and I could not move my legs.

Luckily, Sally grabbed my arm and yanked me out toward her rambling on about the horrors of being trapped in a lift. Her expression, however, told me she did not consider it a horror to be stuck in a lift with an Adonis. I had to agree, as lift failings go that wasn't the worst.

I went home and phoned my best friend Dallas. She was my only real friend and she knew I was a witch. She wasn't magical but thought it was amazing that I was. We had been friends since nursery and I knew she would never tell my secret to anyone.

I filled her in on the mysterious and gorgeous Michael De Marco and the events of the past week at uni that were going back and forth so much, it was giving me whiplash.

I could not believe it had only been a week, it felt like much longer.

Dallas suggested going out but I had an essay to finish and wanted it done before I completely lost all cognitive ability to think, and besides, it was due in on Monday.

We decided to hit the town tomorrow night instead because I needed time to sort my head out and to stop seeing Michael everywhere I turned. Having a fun, crazy night with my best friend seemed like as good a way as any to accomplish that.

I had to figure out how to control my spiralling feelings for him and to do that I had to figure out what it was that he wanted from me because it could not possibly be me.

I wondered why I was so caught up with someone I had only just met; was it just because he was so beautiful? Or did the mystery he presented accelerate my budding obsession?

I went downstairs and found my dad. I wasn't very hungry again so I was avoiding my mum. The last thing I needed tonight was her suspicious stare when she found out I was only snacking instead of eating meals.

Maybe I should just tell her I'm on drugs to stop any further questions on the matter, however, she would take one look at me after today's lift antics and know for sure it was a guy. Best just to avoid her altogether.

Dad was in the lounge watching a football game on TV so I went skulking in and told him I had an essay to write so I wouldn't be taking a break for dinner and would eat when I was done.

I was walking out the room when the thought occurred to me that we might get a Demon attack. "Dad, if we get any Demons attacking tonight, can you deal with it so I can get this paper finished? If no one else is home, then by all means shout me but other than that I need to concentrate."

"No problems, Angel. You finish your work I'll make sure no one bothers you."

"Thanks, Dad," I said. Good, that means I will get peace to work and I don't have to see Mum.

I went back to my room and closed the door. I got my books out, switched on my laptop, and got to work. My desk was placed away from any windows so I couldn't get distracted by looking out and dreaming when I was supposed to be studying.

My mind kept wandering to Michael and the whole lift and singing situation. I resolved to play the song after I got this paper finished so I got back to it. My head wasn't really in it and I honestly could not have cared less about the social and moral implications of *A Doll's House*. I wrote as best as I could but I knew it wasn't my best work.

The second I hit print, I had my Spotify on and lay on my bed listening to that ballad, of which, I now found myself inappropriately referring to as 'our song'. I couldn't stop picturing Michael singing the song. I remembered him looking wistful almost in pain as he sang the lyrics. Maybe it reminded him of someone. It was such a beautiful song, it wouldn't surprise me if it did. That was a painful thought so I banished it from my warped mind. I was thrilled he liked the band though, at least that meant he had good taste in music.

Music was so important to me, I couldn't go a single day without listening to it; and for me, it was the single most compelling evidence life had of showing us it was all worth it.

I truly believed music could change the world; it could touch people in ways nothing else could.

I had wanted desperately to be a musician, but I was told an emphatic and final NO! no chance could be taken, however slight, of becoming famous since our secret had to be protected at all costs, it was adios to a musical career because being famous with lots of media attention wasn't exactly conducive to being a secret witch with magical powers.

I had cried for a long time over that one, but I had to accept it wasn't going to happen for me, and now I just play the piano or guitar for fun or when I needed to think.

I took my jewellery box out and got my amethyst ring from it, Michael's eyes were almost the same colour.

OK, enough of this, it was bordering on fanaticism and it was time for bed, a good dose of crazy tends to make you tired. Maybe my own eyes would dull down a bit when I woke up and my mum wouldn't notice my madness.

I got into my long t-shirt and went under my covers, snuggling the duvet around me. I was suddenly so tired; the emotional rollercoaster of today's events had exhausted me.

I put my lamp out and instantly fell into a deep sleep.

Something woke me in the middle of the night, I had no idea what, but I felt strangely uneasy.

As I took a long drink of water, I knew I had been dreaming of Michael. Of his face, his hypnotic cool voice, and how his powerful body felt against mine.

It made me ache with wanting him, it actually physically hurt me now when I remembered how it felt when he touched me, when his body was brushed up behind me as he lifted my hair and whispered in my ear, how my skin scorched under his cool fingers.

I wanted so badly to be able to rip him from my dreams and into my reality, I was thinking of that as I fell back into a troubled sleep.

My unconscious was telling me there was something not quite right about the whole thing, and that is quite possibly what woke me and gave me the unease. It was alerting me to the fact that there was something big I wasn't seeing that I should be. Something I would never normally have missed, but in my waking state, I was completely oblivious to it.

I guess I should have been looking more closely, paying more attention instead of being staggered by the sheer magnetic force of his sexuality, his personality, and his outwardly dazzling shell.

Chapter Four

Night Out

The next day I got up and forced food down my throat, my middle of the night unease forgotten.

I had slept through breakfast and it was now late lunchtime.

Mum wasn't home so I made some toast and took it into the conservatory to enjoy the tranquil view.

It tasted like cardboard but I knew I had to have something in my stomach if I was going drinking tonight, so I made myself choke down every last bite. I made it easier on myself by washing it down with a lovely cold can of the ultimate Scottish soda Irn Bru. We always had about forty cans of it in our fridge because everyone drank it.

If whiskey was the Scottish national drink, Irn Bru definitely the other one.

Not that I drank whiskey, I couldn't stand the stuff. I was a vodka drinker.

Dallas came over at four and we spent ages trying on clothes. We wore the same dress size so it was like doubling our wardrobe.

Dallas was a beautiful blonde girl and I loved her in red, I thought she so suited it. She picked out a stunning red dress that had a halter top and pencil skirt. She teamed it with a pair of killer Louboutins and my red Dior saddlebag. I decided on a black micro mini dress with four-inch Manolo Blahnik Mary Janes that made my long legs look endless, and a small black Prada bag.

I so loved to dress up and be glamorous, there was nothing that made you feel better as quickly as an awesome pair of killer heels.

Outfits decided on, we sat listening to music and discussing my unhealthy obsession with Michael De Marco.

Dallas was having trouble believing just how beautiful he was, and said she was going to meet me for lunch at my uni one day so she could get a look at him.

We both agreed that my taking a picture of him on my phone would be far too obvious and he might think I'm stalking him.

Which I wasn't bloody far off doing if I didn't get a grip.

At seven we got our showers and started to get ready, blasting kick ass rock and jumping around like kids playing guitar and drums with my pillows.

Dallas said her boyfriend Brian and a couple of his friends were going to the club tonight. OK by me, I got on well with them all and we always had a laugh together.

Dallas had just finished drying her hair, she turned and asked for my straighteners, as I was in the middle of applying mascara, I just waved my hand across them and sent them over to her.

"That is awesome. I wish I had the power of telekinesis." Dallas was forever convinced if I gave her some of my blood, she would somehow get it.

I constantly told her she didn't want it because it would mean Demons would come after her.

"I would be great at kicking some Demon Arse," was always her standard reply. She made me laugh.

Once we were ready, I added my amethyst ring. It was pathetic but it made me feel closer to Michael. What a fool I am, I thought, irritated at myself. I still wore it though.

We didn't bother with a taxi because neither of us could be bothered with the journey into Glasgow city centre so we transported, arriving within a second, in a toilet cubicle of our favourite pub.

We came out the toilet and hit the bar, drinking and talking, and knocking back over eager losers with lame chat-up lines no female should ever have to hear.

At eleven we left the pub and headed up to the club. That was the name of it, The Club. It was our favourite nightclub in the city.

We were both a bit tipsy as we checked our jackets and went once again to the bar.

It's not hard to find us if we get separated in a crowd, the bar would always be a good shout for the first port of call in a search.

Brian and two of his friends were already there and ordered our drinks for us.

I was chatting away to them when I felt strange all of a sudden, not anything I could put my finger on just a pulling sensation like I had to look somewhere, it was incredibly weird. Coming from a magical background it took a lot to weird me out.

Just as I began to wonder if my drink had been spiked, I looked up to see a dark figure elegantly lounging on a stool, looking at me.

My heart stopped. "Michael," I whispered. I needed a second to re-start my heart before deciding on a course of action.

He didn't give me much chance to recover as he stood up and slowly walked across the floor to where I was standing.

I loved how he moved; he was so elegant and graceful like a black panther stalking its prey. I had never seen anyone move the way he did, it was hypnotic to watch, and I could not take my eyes off him.

He was wearing black trousers with a black open collar shirt, it looked striking next to his translucent skin, and I did not think I had ever seen anything quite as beautiful as he was right now. Was it even legal to look as good as that?

He looked down at me. "Hello, Angel." And the whole world just disappeared. He took my arm and pulled me out from between my friends. "I want to get a proper look at you." His eyes travelled very slowly down my body to my toes and slowly back up again.

Every nerve ending in my body was on fire as his gaze leisurely swept the length of me once more. His amethyst eyes were bright as he drank in every inch of me.

His expression as he looked back at my face was one of wonderment. "You're taking my breath away, you look so incredibly beautiful."

I looked beautiful? Had he looked at himself in a mirror lately? I couldn't believe my ears. He thought I was beautiful.

My heart was racing and my knees felt weak as I locked onto his lilac eyes.

We stared at each other for a while and he lifted his pale, cool hand to my face and moved a lock of my hair away from my neck.

He then, very gently, traced the back of his fingers slowly down my cheek, grazing over my lips and onto my chin where he tipped my head up and let his fingers slowly come to rest just at my throat.

It wasn't the alcohol I had consumed that was intoxicating me now; it was him and my head was swimming from it.

Neither of us spoke as his fingers lay against my neck; his thumb resting on my pulse just under my jaw, then he moved both hands down to my shoulders and leaned in closer. "Would you like a drink?" he asked softly. "I am completely forgetting my manners due to being so spellbound by you. It seems I am quite unable to take my eyes off of you."

I managed to choke out a "Yes please, I will have a vodka and orange juice."

He turned to my friends who were all staring at him in amazement and asked if they would like a drink. The world came back into focus again as Dallas gave him their drink requests and he turned to the bar.

I looked at Dallas and she was mouthing WOW at me. She came over to my side and whispered, "He is stunning. You weren't bloody exaggerating a thing about him. I cannot get over it. Did you see the way he looked at you? He definitely likes You. When he was touching your face, we all felt like we were intruding even though it's a public place. It was just so intimate and so damn hot." She was shaking her head at the memory.

"He stuns me to the point I can't move when he's near me. It's like I'm rooted to the spot just trying to remember how to breathe," I answered her.

Michael was handing the guys their drinks, then he turned to us. "I am sorry not to have introduced myself before now please forgive my rudeness but I am simply mesmerised by your friend. I am Michael De Marco. Pleasure to meet you." He shook hands with them all as they introduced themselves.

"I have to apologise but I shall be monopolising Angel's time this evening, I hope you won't be put out by that?" he said to the group.

Dallas giggled in a very girlish manner and said it was not a problem, that in fact, she thought it was a wonderful idea.

Ava appeared out of nowhere and smiled at me warmly. "You must be Angel? I have heard a lot about you. My brother seems quite taken with you so it's lovely to be introduced." There was no sarcasm in her voice just openness and a look of curiosity on her lovely face.

"Hello, Ava, I am very pleased to meet you too," I said smiling at the beautiful girl. Now I knew she wasn't Michael's girlfriend I could appreciate her beauty.

Introductions were made and Brian's friends were openly gawping at her and falling over themselves to buy her a drink, but she politely declined and said she was going to find her boyfriend who was around somewhere.

Michael took my hand and walked me onto the dance floor.

The music had mellowed a bit so he pulled me close to him and I felt that deep spiritual pull from my soul again as he wrapped his arms right around me, holding me tightly.

I put my arms around his neck and leaned my head on his shoulder. "It is really surprising to me how natural it feels to be this close to you," he said. "I don't find it easy to be close to people outside of my family, but with you it somehow seems like the easiest thing in the world and I like it... I like it a lot."

I was ecstatic. I couldn't remember when I had ever been this happy.

I looked up into his smouldering eyes and was lost, completely and utterly lost for all eternity.

We spent the rest of the night on the dance floor with our eyes locked together, I don't think we looked away once, neither of us was inclined to break the stare and it was the most wonderfully intense experience.

I couldn't even identify what songs came on the entire night as I was so wrapped up in him and how he made me feel, until that is, the last song of the night came on and it was our ballad. I had no idea how it came about as he hadn't left my side to ever ask the DJ to play it but I just knew he had to have been involved.

This wasn't a rock club so it isn't like they play this kind of stuff normally. He smiled at me, his expression softer than I thought possible and pulled me in even tighter, something else I didn't think was possible.

We were so close together there wasn't an inch of space anywhere between us; you wouldn't even have been able to get a beer mat between us.

It felt amazing, he felt amazing.

I could feel every slight movement of his entire body against me and I couldn't get enough.

When the lights came up, we were still holding on to each other. Neither one of us wanting to break the spell.

Reluctantly we moved apart only to see my friends trying not to stare at us with their mouths agape. We both laughed and he took my hand, leading me off the dance floor.

I couldn't help but notice every girl in the place was staring at him in wide-eyed wonderment. Even the guys were staring at him.

Dallas collected our jackets and told me she was staying at Brian's tonight. Brian had a flat near the city centre and he invited anyone who couldn't be bothered travelling home to stay at his. We declined, and as they left, Dallas was shooting me knowing looks over her shoulder.

Michael asked me how I was getting home and I couldn't exactly say transporting so I told him I was planning to get a taxi.

"No way am I letting you get a taxi alone at night." His tone was serious. "I will drive you home myself."

"Don't be silly, Michael, you don't have to do that it'll be miles out of your way and I will be fine in a taxi." My protest was weak at best.

"Absolutely not. I am driving you home and that's the end of it." His voice invited no further argument. Fine with me.

We got to his car, and he opened the passenger door for me. He helped me inside and closed the door before going around to his side. The doors on this car opened upwards instead of outwards, very cool.

His manners were impeccable. I couldn't remember the last guy to ever open a door for me let alone a car door. I was stupidly pleased that he was such a gentleman. It was really nice.

As he drove, he kept looking at me and I was looking right back at him. I wanted to touch his face so badly, feel the thick black eyelashes beneath my fingers, and skim the surface of those high cheekbones.

His driving was mental; he drove even faster than I did, which was saying something considering I had never stuck to a speed limit in my life. We would be at my house in no time.

He drove this dream machine like a pro. This car was made for high speeds. It would be a grave insult to drive it any other way.

"I have to say something to you and I want you to listen very carefully Angel." His silky voice was serious, as was his expression. "It really isn't good for you to be with me. I should have left you alone and not allowed myself to get as involved with you as I have. I always only want you to be safe and you may not be if you're with me."

I was crushed. Did he not want to see me anymore? What was tonight about then? I knew it was too good to be true.

I didn't answer him I just turned my head away and looked out the window. The rest of the drive was in total silence.

He turned into my driveway and we made the mile in seconds.

He pulled the car to a stop right outside my front door and got out. He came around to my side and opened the door for me; he took my hand, and helped me out. He walked me to my door as I retrieved my keys from my bag.

"This is a beautiful house. I like it a lot," he said, breaking the silence, and admiring the three levels of beautiful white sandstone that was my home.

"Thanks," I said quietly. I didn't trust my voice to speak any louder in case it broke.

"What I said before, I didn't articulate myself very well. I seem to do that a lot when I'm around you. I did not mean I don't want to see you, I meant you may not want to see me, not if you wish look after your best interests that is. Believe me when I tell you, that does not involve being with me" – he looked away, looked back and sighed – "If you believe in any kind of self-preservation, you should run as fast as you can for the hills right now." His tone was sharp.

"Well let's say for arguments sake that I think self-preservation is overrated what then?" I asked him.

"Then that would be your decision but I had to give you some kind of warning so as not to be a completely selfish bastard." His tone had softened as had his eyes as he reached up and softly swept my hair from my face. "I am physically not able to stay away from you on my own, believe me I have tried. So if you want to see me there is nothing I can do about it, but we will need to talk at a more sensible time as you may yet change your mind." He smiled at me sadly.

"I won't change my mind, Michael," I whispered.

He put his cool, pale fingers to my cheek again brushing it ever so lightly. There was a sad frown on his perfect face as he gazed into my eyes. "You are my Angel." His voice was like satin caressing my skin.

My whole body shivered and it was nothing to do with the weather being cold.

He slowly and deliberately moved in closer to me, lazily pressing his hard body against mine. His head moved slowly downwards… getting closer inch by exquisite inch. I didn't think I could stand the anticipation much longer. I wanted him to kiss me more than I had ever wanted anything, ever. Then my front door opened.

Shit, I thought; I hoped it was my brother or sister. Of course it wasn't, it was my mother.

Michael moved back and we looked at her. What the hell was she doing hanging around the front door anyway? Spying on me? How did she know I was here let alone with a guy? This was all I needed.

"I thought I heard voices," she said looking at Michael with curiosity. "Hi, I'm Angel's mum, Lana," she said ever so politely.

"Hello, Mrs Phoenix, my name is Michael. It is lovely to meet you." He smiled brightly at her, not by a single flicker did he show any surprise or discomfort at her being there at 4 am.

"Would you like to come in, Michael? My daughter appears to have forgotten the manners," she said.

He smiled brightly. "Thank you, but no, I was just leaving. Another time perhaps." He was polite and charming. He turned to me. "I'll see you later, Angel."

"I'll walk you to your car," I said, irritated as hell at my mother's interruption not to mention her still being there. I glared at her as I turned away towards the car. She got the hint and said goodnight and closed the door.

"How embarrassing. I'm sorry, Michael," I said sheepishly. I looked up into his eyes instantly forgetting what I was going to add.

He laughed. It was such a gorgeous sound, and silky like his voice. "It is no bother at all. I know how mothers can be."

He captured my eyes. "I should be leaving anyway before I am physically unable to drag myself away from you, and that really would not be proper." He had a flirty tone in his voice. "Will I see you later or are you having a lie in?"

"I was planning to stay in bed actually but if you want to see me that just might be worth being tired for," I said lightly. I didn't want to sound too desperate to see him even though I was.

"You don't have to get out of bed on my account, I would be more than happy to keep you company." He gave me a cheeky grin. "Bet you look cute in your pj's." I hit him lightly on the arm. "Tell you what, why don't I pick you up at noon and we can go for a drive and find somewhere to talk?"

"Drive all the way out here again? Don't you want me to just meet you somewhere instead and save yourself the journey?" I asked surprised at his offer.

He laughed. "Haven't you figured out yet that it takes me less than half the time to drive anywhere than it does other people? Besides, I want to pick you up, it's proper and to be perfectly honest, I would drive anywhere if it means I get to see you. I promise I'll even drive you crazy given half a chance." The double entendre was not lost on me and he knew it.

"Well, in that case I would love you to pick me up." I was ridiculously happy at his offer.

"Right, it's settled then. I shall be here at twelve on the dot. Should I wait in the car or would you rather I get the parental interrogation over with instead? I do not mind, I have a feeling your family will be meeting me soon enough. May as well be tomorrow."

"I think I'll spare you the brutality of it for now and just get you in the car." Irritation at my mother's blatant interruption flashed upon me again.

He opened his car door but didn't get in, instead he took my chin in his hand, put his lips to my ear and gently whispered, "I can't wait to see you again beautiful." He let his head rest against the side of mine for a minute and I could feel him breathing in my scent.

He looked at me with an expression of something, I didn't know what, on his perfect face and said, "I am not used to feeling this powerless." And then he was in his car before I even realised he had moved.

I watched him drive away, a dreamy smile on my lips and my head buzzing with the mystery he presented. I then went inside to ask my mother what she was all about opening the door.

She wasn't there; I was surprised because I figured she would not be able to wait to question me about this one and point out she knew there was a reason I was off my food. Given how beautiful Michael was, I definitely thought she would be waiting. Oh well.

I went to my room, took off my make-up, crawled into my big, soft bed, and dreamt of him again.

Chapter Five

The Talk

I woke at ten too excited to sleep anymore so I got up and had a shower, washing my hair and singing.

I turned the water onto cold and let it blast me awake. Not that sleep was on my mind, furthest thing from it but the cold water felt good regardless.

I decided not to go downstairs until twelve so I could avoid any questions. I put on music and tried to contain my crazy happiness.

I felt like my whole body was a live wire and one more touch from Michael would make it spark and explode into a firework display of electricity.

I dried my hair and applied make-up. I always liked to wear dark eye make-up because it enhanced the green of my eyes.

I was having trouble deciding what to wear because I didn't know where we would be going.

I decided that jeans were the safest option and put on my skinny Levi's with a white tank top, which I planned to pair with my favourite fitted black leather jacket. I put on black knee-high leather boots over my jeans to complete my look.

My brother Dylan came into my room and took in my being dressed up on a Sunday morning with curiosity.

"So I take you're going out with the mystery bloke Mum caught you with last night?"

"She didn't catch me, Dylan, I wasn't trying to hide. I only met him this week and everything has happened faster than I thought it would. And yes, I am going out with him today." I snapped.

"I'm not having a go, Angel; I was just repeating what Mum said. Anyway, I think it's great cos I heard her say he was too good looking and dynamic. Sounds like he's everything Jason isn't. To be honest, Jason isn't good enough for you plus he's *really* boring."

"Sorry for snapping, D. I just thought you were sent up to grill me cos Mum wants me to go out with Jason." I hugged him and ruffled his hair.

"Angel, it's your life and you should be with someone who makes you happy and if this guy makes you happy then it's a no brainer, regardless of Mum's feelings about it. Plus, I hear he has a supercar, do you think I can see it?" he asked with his boyish enthusiasm.

"Of course you can, babe. He's picking me up at twelve so you can come out and meet him and see his car." I loved my brother a lot; he was always on my side.

"Awesome," was his happy reply.

Dylan sat with me listening to music until twelve and then we went down stairs.

I opened the door and there he was; impossibly pale and striking in a black leather coat, lounging casually against the black backdrop of his car with his arms folded, and holding a red rose.

I caught my breath as it hit me again, the sheer pull of him.

He was right on time; somehow, I just knew he would be, not because of me, but because I just knew he probably wasn't late for anything, ever.

He wore a big expensive watch, but I was sure he didn't need to; he probably decided what time it was.

I stood looking at him, thinking that he looked more sexy and dangerous than anyone ever should.

He pushed himself off of the car and came toward me. "Well, if you're not going to come to me, I will just have to come over there and get you." He smiled a slow, devastating smile, as his amethyst eyes lazily travelled over me.

He leaned in almost motionless and handed me the rose. "You look unbelievably appealing, you have no idea how appealing. Although, I am kind of disappointed not have caught you in your cute pj's." His grin was irresistible and I found myself putting my arms around his neck.

"Well, that's certainly not the worst greeting I ever imagined," he said, putting his strong arms around my waist.

A cough from beside us alerted me to the fact that my brother was standing there.

I had actually forgotten he came out with me. This was the effect Michael had on me, once I looked at him everything else ceases to exist.

I just laughed. "Michael this is my little brother, Dylan. He's been pacing about waiting to meet you and your car."

"Hello, Dylan, nice to meet you. Here's the keys if you want to take a closer look." He handed him the keys and Dylan looked ecstatic. He ran to the Elemento like a kid at Disneyland.

"So where are we going today?" I asked him.

As long as I get to be with him, I would go sit on piles of broken glass if he wanted to.

"I was thinking I'll take you to lunch. Just because we need to talk doesn't mean I shouldn't feed you. There's a nice place not far from here unless you have somewhere else you like to eat?" he asked.

"No, I'm sure wherever we go it will be great. That is unless we can't get my brother out of your car to actually get anywhere."

He took my hand and we walked over to his car. Dylan looked gutted at having to get out but Michael promised him he could have a go of driving it when we got back. I thought Dylan was going to do cartwheels he was so excited. I knew the feeling well; but it wasn't his car that sent me into convulsions.

He opened the passenger door for me and helped me inside; he was doing the whole gentleman thing again. I knew it wasn't an act though, he truly was a real gentleman. It just added to his already enormous appeal.

He drove like a formula one racing driver, handling the powerful sports car with ease and assurance, like he knew the car would do whatever he wanted it to.

We talked about my friends and he told me he thought Dallas was great and I told him she really liked him too.

The place 'nearby' turned out to be a small village that would take a regular person an hour to drive to.

It was a picturesque little place like you see on postcards; all sweet little cottages with white picket fences and rose gardens. I didn't even know it existed. It was perfect.

It was almost like we had driven into a different time; an age long ago where violent crime and terrorism weren't on the rise and people could leave their doors unlocked; and knew all their neighbour's names.

He slowed the fast car right down as he turned into a small car park and pulled into a parking space.

He turned off the engine and put his hand on my thigh as he unbuckled my seatbelt. I jumped like I had been given an electric shock, not prepared for him to touch me so naturally like that.

He looked at me, surprised, but he didn't move his hand he just studied my face for a few seconds before getting out of the car and coming to open my door.

I could feel myself sweating a little from the sensation of his open and intimate touch and my thigh burned where his hand had been.

This was exquisite torture and I wasn't sure how much more I could take before I spontaneously combusted.

Was he even aware of the great effect he had on me? Or was this how everyone acted around him so he was desensitised to it?

He took my arm and opened the bistro door for me. We walked inside and were seated straight away even though it was busy.

Michael asked for a table by the window and he pulled my seat out for me to sit in. Once again, I was impressed with his manners.

Who said chivalry was dead? It was very refreshing for a guy to be so respectful of a female. I liked it. I liked it a lot. He had a lot of class. Unlike the Neanderthals I usually encountered.

It was a beautiful little family-run place with quaint old-fashioned decoration and the suggestion of great food and a relaxing ambience; topped off with gorgeous views over the lush green hills. I loved it. How did he ever find this place?

"What would you like to eat?"

Eat? I would never be able to choke anything down. "I don't feel very hungry so maybe I will just have a drink." I suddenly felt very dehydrated and nervous.

"I'm not hungry either." He laughed. "Glad we bothered to come for lunch."

That was a good sign if he was off his food too.

He ordered us some water and told me I was going to eat if he had to spoon-feed me himself.

"What about you? If you're making me eat then you should be eating too," I said stubbornly.

He looked me in the eye, but even so, his expression was guarded, his eyes careful like he was choosing which words to use. "I'm on a liquid diet."

I looked at him trying to work out why he would be on a liquid diet. He wasn't overweight, he didn't have a broken jaw and as far as I knew he wasn't sick so why would he need a liquid diet?

I let it go, though; if he wanted to tell me, he would. Besides, some deep part of me did not want to pull a that thread.

He ordered for me, chicken and smoked bacon pasta with a white creamy cheese sauce. It did sound good and I felt a little hungry despite myself.

"So, Angel, it would seem we are both a little nervous of being in each other's company today."

"It would seem so. It feels like we both have a lot to lose if this doesn't go well, which is silly because we hardly know each other."

"I have no idea why this is, but from the first moment I laid eyes on you, I felt like I have to see know you or I'll go crazy. You intrigued me, something no one else has never ever done; and from that first instant I had this inexplicable need for you, and to protect you."

I gulped; feeling like my tongue was too big for my mouth. "Perfect sense." I was starting to struggle for breath. "I think I know what you mean."

It reminded me of something William Shakespeare once wrote:

"No sooner met but they looked; No sooner looked but they loved; No sooner loved but they sighed; No sooner sighed but they asked one another the reason; No sooner knew the reason but they sought the remedy."

He smiled although it did not quite reach his eyes, which were still intense looking, layered with deep messages.

"You look so beautiful," he said. His eyes suddenly softening. "I am quite overcome with a constant need to stare at you. Please don't think me rude when I do this."

Rude? Was he kidding? I was beside myself with joy that he wanted to look at me.

"Can I ask you what you meant when we first met, and you said you shouldn't spend time with me because it was complicated?"

He looked at me with that same strange expression he had used that day we met.

"It is rather hard to explain. I have a… a complicated lifestyle; not one that is very compatible with regular people." His eyes were guarded again, and I knew he had a secret. One I had a subconscious suspicion about.

I decided to be honest. Well as honest as I could be.

"I understand that more than you know, Michael. I have a complicated lifestyle too and I tend not to let people get close to me because it's not good for them."

He looked at me not surprised in the least. Resect took over his eyes as at my honesty. "I know you do, Angel."

His expression became deadly serious as he looked at me. "I have a confession to make, and you may think it weird or creepy, but I *have* to tell you if this relationship is going to have even half a chance of succeeding."

He took a deep breath, almost afraid to look at the judgment he imagined would be in my eyes.

"I cannot stay away from you, Angel. I have never been able to from that first sighting I had of you, even If it was simply just loving you from afar. I *have* tried… you have no idea how I tried, but it did not work, and I concluded that if I couldn't get you out of my head then perhaps you were meant to be there. I can't seem to stop wanting to be with you, nor do I have any desire left to try to stop myself anymore.

"I have well gone beyond the point of no return. I want to be with you now no matter what."

I *had* to ask, "Exactly how long were you following me or watching me before you introduced yourself."

He leaned back in his chair for a minute and studied me. It felt like an hour had passed before he sat forward and the look in his lilac eyes seemed to question my sanity. "That's the only question you have to the fact I was basically stalking you?"

"Yes, and why didn't you introduce yourself faster."

He dropped his head for a second and sighed before looking back at me, his vivid eyes clouding over. "You know the old expression be careful what you wish for because you might get it." His voice was quiet, as he went on.

"I saw you *months* before, and I felt this pull unlike anything I have ever felt in my entire existence, and something told me you were incredibly important and needed to be protected. I still have no idea why despite our how intense our love is, the way it is, like it somehow feels like the stars aligned, almost like universal intervention bringing us together. I am afraid though, once we embark on this there is no going back. You need to know this; to grasp it… there is great danger, and things about me you may not like. Things that you may not be able to accept, and you need to know that now, before this goes any further."

I began to realise something wasn't right. Michael was dangerous; there was no doubt about that. Not to me necessarily but in general. Even so, I just could not feel afraid.

My mind flashed quickly over what it could be, that niggling feeling returned that I was hiding from myself that his secret was be supernatural, that would certainly explain all the cloak and dagger mystery surrounding him. Well, I was supernatural too and I guess we would have to tell each other eventually, but timing was everything in these matters.

"I understand more than you know there are hidden obstacles for both of us, and I know you've been trying to tell me all along that you're dangerous, but I'm dangerous too.

"I have resolved though, that no matter what it is you're so reluctant to tell me, I don't care. Nothing, and I do mean *nothing,* could make me not want to be with you. I guess we just have to take a leap of faith and see where it takes us."

His face was very still and awfully close to mine and we were staring into each other's eyes for what seemed like hours.

My heart was beating faster, having his face so close and wanting to kiss him.

"I can hear your heart beating."

"What? How can you hear my heart beating in this noisy room?"

"I have extraordinarily good hearing. It's part of who I am, and I can hear that your heart is beating very fast."

I picked up my water and took a big drink, trying to figure out this revelation, this hint.

"What else can you do that is part of you?" I asked trying to keep my voice even.

He looked at me for a long moment, deliberating on how much to say. "I can see extremely well and over great distances and I have excellent night vision. I see just as well in the dark as I do in the light." His voice was flat, emotionless; like he thought I was going to run out screaming.

I didn't know how to respond because I wasn't sure I wanted to know what these hints added up to. What was he trying to tell me with these hints? I decided I would think about it when I had more to go on.

He seemed a little unnerved that I was so calm. Normal people do not have extra-heightened senses, not unless they were supernatural of some kind.

A fact he knew I must have been aware of.

He seemed to work out why it didn't surprise me and why I had no immediate questions about it.

As I ate the pasta, I was silently watching the changing expressions crossing his perfect features.

He looked at me now, his voice, when he did speak it was soft, gentle. Like a satin caress.

"You are not surprised in the least because you are used to people having attributes that are not altogether human, aren't you? And I know for a fact you have many of your own, I *knew* the second I met you." It wasn't a question merely an observation of something he knew to be true.

I didn't need to answer him; the questions were rhetorical, so I didn't. I simply looked straight into his eyes. He watched me all those months thinking I was human.

He took my hand in his cool, pale one and brought it to his lips; he opened my hand and gently kissed my palm. It was almost a gesture of acceptance, as if he was telling me it was alright.

I lifted my palm to his face, touching it for the first time; softly and slowly in utter wonder. I touched his chiselled cheekbone and ran a finger over one beautiful eyelid, feeling his thick lashes.

I brought my fingers to his lips and felt the fullness and impossibly soft texture of them before leaving one finger over them in a gesture of ssshhh, and whispered, "Everything will be OK."

He took my hand and pressed it hard against his cheek, holding it there with his other hand and closed his eyes, tortured.

He looked so vulnerable, his cultivated façade gone. Replaced with someone whose whole life was changing, and for the first time, doesn't have all the answers.

I had never seen him any way but in total control.

I think if it was at all possible; I was falling even harder for him.

The waitress came over and asked us if we would like anything else, her expression sympathetic as if she thought perhaps that one of us was dying. If she hadn't, I have no idea how long he would have stayed like that, clutching my hand to his face like a lifeline. He told her no and asked for the bill.

He took money from his pocket and left it on the table, and then he stood up and pulled my chair out, taking my hand and standing me up. I could get quickly used to this kind of old-world manners and respect. It was a dying thing; boys don't even think about opening doors for you these days.

We walked to his car hand in hand, both of us resolved that whatever was going to come next, whatever revelations we were going to shock with, it will not affect our relationship and how we feel about each other. No matter what.

"We will go on a proper date on Saturday," he said. "Somewhere that's just you and I alone. How does that sound?"

"Perfect," I whispered. "Just perfect."

"OK it's settled. In the meantime, you better give me your mobile number because I have a feeling I shall miss you tonight." He took his phone out of his pocket and we swapped numbers.

On the drive back to my house we were laughing about what a pair we were. We were both happy and relieved to have had *that* intense conversation and still wanted to be together.

It wasn't just about us wanting to be together, we *had* to be together.

This was something so powerful that it was consuming us both wholly; and pulling us in, like a black hole pulling in the universe around it. we couldn't *not* be together. What else could explain how quickly this happened? It certainly wasn't normal. It was bigger than us.

Not that either of us had any inclination to try to stop it now but I didn't think we could anyway.

We got to my house and Dylan came bursting out to greet us. Michael threw him the car keys laughing.

"Are you sure you want to let him drive your car?"

"Sure, why not. It's only a car, granted a very good car but if a lot of pretty metal and a powerful engine makes someone as happy as your brother is right now then that's what it's all about," he said smiling that dazzling smile of his.

I melted. "You are so sweet." I took his hand.

He laughed. "I have been called a lot of things in my time but I can honestly say sweet is not one of them. I am pretty far from sweet Angel; I am most people's *worst* nightmare when I choose to be," he said this so seriously.

"Well, I happen to know different and you are sweet," I countered, equally as serious. "Come on, let's go inside, my brother will be with your car a while."

We went into the house and I was relieved to note no one was in.

Michael gave me that flirty grin and said, "So do I get to see your room?"

My heart almost flew out of my chest and I felt dizzy.

"Remember I can hear your heart beating, my Angel, and right now it is off the chart. Does the thought of my presence in your bedroom really affect you so?"

"Yes," I managed to croak. "It does, Michael." I feared my legs would not work for me now.

He scooped me up into his arms and carried me up the stairs as if I weighed nothing.

His movements were fast and graceful and he hadn't broken even a slight sweat by the time we got to my room.

He opened my door with me still in his arms and took me into the room; closing the door behind us.

He carried me across the floor and placed me gently on the bed. I couldn't move, couldn't breathe, all I could do was look up at him with huge eyes and a near coronary.

He unleashed the full force of his magnetic eyes on me; and I thought I was going to pass out.

"You get so much more get appealing by the hour." His satin voice was husky.

I didn't know if my heart was exploding because I thought he was going to take me in his arms and make mad passionate love to me; or because he *wasn't* going to.

His eyes were burning, flashing like a bright amethyst flames and he gave me a look so full of desire that I almost hyperventilated.

"Don't worry, my Angel; I'm not going to ravish you… Yet."

Chapter Six

He lay down next to me on the bed and pulled me into him so my head was on his chest and his arms were around me.

My heart was still beating faster than it should but I was no longer close to needing an ambulance.

I began to feel my head clear a little and the dizziness subside as I calmed down.

It was then that I realised he knew where my room was without me telling him.

He had carried me up here needing no directions and found it first time. My house was very big with a lot of rooms so how did he know which one was mine? I pondered this for a while. I didn't feel uneasy about it, merely curious. Whatever his answer would be I was sure I wouldn't be surprised. So I asked, sitting up on one elbow so I could look at him. "How did you know where my room was when I didn't tell you and you've never been here before?"

He studied me for a minute, looking for something in my voice or my face that would tell him what to say to that. There was nothing, my face and voice were completely neutral.

"I followed your scent," he said simply.

"So, I take it that would be another one of your heightened senses?" I asked curiously.

"Yes, one of many if you want to know the truth," he told me, his face open; not trying to hide a thing now.

"OK." End of discussion. He had given me an honest answer to my question, I didn't need anything else.

I curled back up in his powerful body and he held me tightly. I was once again overcome with a feeling of safety that came with being in his arms.

I began to feel sleepy; my whole body was totally relaxing and melting into his. I felt him kiss my head while he was softly stroking my hair. It felt so nice I closed my eyes.

"Sleep if you want to, my Angel, I will never let you go," he whispered.

I was just falling asleep when my door opened and Jason came in. He looked at Michael and I wrapped in each other's arms with disbelief.

I sat up highly annoyed, who the hell did he think he was walking uninvited into my bedroom. *This* was crossing the line.

"What the hell do you think you're playing at Jason? I know you learned how to knock on a door," I said angrily.

"I came over to see you and Dylan said you were up here with a guy, and lo and behold here you are and here's the guy." He gave me a bitter laugh.

"What of it? It's none of your business who I choose to spend time with and you have no right to question me." I was on my feet and shouting now.

"I thought we were going to get it together soon. Our families expect it and I don't appreciate seeing you with another guy in your bed," he retorted, unrepentant in his undeserved anger. He had always been self-righteous, one of his many qualities I could not stand.

I was furious now. "I don't give a crap what our families expect you bloody worm and as for seeing me in bed with another guy, I have never been, and never will be, in a bed with you so how dare you have the audacity to say that. I couldn't care less what you do or do not appreciate so do not come barging into my bedroom as if you have any right to be here."

"You are nothing but a user. You lead me on making me think we're going to get married and you're sneaking about with some other guy," he shouted.

Michael tensed and sat up his face like stone, anger bubbling beneath his skin.

"Lead you on, LEAD YOU ON?" I was screaming now my temper broken. "How could I lead you on when nothing, and I repeat it again for your half a brain, *nothing* was ever going on? You lead yourself on, you useless idiot. I should maim you where you stand."

Michael put a hand on my arm in a calming gesture.

"Bitch," he screamed at me. "You're nothing but a lying bitch and I should slap your face."

He barley even got to finish the end of the sentence when Michael was across the room, he had moved so fast I didn't even see him. His hands were around Jason's throat and lifting him into the air. His expression was frightening.

The fact he could kill him easily wasn't lost on me.

I ran across the room and put my hands over his and locked eyes with him. "Put him down, Michael, he genuinely isn't worth it," I said gently.

Michael loosened his grip and Jason fell to the floor.

"You ever talk to her like that again and I will kill you, do you understand?" His satin voice was all the more deadly because it was calm.

Jason got up from the floor and stormed out, still unrepentant but not brave enough to argue with Michael.

I knew Michael could have killed him with no problem at all in under a second, he had held back purposely. He turned to me and asked me if I was alright, touching my face gently he said, "I have a serious temper, Angel, mostly it is under control but that really got to me. I'm very protective of you."

"It's OK, baby, you were only standing up for my honour, which I appreciate. Who wants to go out with a wimp?" I smiled.

The crisis was over, Jason was gone, and Michael was back in control.

Dylan appeared looking sheepish and apologising for sending Jason up. He said he done it to get rid of him for me, that he knew if Jason saw me with Michael, he would get the hint I wasn't interested, he had no idea Jason would react like that.

I knew he didn't do it to be malicious, he was just looking out for me because he knew I didn't ever want to go out with Jason.

I told him not to worry about it but to tell Mum that Jason had screamed bitch at me.

That would diminish her matchmaking between us.

Dylan was walking out the room when he stopped and turned to Michael. "You were awesome dude, no one should mess with you. That was pretty kick ass," he told him, admiration in his voice.

I knew Michael had a fan for life now.

Michael sat on my bed, reached over, and pressed play on my phone. He was looking through my playlists of which I had many; and commented that I had almost as much music than he did and he had a lot.

He put on Run and got up and came towards me. I was just standing staring at him, not moving.

He pulled me into his arms. "I love this song; dance with me my Angel."

I loved it when he called me his Angel; it made me feel wonderful.

We began to move slowly, entwined together. The scent of him was making me heady and I just melted into his chest.

He put his face down to mine and we gently touched heads; he placed both hands on either side of my face. I became breathless, forgetting how to exhale as his breath on my lips made my entire body tremble with anticipation. Was this it? Was he going to kiss me? I couldn't think straight; all I could think about was his lips so close to mine yet not quite touching.

Then he was gone. Gone before I even had time to realise it.

I stood on the same spot for a while, waiting as my breathing returned to normal and my heart slowed back down.

I still felt weak and sat on the floor until my legs were able to take my weight again.

As the fuzziness left my head, I lay back on the floor in total frustration and hit my palms against my legs. What was he doing to me? Tantalising me with his luscious lips, coming so close to pressing them to mine but always holding back. What was stopping him? I couldn't figure it out.

I lay and debated this topic for a while; going around in circles in my head not coming up with an answer, any answer.

I got up off the floor, sighing and walked over to my bed wondering when he would kiss me. There was a yellow post-it on my pillow and I picked it up. Written on it in beautiful, swirly handwriting were the words:

'When The Moment is Right'.

I was staring at it with total disbelief.

It was like he knew exactly what I would be thinking at the exact moment when I saw this note.

Wow, didn't quite cover it.

He was undeniably amazing. I didn't even see him write the note, and I never left the room; how could I have missed that? I didn't think I missed anything about him. I was overawed at him; and more than a little impressed. I held the note, smiling in wonder.

It was good to have an answer too, finally. I didn't know when the moment would be right and neither does he, but I knew the anticipation would be heart stopping; every time he comes close to me now, I will be searching for signs that it might be the right moment.

Like he didn't take my breath away enough already now it would be even more intense.

I lay across my bed hugging the note to myself, my heart soaring in total happiness, about to burst with excitement; my body tingling and my head filled with his image. It was the kind of feeling that only comes when you're truly alive… when someone brings you to life.

There was a knock at my door and my mum came in, she surveyed me lying on my messy bed holding a post-it.

I was aware of how this looked but I made no comment.

"Dylan told me about the incident with Jason earlier, I was all set to go over there. I am really angry. He had no right to call you vicious names regardless of who you were with," she said.

"Well, all I can say is he's lucky Michael was there or I might have seriously hurt him, Mum, but I knew even through my rage I couldn't use my powers in front of him," I told her.

"By all accounts it's Michael that could have hurt him. It's curious to me how a mortal could overpower a witch even if he wasn't using his power." My mother missed nothing.

"He's very strong, Mum," I said. "Plus, I think Jason was taken by surprise too."

She looked at me, no not looked, studied. Searching to see if I was hiding something. Which I was, I knew now Michael was some form of supernatural.

"I think he might be supernatural, Mum; he has gifts that humans don't have and he suspects I am too. We talked about it today but we didn't actually tell each other anything." I just decided to tell her, no point trying to hide it because it will come out eventually.

"What gifts does he have?" she asked me.

Something, and I wasn't sure what, held me back from telling her because I knew she would look it up in the book and she might find something, something I was avoiding. I wasn't ready to know quite yet. At the same time, I didn't care what he was. I was in love with him; absolutely and hopelessly in love with him.

"I don't know the full extent of his gifts yet and I don't care."

"How can you not care? What if he's in the Grimoire? Nice creatures do not land in the evil section of the book, Angelica." She used my full name, something she hardly ever does except in certain situations.

"Because I'm in love with him, Mum, alright. I am in love with him and it doesn't matter to me who or what he is, and he is in love with me. Don't you think that if he was evil and wanted me dead, I would be by now? I mean it's not like he hasn't had plenty of opportunities to kill me. We just want to be together. Is that a crime?" I was animated saying this.

"It isn't a crime but it could be dangerous. You really should find out," she said to me quietly. She didn't try to lecture me; she seemed to know she was beaten. She sat down next to me and gave me a hug instead. I was surprised, I really expected her to voice some opinion on how fast it had happened and tell me not to be silly that I couldn't possibly be in love with him this quickly. However, weirdly she didn't. She looked at the note in my hand for a second then left my room.

I got changed for bed completely tired out from the day's activities. Somewhere between that and getting water I had to kill a demon.

He appeared on the stairs when I was on my way from getting a bottle from the fridge.

I just shook my head and threw a destruction ball at him; I really couldn't be bothered finding out what he was up to. It was over in seconds and I trudged back to my room.

I had just got under the duvet and put the light out when my mobile vibrated with a text. My heart leapt and I picked the phone up. It was from Michael:

'sweet dreams baby. I miss you more than you know. You have no idea how much I wish I was with you now. xxx'

I was thrilled he had text, and grinning stupidly to myself I text him back telling him I missed him too and wished he was lying next to me.

It didn't take me long to fall asleep. I dreamt of kissing Michael and it was amazing.

When I woke in the morning and remembered the dream, I knew the real thing would far surpass anything I could ever dream.

I got to uni and turned into the parking lot and saw him straight away, he was hard to miss, leaning elegantly next to his car; pale and spectacular with the morning light catching the gleam of his jet-black hair.

I caught my breath. Would I ever get used to how beautiful he was? He was wearing black trousers and a black cashmere jumper with blacked out aviators. He looked cool and classy. Which he was.

He opened my car door and helped me out pulling me into his embrace tightly and burying his face in my hair like we hadn't seen each other in a week. I was surprised at his eagerness, he usually took his time. Not that I was complaining.

He pressed me against my car with his body so I couldn't move; he removed his sunglasses and looked into my eyes, dazing me.

"I missed you so much, I don't know how I'm going to be without you every night," he said closing his lilac eyes briefly.

"I don't know how I'm going to do it either. Yesterday when you were in my bed holding me it felt so right that I wanted you never to leave," I said touching his face gently.

He put his face to my hair, gently tipping my head back and slid his mouth around to my neck.

He trailed the width of my throat with his lips and kissed my collarbone so softly I thought I'd imagined it.

I stood motionless not wanting to move for fear it would break the connection of his sensuous lips from my skin.

His lips slid back up my throat and came to rest under my jaw, pressing his lips tight against me, his pale hands in my hair holding the back of my head.

I had never felt anything this intense and my whole body was trembling with desire for this glorious creature.

He pulled his lips away and let my head go, looking at me with a mixture of pain and desire on his flawless face. I was sure our expressions matched.

"I wasn't intending to do that but the impulse completely overwhelmed me," he said, his silky voice thick. "Your heartbeat is telling me you didn't want me to stop."

"I didn't want you to stop; not ever." My voice was still breathless.

"Perhaps you and I should keep ourselves amongst lots of people that way we have to behave." His voice was lighter now. "Come on, temptress, I will walk you to class." He took my hand.

"You call me a temptation? You can make people hyperventilate just by walking past them," I told him.

He shot me a look of bemusement at my statement, like I was exaggerating. Surely, he had to be at least a little aware of the effect he had on others.

Sally was wide eyed when she saw us walking along and holding hands. Michael left me at the door saying he will meet me outside the café at lunchtime. With one quick touch to my cheek, he was away.

I walked into the class and felt like everyone was staring at me… no, *I knew* everyone was staring at me. Michael was so mysterious and intimidating looking he captured people's imagination.

As soon as I sat down, Sally was all over me for details.

"So you and Michael De Marco then?" she asked.

"Looks that way," I answered vaguely.

"I was going to tell you what a great night you missed in the union on Friday but by the looks of this it was everyone else that missed the great night. How and when did this happen?" She was bursting to know the details.

"It just happened. It started on Friday, escalated on Saturday and was cemented on Sunday." That's all she was getting, no way was I giving her details; it was private.

"So it's serious then? I am so jealous of you, he is like the most gorgeous guy I've ever seen." Her envy was plain, it was written all over her face.

I just smiled and turned away.

"Did you sleep with him?" A beat. "You must have slept with him… I would sleep with him in a heartbeat… I bet he is *amazing* in bed, you can just tell in the way he moves or something… you are so lucky." She finally stopped for breath and thankfully the professor started to speak.

I could feel her staring at me throughout the whole class; wanting to be told every single detail. She was going to be disappointed because I wasn't telling her anything else.

The morning past quickly, mostly because I was drifting away thinking of Michael. The post-it was in my purse and I took it out periodically to look at it dreamily.

I sat writing Angel loves Michael in my notebook and I didn't even care if it was childish.

I dropped my mediocre essay off on my way to the café. My stomach was doing flip-flops at seeing Michael and my heart was fluttering in my chest.

Michael was waiting for me when I got there and my heart quickened.

He smiled at me and took my book bag off of me.

I looked into his eyes and thought this is the universe; this was divine intervention we be together.

We sat with Sally and the others, listening to them talk about Friday night and talking about everyone who was there. They all seemed uncomfortable to be sitting so close to Michael, their eyes darted to him every now and then and back to the table, avoiding eye contact. It didn't seem to bother him. He was obviously used to people not knowing how to act around him. Sally on the other hand was practically drooling on his arm, a fact he barely noticed but then again why would he? His wardrobe was probably filled with the drool from a thousand girls.

Neither of us joined in their mind-numbing conversations; having no interest in silly gossip and endless bitching about people.

We had better things to be going on with, but at least sitting with them stopped us from getting carried away as we sat holding hands over the table and staring at each other.

I knew it hadn't escaped anyone's attention that we didn't stop looking at each other; the heat between us was almost tangible.

I had no afternoon classes so I was going to a kickboxing class in the university's sports hall. Michael came with me to watch.

I was a black belt; having learned the skill at an early age and I loved it. It was one of my favourite things to do plus it was a great way to relieve some pent-up frustration and I had that by the bucket load.

I was very aware of Michael watching me from the back of the class. Mostly I worked on the martial arts training dummy, I had the same one in our gym at home and it lights up whenever you kick or punch key spots.

I didn't miss a single one as I let rip on it, feeling some release from the tension in my body.

Michael walked me to my car after kickboxing. "When did you learn to do that?" he asked with admiration in his voice. "That was some serious moves you had there. I don't fancy going hand to hand combat with you."

"I learned when I was a child and just honed my skill over the years," I answered smiling. "Something tells me you have no need of martial art skills."

"And you do?" he asked arching his eyebrows.

"No," I answered honestly.

"I didn't think so." He was looking carefully at me.

We reached my car and as he turned to face me. I was so acutely aware of him the fire he ignited in me was boiling my body.

His class was starting in five minutes so I knew he had to rush off now.

He turned to leave and I opened my car door more than a little disappointed I wouldn't see him till tomorrow.

He pulled me back around, leaned into my ear, and whispered, "Drive safe, beautiful, I won't stop thinking of you." He put his lips to my neck and placed a gentle kiss on it.

He lifted his head and so quickly I wasn't prepared for it, his lips brushed mine, so lightly I could have imagined it.

Then he was gone.

I knew I didn't imagine it because I could feel the burning hot sensation where his lips, albeit fleetingly, had grazed mine.

I stood there dazed for a long time, with my fingers to my lips, just staring at the spot where he had been standing.

I was so taken aback at him doing that, I was in bits.

My head was spinning and I actually felt a bit faint. I could only imagine the kind of state I would be in when he kissed me properly.

If this is how I reacted to a simple brief lip graze then the real thing was going to send me spiralling into an abyss.

I drove home in a trance, not really aware of actually driving but knowing I must be because the car was moving.

When I walked into my house, my mum was looking at me, wondering no doubt, if I actually *was* taking drugs.

I had to give myself a shake but I didn't want to; I was enjoying this feeling, it was wonderful. Just when I thought Michael couldn't possibly affect me in any more ways, here I was with a new one.

I lay on my bed and listened to music with my note next to me, just re-living how his lips felt in that brief second they were on mine.

I spent hours fantasising what his real, full on kisses will be like, how it will feel to tangle my hands in his hair as he kisses me with passion.

I didn't even know how long I spent in my daydream until I looked at the clock and it was bedtime.

I changed for bed and got under my duvet just as my phone rang. It was Michael. My heart started its usual racing whenever anything Michael-esque happened. I answered it with a smile. "Hi."

"Have you recovered yet?" he asked me laughing.

"How did you know I was in recovery?" I asked him.

"I saw you from the window, the class I was in overlooks the car park. It was never my intention to render you incapacitated; I simply could not help myself." His silky voice was low and seductive.

"Well, you took me by surprise, I really was not expecting it; not with your anti-kissing rules," I said, not even remotely embarrassed he had seen my reaction.

"It was very sweet, Angel. I'm flattered I have such an extreme effect on you, it means I must be doing something right."

"I miss you," was all I said.

"Baby, I miss you too, all I do is think about you and want to be with you. It is incredibly difficult I had no idea anything could be this difficult." His silky voice had an edge of frustration to it now.

"I cannot wait till Saturday to be completely alone with you, no interruptions and no one to bother us." I sighed wistfully.

"Hmm perhaps you should also feel some trepidation at being with me so completely alone, Angel. I told you I am dangerous and you should feel some fear of that," he said seriously.

"I'm not afraid of you," was all I replied stubbornly to that.

"What am I going to do with you girl? You are impossible," he said frustrated.

I laughed cheekily, my voice dripping with innuendo. "I'm sure you have a few ideas Mr De Marco."

"Go to sleep you little minx, I will see you tomorrow." He hung up the phone quickly.

I lay in the dark grinning to myself that I had rattled his cool control; not something I imagined ever happened often.

I fell asleep and dreamt of Michael and rose gardens surrounded by ominous purple skies and woke in the morning feeling restless.

The whole day at Uni was a complete turnaround; Michael kept his distance, not allowing his body to get too close to mine.

My hand brushed against his arm in the café, and he tore it away like he had been burnt.

I was upset wondering what I had done to annoy him. When I spoke to him his answers were short; usually one worded, and every time I looked at his face it was unreadable, but his eyes… his eyes were very wrong.

On Wednesday things only got worse and I was getting really scared that he was going to break up with me.

He sat nowhere near me at the lunchroom table and barley looked at me and when he did, he just looked furious.

I noticed his eyes were a deep; with none of the softness in them he was capable of. They were hard, and deep with some hidden need. He looked in pain. Even his skin looked paler than usual.

I was going over in my head what I could have done to make him look at me like this way, but I couldn't think of anything.

By the end of the day, I was avoiding him. I didn't want to see the rage directed at me anymore; it was too heart wrenching.

I walked to the car park alone, not going to meet him outside the English building like I usually did.

If he wanted to dump me then he could bloody well come and find me.

I had just opened my car door when he appeared next to me.

I didn't say anything; I just looked at him with tears in my eyes, feeling like there was a real wound I was bleeding from.

He stared at me with real pain on his gorgeous face, his forehead and eyes creasing with undisguised torture.

His now, Amethyst eyes held mine as he kept his arms to his sides so he wouldn't touch me by accident, and his voice, when he spoke, was deeper than I had ever heard it, like it was sore just trying to talk.

"I am so sorry, Angel; I am a total bastard and there is no excuse for my behaviour the last two days, it is more than unacceptable. I am just going through something, which is testing my endurance to the limit, and it seems I overestimated how strong I could be."

"Michael, if you want to break it off with me, just say it please. I can't stand this. It is noticeably clear you don't want to be around me so just tell me now and let me go home," I said, not even angry; just feeling like my heart was going to break.

"Is that what you think? That I don't want to see you anymore? Oh, my Angel nothing could be further from the truth. How could you ever believe that?" He put his pale hands on my arms now.

"The way you've been acting for a start, and I guess on some level I never believed it made sense for you to want to stay with me," I said sadly, looking down at my feet as a tear came down my cheek.

He put his hand under my chin and lifted my face up; wiping my tears away with a soft cool stroke. "I am such an idiot, please forgive me. I want nothing more than to be with you. It's just I have been torn between my natural instincts, and my desire to keep you safe, to not hurt you; that's why I haven't been touching you." He shook his head. "Now I realise I didn't have to worry because I couldn't hurt you, not ever, no matter what my nature dictates about how close you are to me when I'm like this." He looked at me with so much love on his flawless face and pulled me into his arms, crushing me to him like he was afraid I would run away.

His face was in my hair, kissing my head over and over. "I would never hurt you; I will spend eternity keeping you safe."

I wasn't sure if he was talking to me or to himself but either way, I was relieved. I could feel the tension leave my body as I surrendered to his needful embrace.

After a while he let me go and we sat on the grass next to my car. He looked at me for a few minutes, then started to speak, "I won't be in uni tomorrow, or Friday Angel I have to go away with my brother for a couple of days, but I will be back for our date on Saturday, nothing could keep me away from that."

"Where are you going?"

"We go on hunting trips every couple of weeks," he said searching my face.

"Oh," was all I said.

"Promise me while I'm away you will be careful and not do anything reckless like parachute out of a plane or anything." He laughed. "Seriously though, I don't want you in any dangerous situations when I'm too far away to protect you; I will be worrying about you," he said; his expression grim.

"I promise I will not deliberately put myself in harm's way," I said, touched that he wanted to be my knight in shining Armani.

"OK then, I will trust you to keep your word. I will miss you though," he said looking at me with the strange purple eyes.

"I better let you leave then; I don't want your brother mad at me for keeping you back."

We stood up just as it began to rain, and he opened my car door for me, we gazed at each other, and he moved towards me.

I reached up and swept his hair with my hands luxuriating in its softness and texture. He closed his eyes with pleasure and let out a sigh.

As he opened his eyes, I could see hunger in them, and he leaned in very very slowly and placed his lips on mine then pulled away.

It wasn't a proper kiss, but it was longer than the brief quarter of a second of Monday's lip brush and my heart almost stopped, my body shaking, reacting to the feel of his lips against mine.

"I do believe your heart is skipping some beats," he said smiling.

Sometimes I hated that he could hear my heart; I could never hide anything I was feeling because of it.

The rain was really coming down hard now and Michael told me to get in my car, so I didn't get soaked and then he disappeared. His Lamborghini was parked behind me at the back of the car park, and I looked around and saw he was already inside it. How did he get to it so quickly?

I sat for a few minutes just thinking about him and the mystery surrounding him. Something was niggling at the back of my mind, the same something that had been since I met him, the little voice that told me to check the book.

If he was in the book, what then? Would it really change how I felt about him? No. I knew it would not; I had crossed that line a while ago.

I just sat and watched the rain come down on my windshield and let the noise of it hitting my roof drown out the little voice.

The waiting and wondering was almost over... I was about to find out his secret.

Chapter Seven

The Truth

I eventually started the engine. A song came on my cd player that I hadn't been listening to when I drove here this morning.

It wasn't even my cd. What was going on? I listened to the song; it was called *Love Bites*. I loved the song but still couldn't figure out how it got in my car. Until I heard the chorus. It was about someone scared to get too close to the person they loved because it could all end very badly. I repeated the song title over and over in my head, *Love Bites*... love bites as it began to swim, the scenery around me swaying before my eyes and the cold icy hand of fear griping at my insides as waves of reality crashed over me telling me what my subconscious had known all along.

I was stunned. I could feel the emotions in me bubbling over and I wanted to cry. Michael was telling me, through the medium of music, exactly how he was feeling, and his fears of our relationship and that he loved me.

He was also telling me love bites in a much different way than I'm sure the song was ever intended.

The tears fell silently down my cheeks as I listened to the song again.

Words from our Grimoire was flashing through my mind...

Speed, strength, agility, beautiful, heightened senses, vivid eye colour, pale skin.

It was at that exact moment I finally admitted what Michael was.

A vampire.

I closed my eyes, powerful emotions overwhelming me. I was in love with a vampire. The repercussions of this were not lost on me and I knew I was about to make a decision that would rock the magical world forever. It was out with my control, destiny had intervened.

I knew he was still there, watching me. Waiting for my reaction.

I threw open my car door and went running across the lot towards him, tears streaming down my face in violent succession.

He was next to me in an instant and I hurtled myself into his arms.

His lips came crushing down onto mine in a no holds barred kiss, our hands gripped in the others hair; holding us tightly pressed together; turning around and around with the force of our bodies clashing together in urgency.

The tears were still streaming from my eyes as we kissed on and on, while the rain lashed heavily down on us.

It may not have been the perfect moment, but it was the right one.

When we finally stopped kissing, he put his hands on either side of my face looking at me in utter anguish, tears in his eyes. "I will spend forever doing nothing else but loving you; I promise you that."

"I love you, Michael," I said forcefully, kissing his face over and over.

"Oh, Angel, I love you too… you have no idea." He fastened his lips to mine again, kissing me harder than I had ever been kissed in my life.

My breathing was laboured, and my heart was close to just exploding in my chest. If I died at this moment, I would die happy.

He let me go, laughing, and said, "I think we better halt this now before you have a coronary. As much as I never want to stop kissing you like this, I would rather not have you collapse and die."

As soon as he let me go, I felt my legs give way and folded to the wet ground in a sitting position.

He sat down next to me looking at me affectionately as I tried to catch my breath.

"I don't want you to, but you should go soon Michael you need to feed. That's why you've been keeping your distance? It only happens when you're thirsty," I said looking into his hungry, purple eyes.

"Yes," he answered. "That's why I was afraid to come too close to you the last two days, I was afraid of losing control. I knew I would be all right so long as we were not actually touching or sitting too closely. I'm used to being around humans when it's nearing time to hunt but I've never had one so close to me in proximity as you are and never one with magical blood," he explained.

He smiled at me. "But I realised after we were at your car and standing so close together that it didn't matter, no matter how thirsty I am; I could never hurt you. I could have you in my arms with your throat exposed to me and I would never ever kill you. So, I guess I must be stronger than I thought." He shook his

71

head and looked at me perplexed. "How can you be so alright with this? I kill people and drink their blood, Angel."

I put my hand onto his wet face. "I don't care, Michael; I don't care what you are. I love you and that's all that matters. You're not evil, you kill to survive and I'm OK with that." My voice was insistent, and he shook his beautiful head in wonder at my total acceptance of who he was.

We were sat there in the rain, soaking wet like a couple of escaped mental patients and we didn't even notice, or would even care if we had.

If anyone was watching this whole scene, I couldn't even imagine what they would make of it, again I didn't care, because for me; this was the most intensely romantic moment in the history of the world. I hadn't even seen anything in a movie that would even come close to this.

Michael finally stood up and lifted me effortlessly to my feet as though I weighed no more than a sheet of paper. As I looked at him, standing there absolutely drenched through, his hair dishevelled, with water running off him and his wet top clinging to every contour of his hard chest; he was simply... glorious.

He quite literally took my breath away.

"I have to say, Angel, you look so incredibly tempting standing here in the rain, dripping wet. It is going to take me a lot to leave you here now, but I must, I have to hunt," he said with a regretful tone.

"I was just thinking the exact same thing about you," I said surprised how in tune we were.

"In that case I have a request, I get to kiss you in the rain again soon when I don't have to leave and perhaps under slightly less dramatic circumstances?"

"Absolutely, any time it's raining, feel free to come and get me." I laughed. I would kiss him during a tsunami if he asked me.

He put me in my car and leaned in to switch on my heater for me. It just occurred to me I had left my keys in my car, with the engine running and the door opened when I ran out to get Michael. Anyone could have easily stolen it.

I said this to Michael, and he just laughed and said no one would ever get further than six feet before he stopped the car.

He kissed me gently and told me he would miss me and reminded me I promised not to get into any dangerous situations, natural or supernatural while he was gone.

He turned to go back to his car, and I stopped him. "Michael? You knew I was a witch all along, huh?"

He just smiled and pointed to his nose and went into his car.

When I got home, I sat in my car for a while wondering how I was going to explain how wet and, undoubtedly, flushed I was.

I was sure without a shadow of a doubt my love for Michael would shine from me like a stadium light and it would be obvious to my family that something major had just happened between us and that I was altered forever.

I had gone from being Good Angel, to Fallen Angel in less than three hours.

The witch and the vampire, it goes against everything white Wicca is about and no one is going to be happy about it, not good or evil.

People like me do not get to choose their life; it is chosen for us at birth. We are brought up knowing we have a higher destiny to fulfil, that our powers are not just gifts, they are responsibilities that we have, to fight evil.

Falling in love with a vampire pretty much breaks every Wiccan rule there is.

There is no precedent for this so I have no way of knowing what the outcome of my actions will be.

As far as I was aware, this is the first time anything like this has ever happened since the dawn of witchcraft.

The Wiccan consul is the governing body of witches, they make sure no one misuses their magic or exposes magic, and they punish Wiccan rule breakers. In my opinion, their ways were seriously outdated and set too much in concrete, there was no room for evolution. Charles Darwin published *The Origin of the Species* in 1859, evolution by natural selection, and if the Wiccan consul did not evolve, they too would be unseated.

Not everything could be viewed as black or white, there were many grey areas; and not everything was clear-cut good or evil.

The Wiccan consul will have to decide what to do with me themselves since they have no point of reference, and I had no clue what they would do.

As far I was concerned, they could do their worst to me, nothing they could do to me would ever be worse than losing, Michael.

I remembered how my heart was breaking earlier just at the prospect he might break up with me. I didn't intend to fall in love with a vampire, but I knew if I ever lost him, I would be broken, irreparably and irreversibly broken, and this life would have no appeal left for me. My whole meaning for living would be over. Higher purpose or not.

So how much did they expect me to give up for the greater good? If fighting for the greater good meant having to give up the one truly pure thing in my life, then it wasn't so great or so good in my eyes and they could shove it.

I decided to transport into my room, change my clothes and go for a drive, that way maybe everyone would be in bed when I got home.

No such luck, there was demon fight going on downstairs and I didn't know who was home so I had to go and help.

I transported down and it was chaos. Demons everywhere throwing some form of red liquid from their hands that was like acid. It was only my brother and sister fighting them, my parents weren't there.

I jumped behind a couch as one of them attacked me with it and watched half the couch disappear. This was not good; we were outnumbered and who knew if that red crap would burn through our protection shield? I didn't care to test it.

I was throwing demons left, right, and centre across the room, with my mind because I had to keep my hands free to blast them.

My sister's light bolts were not even fazing them and the spell to paralyse them didn't work they seemed to be immune to it.

I tried to blast a couple and that didn't work either. My brother managed to take a couple out with destruction balls but there was a lot more of them coming at us.

I was using telekinesis to divert red stuff from my sister as I told her to see what potions we had and look in the book.

My brother yelled at me to divert the red stuff towards the demons, so every time I saw some, I threw it right at a demon. It worked, they melted. There was lots of red stuff coming at us and I managed to divert all of it, while my brother took out the rest with destruction balls.

Finally, it was over but the whole downstairs looked like a bombsite.

My sister was looking them up in the book, while I was making the room tidy itself, but that did not fix the half-melted furniture, so Dylan said a spell that restored the room and everything in it.

It was a spell written by some long-ago ancestor and it was a good thing they did, otherwise all our time would be spent doing nothing but shopping for new furniture.

"Have you found them yet?" I asked Kennedy.

"Yeah."

"Let me see it, I am going to take out the rest of those red acid throwing freaks if it's the last thing I do."

I had already broken my promise to Michael about staying away from danger so I should beautifully finish the job.

"It says they are immune to a lot of which powers; you're not kidding; but at least we know they are defenceless against telekinesis and destruction balls so all we need to do is make a batch of kick ass destruction ball potion and go get them." My tone was one that no one was going to argue with.

"Why are you all wet?" Dylan asked me amused.

"It's a long story but the short version is Michael and I got caught in the rain." That's all they were getting told.

"You are positively glowing, Angel," Kennedy observed as we made the potion.

"I'm in love, babe, and that's what happens, you glow," I said happily, I was unable to keep the smile from spreading across my face and even though we were demon fighting I thought I would burst with joy.

"Did someone phone the parentals to come home? No way are we taking on these particular demons short-handed," Kennedy asked.

"Yeah, I called them; they should be here about now," Dylan answered.

My mum and dad transported into the room, and we filled them in as they looked at the book.

We debated whether it could be a trap or not as we filled potion bottles and decided it didn't matter because we had enough firepower and potions to take hundreds of them out.

My dad decided it was safest if he transported to their lair invisible to get a look at how many there were, so we weren't going in blind.

When he came back, he told us there was about one hundred and fifty of them.

No problem.

Dad and Kennedy took the potions since Mum, Dylan and I could all throw destruction balls.

We transported to their sceezy lair, and they were all surprised. Good to know since that meant it wasn't a trap and they were unprepared. We split up around the room, so we had every angle covered and just started taking them out before they knew what was happening to them.

I stuck to making their own red stuff hit them, while Mum and Dylan threw destruction balls, and Dad and Kennedy were throwing the potions.

It was all over in about ten minutes, and we didn't even have a scratch on us.

I was so tired when we got home that I went right to bed. I couldn't sleep though because I couldn't stop re-living the kiss with Michael, not to mention thinking about the fact that he is a vampire.

I finally fell asleep at 3 am resolving to think about it at leisure when I got up since I had decided to skip uni.

Right now, education seemed very insignificant to me.

When I woke up, I knew I had to read what the book had to say about vampires. I had to know everything now.

I climbed the stairs to the loft, which was the place where we kept not only the book at a protected alter, but also where we kept all our Wiccan gadgets and materials like potion ingredients, steel bowls to make them in, vials for storing them, spell casting candles and incense, sacred drinking goblets and other important ritual things.

We also kept trunks filled with demon's clan symbols and weapon leftovers up there and had trunks for ancient powerful Wicca weapons that can kill evil.

I approached the book with trepidation, wondering what I would in find there. Usually, I loved spending time in the loft, surrounded by my family's magical inheritance, but today I just felt conflicted. I was about to read about the person I loved in my magical book. If anything was going to cause some anxiety it was that.

I picked up the huge, heavy black book, sat in the rocking chair, took a deep breath and opened it to the vampire section and began to read.

Vampires are blood drinking immortal creatures with super strength, and incredible speed and agility, they can move and fly faster than the speed of light, making them invisible to the naked eye. They have incredibly heightened senses such as hearing, smell, sight, and hyper awareness. Their instincts are second to none, and they have unparalleled senses. Most of them have extra gifts, usually involving powers of the mind like telekinesis, mind control, mind-tracking capabilities, seeing the future, telepathy, and strong mind reading abilities. There is a power known as vampire magic, called such because they can seduce humans into doing what they want. It is the power of persuasion.

Vampires have no vulnerabilities or weaknesses and cannot be killed except by another vampire.

There is however, a sacred dagger that was fashioned by a vampire hunter in the fifteenth century, which is said to be the only weapon known to be able to kill a vampire. Anyone using this dagger would still have to have powerful gifts in order to get close enough to attack the vampire; even then, it is unlikely they would succeed. The dagger is said to be passed down to the sons of the hunter who made it but would need to be blessed by a powerful witch before they could use it.

Vampires are inhumanly beautiful with pale, cool skin, flawless bodies and vivid eye colour that occurs when they are thirsty for blood.

They are usually extremely charismatic, graceful in movement, elegant and sophisticated and they are extremely sexual, having many vampire partners throughout their eternity, but once a vampire falls in love, they mate for life and this union is sacred.

They are governed by rules they must follow, and a higher body of vampires, known as the immortal leaders, are the ones that punish any vampires who break these rules. It is not known all the rules they must follow, but some include keeping their secret at all costs, which would involve no hunting or obvious vampire behaviour in the daylight hours, never falling in love with a mortal unless they are willing to turn them and no killing another vampire without having good reason.

Vampires are unstoppable killing machines, extremely feared by all magical creatures and mortals alike, and who, if they so wished could take over the underworld due to their indestructibility and the fact they are more powerful than any other species on earth. However, they chose to live above ground among humans and usually have jobs, houses, and cars, picking their hunting grounds nowhere near, where they live and work.

Vampire teeth are deadly; the teeth are incredibly strong and can tear a limb or head off as easily as ripping out a throat. Vampires in a fight can simply slide their teeth across their opponent and it would dismember them instantly.

Contrary to many myths and legends, a vampire must be sired, either by being born to vampires or being turned by one.

Transforming into a vampire can only be done with a vampire bite, it is a blood exchange, the mortal and vampire will drink each other's blood until the mortal's heart stops beating, then they awake a vampire. This is commonly known as an 'immortal kiss' as it is termed in vampire circles due to the warmth and pleasure both parties feel doing this bond.

This is done by using their retractable fangs when extended. Once retracted, a simple bite would not turn a mortal into a vampire as they have not transfused both sets of blood. Their fangs extend only when a vampire is ready to bite, the preferred spot vampires used for feeding is the carotid artery but to turn a mortal the bite can be placed anywhere that doesn't have a major artery, although the base of the neck at the collarbone is usually the popular choice.

Once bitten, the change is said to take a few hours for the new vampire to awaken, in which the unconscious human goes through the change.

New vampires known as cubs, awaken to what is called sordoinia, which is the transcendence into vampirism, and the ensuing struggle to master the beast and balance opposing urges and principles. cubs must always be supervised so as not to let their new powerful blood lust get out of control.

It is undetermined how long it takes a cub to control their bloodlust.

Vampires need blood to survive and can feed on both human and animal blood. Human blood is preferable but animal blood works just as well.

They are not inherently evil and only kill to survive, defend, or avenge, not for sport, however they are never to be underestimated because they will kill any witches that attempt to stop them, and a witch's blood holds a lot of appeal for them.

There is also a section of certain vampires who are known as roamers, these vampires have no family ties, no blood ties and no coven to belong to and roam the world killing whoever crosses their path. This particular species are vile, disgusting killers that have no shred of goodness and will do a great evil just for the sake of it. They have no shred of their previous humanity and behave more like demons.

There are no defences against any vampire attack, and everything said is myth or speculation.

Some vampire myths include…

They are unable to walk on consecrated ground.

They cannot enter a church.

They live in graveyards.

They cannot enter a house unless invited.

They cannot go out in sunlight because it will kill them.

They turn into bats.

Garlic repels them.

Holy water and crosses will hurt them.

They can be killed using a wooden stake to the heart.

They are vulnerable to silver, especially bullets.

They sleep in coffins during daylight.

They have no reflection or shadow.

None of these myths hold true; vampires can go anywhere and do anything humans can which makes them harder to spot.

They are very human in their appearance and emotions, with most turned vampires retaining shreds of their previous humanity even though they are no longer mortal and have more power than can be determined to an exact.

There are certain vampires who, if born to two immortal parents, are more powerful than most others.

Their birth right makes them second only to vampire royalty and as such an ancient law was passed where the immortal leaders were not allowed to kill them unless absolutely necessary.

Any vampire born to two immortal parents at midnight on the eve of a new millennium is said to be Lumia Regius, which is Latin for vampire royalty, usually being known as prince or princess. These vampires are the most powerful of the species, with a direct lineage to the throne, making them destined, if they so wish, to rule all other vampires.

Their power over the immortal leaders is absolute and they cannot be killed by them or overruled by them.

This birth right is called fedictus and is sacred to all vampires and as such, they are revered by their kind.

I was impressed by the vampire world despite my Wiccan ways, yes, I understood that they killed humans, but it was done for survival, and they rarely turned a human unless asked to do so by the human.

Humans kill animals to survive, and animals kill other weaker animals for the same purpose. It was Darwinian, the evolution of life, survival of the fittest.

Humans can't stand that vampires are higher up on the food chain than them, that there was a superior species that were smarter and stronger than they were.

Much the same way, witches are scorned as make-believe stories.

Humans kill animals not just for food, but for sport, fashion and decoration whereas a vampire only kills to survive.

Why does that make them worse in the moral high ground stakes then? You never see vampires wearing human skin for fashionable purposes, they do not hunt humans and call it sport, and they do not keep human heads mounted on the walls of their houses, as humans do with animals.

Yet it is vampires that are forced to hide who they are.

I sat for hours pondering these facts, harsh facts most people would never admit to.

I didn't fool myself into believing that all vampires were good but nor did I believe they were all bad. Even the book said most were not inherently evil. They could cause utter havoc and destruction, but they didn't.

I thought of Michael and his complete anguish at the thought of harming me, trying to distance himself away from me because he was thirsty and fighting against his nature to kill me and drink my blood.

My eyes filled with tears at how much I loved him, how even though he was a vampire he made me feel safer than I had ever felt in my life.

I was happy he had the inner peace of knowing now that he could never hurt me; that must have been an awful lot of torture for him; I could only imagine the horror of going through that.

I thought about how he tried to stay away from me, even though he had fallen in love with me and how he kept warning me not to be with him because he thinks he is a monster.

He was always putting my needs above his own, never wanting me to be anything but safe and he would have allowed me to walk away from him, even though it would have broken his heart to lose me in order to keep me safe, to be with someone a lot less dangerous.

Michael wasn't a monster in my eyes. He was my saviour, he rescued me, and my life only became truly worthwhile when I met him. My magical destiny paled in comparison.

I looked in the book for other ways to become immortal. I figured if the answer was anywhere, it would be in our book but there was nothing that didn't bring me back to the vampire entry.

My parents came in then, and I quickly shut the book so they wouldn't see I was reading about vampires.

"What are you reading, Angel?" my father asked mildly.

"Nothing in particular, Dad, I just felt like some peace and quiet," I said in what I hoped was a normal tone. "What are you two doing up here?"

"We're going to make some potions, we're running a bit low, and with all the demon attacks around here we don't want to run out," my mum said eyeing me suspiciously.

"Oh, right, well you better take the book then. I'm going for a hot bath unless you want me to help?" I asked hoping they would say no because I wanted to be alone. I had a lot to think about.

They did say no and told me to go and enjoy my bath.

I went to my bathroom and ran the hot water. I got my phone speakers and put them next to the bath.

When it was full, I got in and put on my Bon Jovi playlist, I was in serious need of Jon's voice tonight.

I lay there thinking about my vampire.

I knew I should be more concerned that I was in love with a vampire, but I just could not find the guilt or fear over it that any other person would. I was well aware of how wrong it all was in the eyes of the magical community, but I just could not bring myself to care. If loving him was wrong, then I never *ever* wanted to be right. I chuckled; I was turning into a cliché with statements like that but it fit.

How can the way I feel when I'm in his arms or when he is near me, ever be wrong? when he kissed me, oh… when he kissed me, the whole world stopped spinning. Who could ask for more than to live in a moment they would be willing to die for?

To say I love him more than the whole universe was a serious understatement.

My phone buzzed and I looked at it. It was a text from Michael and my heart crashed wildly.

I hope you aren't doing anything dangerous. I miss you. xxx

I texted him back.

Unless you consider hot bubble baths to be particularly hazardous then I am most definitely not doing anything dangerous. I miss you too. xxx

He replied to me a minute later.

Sleep tight Angel, I love you. xxx

I smiled dreamily and text him that I loved him too. I put my mobile back down and layback with my eyes closed and sang along to music.

On Friday, I spent the day looking at my clothes, wondering what I should wear for the big date the next day.

Nothing seemed right because I had no idea what he had planned. My stomach was in knots and my heart was.

Michael text me when I was in bed and told me he would pick me up at 6 pm. My heart missed a few beats, I could not wait.

Chapter Eight

The Date

I awoke on Saturday so hyper about seeing Michael and being completely alone with him, that I thought I might need a tranquiliser or an ambulance. Either way I had to try to calm down to a small frenzy.

I spent forty minutes in the shower, just letting the water cascade over my head and trying to breathe evenly.

My mum came in about an hour later, with a dozen long stemmed red roses that had just been delivered for me.

The card read, about love, the truth and what you mean to me.

It was a line from *Bed of Roses*.

I got such a head rush that I thought I was going to pass out.

Once again, he had successfully overawed me.

It took me an age to do my make-up because my hands were shaking so much. Luckily, I had allowed myself plenty of time to get ready because I kept smudging my eyeliner.

I couldn't stop thinking about kissing him again, the mere thought of it was making me warm and dizzy.

He was like a drug to me, only much more potent and much more addictive. I giggled at the thought of going to an addicts meeting and saying, "Hi, my name is Angel and I'm addicted to a vampire." Maybe they do vampire medication that helps wean you off your habit. I was laughing at my own silliness now. I was probably a bit hysterical with nerves and excitement.

By the time six o'clock came, I was jumping out of my own skin at every little thing.

I made my way downstairs, my legs shaking and my heart racing like a 747 at take-off.

I opened my front door and there he was gorgeous and classy, sitting casually on the bonnet of his Lambo and holding a single long stemmed red rose.

I literally forgot how to exhale as my heart almost stopped at the sight of him; my memories didn't do him justice; he was a masterpiece.

He came towards me slowly, as if he were not quite sure how to approach me, almost like he was afraid to startle me. His eyes searched mine for signs I wasn't sure about him.

He held out the rose and just simply said, "I missed, you my Angel, you are devastating me with how beautiful you look."

I took the rose from him and locked onto his gaze; his eyes the vivid, stunning lilac shade that captured my soul. I inhaled his scent that nobody could recreate and bottle.

He was breath-taking in a tailor-made black suit with a white shirt that he wore with no tie and a few buttons undone at the collar.

It was sexy and sophisticated and showing to perfection his unbelievable body.

"Forever starts now," he whispered, his eyes were fiercely beautiful and deadly serious.

I threw my arms around his neck and pressed my body into his; he buried his face in my hair and inhaled my scent, holding me in a vice like grip; sighing in relief that nothing and everything between us has changed.

He picked me up in his strong arms and twirled me around and around until we were both laughing.

He put me down and as we walked to the car, I saw the curtains move in one of the downstairs windows. I shook my head in amusement because I knew my whole family were trying to sneaky peek and failing miserably since I caught them.

We drove away, staring at each other in wonder.

I was curious where we were going as he shifted the powerful car and hit the motorway.

"So are you going to tell me what we're doing tonight?" I asked him.

"No, why on earth would I do that?" he asked perplexed.

"So that I will know what to expect."

He laughed. "I don't want you to know what to expect, it ruins the mystery."

"Give me a hint then and I'll try and guess," I asked hopeful he would cave in and tell me.

"No, now stop it. I'm telling you nothing."

"OK, well, at least tell me where we're going."

"You are making it shockingly difficult to please you with a surprise, Angel. We'll be there soon, and you can see for yourself where we are." He looked at me like I was an impatient child.

I was impatient, I knew we wouldn't be going to a restaurant because I'm sure he was aware I wouldn't be able to choke any food down if my life depended on it, and he didn't eat food so that left... Well, things that don't involve food.

We were both dressed up so anywhere that involved casual clothing was out, bowling, ice-skating, and the movies.

What was left? I was out of ideas, and he wasn't telling me anything. I looked around we were on a busy motorway which told me nothing, but five minutes later I felt the car slow.

We were at a private airport turn off; this was weird why would he bring me here? Instead of getting less mysterious once we reached our destination this was getting more mysterious.

He didn't take the road to the car park; instead, he followed the roundabout straight through and went in the opposite direction.

Michael stopped the car at huge iron gates and a security officer came out. He pulled a plastic card out of his pocket, which I saw had the words security clearance on it, and handed it to the officer, who scanned it and opened the gates.

He drove inside and within a few minutes stopped the car outside an aircraft hangar building and got out, coming to open my door for me.

I looked around and saw a sleek gulf G5 and smaller red plane. Both aircraft were outside the hanger building but there were more inside. What was going on?

"Come on, impatient girl, we're going flying," he said taking my hand.

"What? Did you hire a plane?" I asked baffled.

"These planes belong to my family, and I am going to take you up in one of them. I wasn't sure which you would prefer so I gave you a choice." His voice was utterly casual, as if having a fleet of airplanes was the most normal thing ever.

"You can fly a plane?" I asked in surprise, although I don't know why I was as I was sure there wasn't much he couldn't do.

"Yes, Angel, I can fly a plane, I promise not send you plummeting to your death." His tone was amused. "So, which one would you like to go up in?" he asked as his arm waved towards both planes.

"Whatever one you think," I stammered, not being able to choose.

"OK, we'll leave the jet since we're not going far, and the smaller one is the best one to see everything. The jet is more for travelling, although I do have to admit flying you off to somewhere exotic had crossed my mind." His satin voice slid over my skin like the softest negligee.

I was so impressed I could barely speak; just when I thought he could not possibly get any sexier, he tells me can fly planes.

"I don't think I would have minded one bit if you flew me away somewhere," I managed to croak.

"Yes, but I may not have brought you back," he stated simply.

"I don't think I would mind that either." I looked into his beautiful eyes and was completely lost.

He helped me into the plane and got into the pilot's side, pressing buttons and lighting the board up. He spoke into his headset and told someone he was ready for take-off. My heart was hammering in excitement as he taxied the aircraft to a nearby runway and waited until a voice came over and told him he was cleared for take-off. This was it.

I was nervous and excited at the same time. I didn't know why I was nervous because it's not like I didn't trust him to fly the plane; yet my stomach was fluttering.

He revved the engine, and we were off like lightning, speeding down the runway and soaring into the air.

It was amazing and exhilarating and I couldn't ever remember feeling this free, this unencumbered and so completely alive.

I could not even begin to describe how sexy he looked handling an aircraft with such ease.

"I know you don't scare easy so I'm going to flip the plane," he told me, and before I could respond we were flying upside down and it felt insane to be moving whilst looking at the ground from the wrong way around.

He started doing figure of eights and then making the plane vertical and dive bombing towards the ground and pulling back up at the last second, it was better than any rollercoaster ever invented, and I was screaming in total delight and complete abandonment.

He was enjoying my pleasure and was watching my face with his eyes wide and alert not wanting to miss a moment. "You look so delectable with your cheeks flushed like that," he said smiling.

After a while, he levelled the plane off and we flew around, looking at the scenery and talking about what it was like to be a vampire and a witch. "I knew you were a witch from the fist second we met." I looked at him questioningly and he went on, "Your blood is different to a human, its richer, more powerful and almost irresistible."

I laughed. "Almost?"

He grinned at me. "The loving you part makes it almost."

"Good thing I've never bumped into a vampire who didn't love me then," I joked.

His amethyst eyes went dark. "I will kill any vampire who even thinks about drinking your blood, I would rip them apart piece by piece."

I remained quiet since there was a distinct possibility that situation may arise.

He was showing me landmarks of where we were, and he pointed out his house. It was an old gothic-style castle it looked romantic and spooky all at the same time.

It had an actual moat and drawbridge and had turrets and towers and huge windows. It was massive.

It was beautiful in an old worldly kind of way and captured my imagination of a time long ago when historical figures were alive, and I could easily see William Wallace or Robert the Bruce spending time in it, making love to beautiful maidens, planning attacks and fighting for Scotland's freedom.

"Wow, Michael, it is so romantic looking and lovely," I said gaping at it.

I noticed people hanging about the roof, playing games with each other. "Is that your family?"

"No that's our guard."

"I didn't realise vampires needed guards."

"We don't, but we have them anyway because my birth right makes us royalty and as such must be guarded. It's a bit silly to me though because they never have to do anything." He shook his head.

The book was coming back to me as I remembered it saying vampires born on midnight on the eve of a millennium were royalty, making him was a prince.

"You're a Fedictus?" I asked him, wondering if he would ever stop surprising me. "Revered by all vampires and more powerful, with a birth right that gives you direct lineage to the throne." I waited a beat. "So you weren't born in the year 2000, which millennium *were* you born?"

He looked at me intently. "I was born in 1000, and I have no desire to take over and rule I'm perfectly happy leaving that to the immortal leaders. Your Grimoire must be truly knowledgeable, I am impressed," he said looking at me with surprise.

"Wow, you're over 1000 years old and yes, it is the most powerful magical book there is," I told him simply, "so there isn't much that isn't in it."

"So, it would seem. You are much more powerful than I imagined you to be." He looked at me evenly, not really surprised.

"Yes, I am the most powerful of our kind." I shrugged my shoulders and looked away, but I felt him study me for a few minutes wondering, no doubt, why I didn't sound pleased about that.

We flew around a while in silence, it was dark now and the lights below were stunning.

I loved to look at views at night when the city lights allowed you to dream as you got lost in them.

I realised that all my life I had been dreaming about one thing or another and feeling so resentful I couldn't have any of the things I wanted because of what I was.

Now I had this epic love, and it was better and more powerful than anything I could ever have dreamed up; that it was him I had been dreaming about all along and never even knew it. It made everything else I had wanted mean nothing.

I wanted him more than everything else I had ever dreamed combined and no one and nothing was going to take it from me, magic does not get to mess with this, not now and not ever.

"Prince Michael of Scotland," I said suddenly. "I like that a lot, it suits you very much."

"Thank you, I'm pleased you like it." He smiled that mesmerising smile and I found myself quite unable to catch my breath. The effect he had on me was going to kill me one of these days, but what a way to go.

I was mulling his age over, it was so hard to believe even for me. "In over a thousand years you never married, fell in love?"

He reached out and stroked my cheek softly. "Oh, I've been in what I thought was love many times, but not until you that day, did I finally feel a strange pull from within my chest or soul and I knew you were the one I had been waiting for."

I thought about that for a minute. "That means we have a purpose together besides this unequalled love we both feel."

He landed the plane and taxied to the hanger, and I was almost suicidal at the thought of the date being over, or at least the part of it where we were alone, because we would probably go to a club now.

Michael lifted me from my seat on the plane and kissed me as he put me to my feet, a gentle but firm kiss that had the promise of getting carried away into a passionate one. Which it did, as his hands ran up my back and into my hair and his body pressed me against the aircraft.

My whole body shivered as I gripped the back of his neck tightly and wound my hands into his luxurious hair, surrendering to the wonderful sensations flooding over me.

I wanted to stay right here with him, in this moment being kissed like this until the end of time.

Alas it was over as he pulled away and sighed. "As much as I hate to end this kiss, we have somewhere else to go tonight."

"What? I'm not sure my heart can withstand another of your surprises, this one was so mind-blowing you've already far surpassed yourself." I looked at him with amazement.

"Well, I'm not done yet so let's go co-pilot." He grabbed my hand and we got in his car.

Back on the motorway, I was still totally buzzing from the incredible flight and incredible kiss, I could barely keep still and kept fidgeting with my hair.

I knew better than to ask where we were going because he wouldn't tell me, but I couldn't help wondering what he had in store next.

"That was amazing, Michael, you continue to stun me senseless. Thank you for taking me flying; I loved it," I said still feeling breathless.

"I hope I will always stun you, baby; I want nothing more than to make you happy." He turned his amethyst gaze onto me, his silky voice was so full of sincerity it rendered my heart still.

"You make me happier than I ever dreamed was possible, Michael. I moment I met you, I stopped just existing and started living. You brought me to life; between the times when you say hello and goodbye, I understand why I live."

I was looking at him with unconcealed need now because I did need him; I needed him more than the oxygen I needed in order to breathe.

His gorgeous face was intense, his eyes bright with love. "You captured my soul the first second I heard your heartbeat. Eternity means nothing to me without you and if it were at all possible, I would become mortal for you and I would do it in minute. My love for you is so powerful and uncontrollable that it has a life of its own, I would do anything for you."

"I would do anything for you too, Michael, anything. I feel like I'm standing on the edge of a mountain that could give way any minute and yet somehow, I have never felt safer. I really want you to know that there isn't anything… anything at all that will ever break my faith in you." I reached over and stroked his dazzling face.

His eyes softened to molten liquid. "Your total trust and acceptance of all I am is heart-breaking and I will never let you down, never cause you a single moment that would make you regret your decision to be with me. I promise you that." He stroked my cheek gently and looked back at the road.

I noticed we were in the west end of Glasgow now and wondered again at where he was taking me, until he drove into Kelvin Grove Park and stopped the car.

This was weird; the park would be almost pitch black, was he forgetting I didn't have perfect night vision like he did?

As he took my hand and led me further into the dark deserted park he asked, "Are you afraid?"

"Only of getting lost," I answered flippantly.

He laughed. "You really are insane do you know that? There isn't a single other person in the world that wouldn't be afraid of walking into somewhere dark and deserted with a vampire."

"Well, the way I see it, if you're going to kill me there would be pretty much nothing I could do about it, plus you would have done it by now, and you certainly wouldn't have to wait till we were here. Besides having a vampire next to you is the best protection ever, I mean who in their right mind would try to mug a vampire?"

"Probably you," he grumbled.

I laughed and so did he, we turned the corner, and I was met with thousands of fairy lights surrounding the bandstand, there was rose petals everywhere and a huge blanket on the ground.

Music came on from somewhere and filled the bandstand.

I was speechless, and as he took my hand and led me onto it to dance, tears filled my eyes, and I was completely overcome with emotion.

He pulled me into his strong arms, and we began to dance to the most beautiful song.

As he twirled me slowly around the floor, gazing into my eyes; I knew there was never a moment in the history of the world that was as perfect as this one.

He leaned in and kissed me, and time just stopped, I was completely swept away.

He kissed me on and on until I thought I was going to faint, he must have known that and pulled gently away from my lips.

"My heart is ever always yours, Angel, you are the only one who's ever reached it," he sighed.

"I give my heart to you forever, Michael. Please don't break it." My voice was unsteady, and he stopped dancing.

He looked deep into my eyes with a serious look on his lovely face then he put his hand slowly to my chest and rested it at my heart, feeling it beating with wonder as he said, "Your heart is my most precious possession and I promise to protect it always." His silky voice was a reverent whisper.

I hadn't even moved a single muscle, I couldn't breathe I was afraid to in case it made him take his hand off my heart; we stood like that a while, eyes locked, in our own world where nothing else existed but here and now.

My breathing quickened at the desire in his lilac eyes, and I never wanted him to stop looking at me like that. I whispered, "Kiss me and make me immortal."

He didn't say anything, he just pulled me in, and danced with me again, after a while he said, "I won't stop your heart, Angel."

I didn't look up I just held on tighter as I said quietly, "Time will prove my love to you and cement my place in your heart forever. Time will give me the believability that I need to convince you to want to spend the rest of eternity with me. That I am worthy of you."

He pushed me gently away from him and looked at me in utter despair. "You think you're not worthy of me? That is why I won't end your life for you? My Angel it is I who is not worthy of you, and I will not condemn you to eternal damnation. You are better than that, you have a higher purpose."

I didn't answer him, we didn't have to talk about this right now but we both knew it would have to be addressed eventually.

We continued to dance in silence, holding on to each other as if at any minute we could wake up and find this had all been a beautiful, perfect, unattainable dream.

Most people only acted on a forbidden love in their dreams, and if he only loved me in my dreams then let me be asleep forever; if this *was* a dream, I never wanted to wake up.

He led me off the bandstand onto the grass where he sat me on the blanket and sat facing me. We stared at each other for a few minutes when I noticed a black velvet box next to me. "What is that?" I asked him stupidly.

He smiled. "Why don't you open it and see?"

I picked the box up with shaky hands and opened the lid; I gasped as I saw the most stunning majestic emerald heart surrounded by a platinum setting and chain.

It was the most stunning piece of jewellery I had ever seen. "I don't know what to say Michael; you really shouldn't have done this but thank you." I was trying (and failing) to form the right words.

"It's the colour of your eyes and my small way of trying to show you how much I love you," he said simply.

"I love it, I am completely overcome. I love you so much, Michael," I said throwing myself into his arms, kissing him hungrily.

He pushed me back, lying me down and kissing me with so much passion I could almost touch it in the air, his lips made my heart stand still and the feel of his body on top of mine, hard muscles moving with every movement of our lips felt utterly amazing.

His hands were moving up and down my sides and my hands were running all over his back; both of us urgent but hesitant because, as perfect as this date was, it wasn't time yet to make love.

We finally gained some control and lay side by side, holding hands and gazing at each other.

He reached over and placed the necklace around my neck and lazily moved his head down, my whole body was trembling as his lips on my throat stopped my heart, breath and brain.

He softly kissed the spot under my jaw beneath my ear, leaving his mouth there for a few minutes feeling my pulse beat against it.

I lay completely still; part of me wondering if he could keep control and not sink his teeth into it, and the other part of me knowing he wanted to but would never do it.

It was the headiest feeling; the danger he presented mixed with his love for me; it was the greatest aphrodisiac possible, well at least for me it was.

I was aware of how sick that sounded but I really didn't care.

He gave a half laugh in disbelief at me, shaking his head. "Either you are utterly fearless, or you really do have complete faith in me to not lose control. Some might say that is ill advised."

"I do have complete faith in your control, Michael. Do you think I don't know that you want to do it, blood as rich in magic as mine? I just know you never would." I smiled easily at him and went on, "My book said most vampires have extra gifts, what is yours?" I was genuinely excited to know.

"I am telekinetic which means I can move things by just thinking about it." He smiled, but you already know of all magical gifts. "I also share telepathy with my family and Ava can read minds so whatever she reads in people's minds I can hear through her."

"Wow, so that's how the DJ played Bed of Roses in the club last week, you telepathically told Ava to ask for it?" I said with wide eyes. "That is so cool."

"Busted." He laughed. "And here I was hoping to keep it a mystery so you would wonder how I do some things."

"I have the power of telekinesis too, I love it, and it's my favourite power," I told him.

"You do?" he asked in surprise. "I wondered at what your powers were, but telekinesis wasn't one of my main choices, and to what do refer *one* of your powers?"

"Oh, I have many, I *am* the most powerful of my kind. Ava can't read my mind, can she?" I asked him knowingly.

"No, as a matter of fact she can't, and I assume you know why?" He raised his eyebrows.

"It's because I have a magic shield that protects me from most physical and mental attacks, all of my family has one."

"That is pretty amazing, Angel, and highly unusual," he told me; his voice sounded overly impressed. "I've come across many witches in my time, and they never possessed more than one or two physical powers, mostly spells and potions."

93

"Well, I have a lot of other powers too, my mother's side of the family has the lethal powers and my father's side has the non-lethal powers and I inherited most of them." I was sitting up looking at him now.

He sat up too, intense interest on his face. "So what else can you do?"

"Well, my fire power includes a blasting ability which means I can blow things up, big or small; I can blast a building as easily as a door and most demons are vulnerable to it, but for the ones that aren't I can throw destruction balls and I can shoot light bolts from my hands, but I don't use that one much, telekinesis which you know and I can stop time."

He sat staring at me wide eyed. "I have never known of such power in one witch, wow, and what about your non-lethal powers what are they?"

"Well, the shield I told you about, I can heal wounds including my own, I can become invisible and I can transport from place to place in seconds, I supposedly have other mind powers like reading, control, controlling the elements, and seeing the future; but I'm not very good at any of those, and to be honest, I have all the power I need and for everything else there's a spell. It would be really cool though to mind read but I would imagine it to be really hard to get control over it, so you don't go crazy."

He was just staring at me in awe for a few minutes; when he spoke, his voice had pride in it. "You are utterly amazing, you are a walking weapon of mass destruction. Will you show me how your powers work? And what do you mean, in terms of controlling the elements?"

"Yes, but not here; I'm intensely paranoid of openly using magic outside unless it's absolutely necessary. I'll show you when we're not in a public place. Elements of nature like control of fire, water, land, air and spirit."

His way of speaking was rubbing of on me, I would never have said intensely paranoid before, I would have said totally paranoid. I loved his ultra-polite, old fashioned diction and grammar; it sounded so nice and classy. I spoke politely but he was upper class.

He shook his head in wonder. "We learn so much about physics yet, both our worlds are not of this world, we defy the laws of physics and science… I wonder often why that is." He stopped a second and took both my hands. "Your Wiccan leaders are not going to allow you to be with a vampire, Angel, you do know that." His eyes were sad.

"The Wiccan consul has no say in the matter, they can either accept it or I quit. I made up my mind on that. I've given up everything I ever wanted to fight for their precious greater good and I will not give up you, not ever, that's too high a price to pay." My tone was deadly serious.

"But you have a higher destiny, Angel, like it or not you're not a normal person with the freedom of choice normal people have and I don't want to be the cause of you giving up a greater destiny." His stunning face was torn now.

"My destiny is with you, Michael. My family has always married other powerful witches for thousands of years to ensure greater power in future generations, but how much bloody power do we all need? I don't want to just spend my life with someone I can live with, I want to spend my life with someone I can't live without, and that's you. I don't care what anyone has to say in the matter, it's my choice and I've chosen you and to hell with it." I was animated now, my voice rising to get my point across.

He pulled me into arms, embracing me tightly, his body was tense, and his voice filled with pain at all the many complications and trouble our relationship was going to cause. "It's not going to be easy, Angel, no one will exactly be amused at us being together and they will do everything they can to stop it."

"I know, I *know,* and I don't care, no sacrifice is too great as long as I'm with you." My hands were clutching at his, my desperate need for him almost making me crazy.

"I love you, Angel, and if I have to take on the whole world in order to keep you, then bring it on." He was stroking my hair and kissing my head.

The relief that he wasn't going to get all moral and send me back to my greater good was almost overwhelming, I felt the pain in my chest subside and the intense knot of fear in my stomach disappear as the tension eased from my body.

We had been in the park for hours; I looked at my watch and was shocked to discover it was past 2 am. It was amazing how time both, stood still and flew past when I was with him. He pulled me to my feet, I didn't really want to leave but without the scorching heat I felt whenever he was close to me, I realised how cold the weather was.

"I'm taking you home before you catch a chill, I would feel incredibly guilty if you got ill because I kept you outside."

"You're not exactly holding me against my will, besides it will give me a good opportunity to work the elements and heat up with fire." I mumbled as we walked to the car.

"I have no idea how on earth I am going to take you home and be able leave you; I only have so much strength." He was shaking his head and the moonlight streaking across his exquisite face was cinematic.

"I think I have a solution; my parents are going on holiday. In a few hours so why don't you drop me off, get some sleep, then pack some clothes and come and stay with me for two weeks?" I asked him excitedly. I had no idea why that that thought was just occurring to me.

"That may just be the greatest idea I have ever heard, what heaven not to have to spend my long nights away from you," he said, lifting me up and swinging me around.

"OK it's settled then," I said laughing as he we reached the car.

On the drive back he reached over and put his hand on my thigh, where it stayed, even when he spun the speeding car around corners. My whole body was tense with being so unbelievably aware of him touching me, he could feel it too; the heat between us was electric.

When we pulled up outside my house he walked me to the door, both of us grinning with our plan of staying together for the next fortnight.

"Thank you for the most wonderful night of my life Michael, it was magical, and I am so blown away by the whole thing; the flying, the fairy lights, your kisses, our conversations, and the gorgeous emerald necklace. It was perfect," I told him softly.

"It was my pleasure my darling." His lilac eyes soft and dreamy as he looked at me.

I forgot to inhale, his eyes devastating me in their power, and he gave me *that* look, the one that rendered me breathless. I lost my train of thought and just stood there dumbstruck, staring at him like the village idiot.

He didn't let me recover as he leaned in and kissed me; his hands gripped my waist and held it tight. I pressed myself closer to him wishing I could somehow fuse with him and become part of him forever.

"My parents are leaving at nine so come over when you get up," I told him quietly in case anyone was eavesdropping.

"Nothing will keep me away," he said, giving me a gentle kiss.

He walked to his car and opened the door, winking at me. "See you soon, my Angel." And he was gone.

I floated inside, unable to take the smile off my face, I went to the kitchen and got a bottle of water from the fridge and wrote a note telling my mum and dad to have a great holiday and not to worry about a thing because Dylan, Kennedy and I could handle it.

I went to my room and got changed for bed, I felt like I was levitating about my room and my head was light and disconnected from everything in the world except him.

I got under my covers and lay luxuriating in my thoughts of him and my memories of tonight, reliving it till I fell into a deep sleep.

Chapter Nine

Two-Week Sleepover

I woke up at ten too comfortable to move, I was curled up on my side and cuddling my pillow as events of yesterday began flooding my mind making me smile.

I still had my necklace on; I was never planning to take it off unless I had to. I twirled it in my fingers, and I realised I had better think about getting up and showered before Michael arrived.

I felt my duvet move and froze; I knew it was him, even though I never heard him come in. I never hear Michael moving, his movements are always so silent and graceful.

I could smell his lovely, intoxicating scent. My heart began to beat erratically at the thought of him under my covers with me.

"You won't need to hold that pillow anymore in fact you won't be holding anything but me," he said in my ear as he cuddled into my back, sliding his arm under me and the other over me.

I leaned my head back into his neck and allowed myself to sink into this incredible embrace.

I was more aware of his closeness than I had ever been, maybe because he was in my bed and under my covers with me and it was making my imagination run away.

We lay like that for around an hour, neither of us in any hurry to move, just enjoying being together like this.

I allowed myself to wonder what he wore to bed, a top and bottoms? Just bottoms with no top? Nothing? I gulped heavily at that last one, and felt warmth spread over my body as I tried not to picture him naked. It would be a futile exercise anyway because I was sure whatever I imagined it would not even be slightly close to the real deal.

Still, it was not the worst thoughts I ever had.

I smiled to myself as I snuggled in deeper to his body and he squeezed me tightly to him.

There was a light knock at my door, and I shouted come in, there was no point in trying to hide from my siblings the fact that Michael was staying here while our parents were away.

Both were there and they came into my room wide-eyed and curious. Kennedy was openly gazing at Michael with disbelief and unconcealed admiration of his looks.

We sat up and Michael's arm was still around my shoulders as I asked them what they wanted.

They made up some lame nonsense about seeing if we wanted any lunch. Never in my life did these two come into my room and offer to make me lunch out the kindness of their hearts; they were here to find out what was going on.

"OK, here's the deal, Michael is going to be staying here with me while Mum and Dad are away," I told them.

"Oh, OK cool," was Dylan's response.

"What all the time?" Kennedy asked.

"Yes, all the time and neither of you better not even think about snitching to Mum and Dad or I will give the pair of you a cuffing," I said sternly, eyeing them both with narrowed eyes.

"I would never snitch to Mum and Dad, Angel, you know that," Dylan said.

I did know that my little brother was my star.

"I won't tell them anything, I swear," Kennedy said with wide eyes, she knew I was aware she wasn't above sticking me in if it served her own purpose, but she also knew I would paddle her arse if she did.

"OK then, well get out the pair of you, we want to be alone." I did not consider it rude to kick my siblings out of my room, neither did they; they sloped off grinning at me.

Michael was laughing his head off when they closed the door. "They were so obvious coming in here on a fishing expedition, they didn't even think up a decent cover story." He was laughing even harder when he said, "It was so funny when you threatened to cuff them, I don't know how I kept a straight face."

I laughed too, shaking my head at them and saying they would make terrible spies with shady cover stories like that; that it was in fact a miracle they hadn't got us all discovered as witches. They were not exactly stealth.

When we stopped laughing at dumb and dumber invading, I told him I was going for a shower. I got out of bed and Michael's arms were behind his head casually as he lazily trailed his eyes over the skimpy shorts and top I had worn to bed. The sunlight dancing across his face was illuminating the sparks of desire in his eyes.

I felt short of breath again, he always had this effect on me, would it ever end? Would there ever come I time when I could look at him, or have him look at me when I wouldn't require an oxygen tank?

"When you look at me like that I... I..." I could not find the words to finish the sentence because his eyes were penetrating mine and I just couldn't remember what I was going to say.

"You're not coherent, Angel, perhaps you should go and have a shower and gather your thoughts without me distracting you." His smile was understanding. He was probably used to rendering people speechless.

I nodded and padded into my bathroom and spent twenty minutes just standing under the hot water, letting it clear my head.

I got out and brushed my teeth and tied my bathrobe around me and went back into the bedroom.

Michael was standing looking at my wardrobe and turned around when I came in. He stood completely still as he took in me with my just out of the shower appearance and then he came towards me.

He reached out his hand and pulled the towel from my wet hair, watching it fall around my shoulders. He ran a cool finger through my black hair, down my damp neck and down the front of my robe to the belt that was holding it closed.

His fingers went up and down on it, playing with it for a minute as he looked at it, deliberating.

I was rooted to the spot, wondering if he was going to untie it and let it fall open. I knew he was struggling with himself.

He looked up into my eyes and I could read the wish in them mixed with the battle for control. "You have no idea how much I want to untie your robe right now." He squeezed his eyes closed and turned away quickly.

I realised I hadn't been breathing as I watched him cross the room away from me, watching his top caressing his well-defined back as I exhaled loudly.

I went into my walk-in wardrobe and got dressed. As I thought about what almost could have happened I noticed my hands shaking when I tried to fasten my jeans.

I sat down on the chair I kept in there and tried to slow my heart. I put my head in my hands and wanted to scream in frustration. This was going to be hard, him staying here, and us having to keep the heat to a minimum.

I imagined it was even harder for him though, judging by the utter struggle to restrain himself that I saw in his eyes.

I figured though if he could stop himself killing me then this was a breeze in comparison, plus it was much better than the alternative, which was, he didn't stay here at all, and neither of us could handle that.

We would just have to be more careful with things is all.

He was lying on the bed and I noticed that he had made it, I smiled at him and lay down beside him, careful to not touch yet.

"I am sorry about that, Angel, I overestimate my restraint, then something catches me off guard, and I realise how weak I really am around you." His voice was low.

"No, I'm sorry, babe, I should have thought about things like that; so, from now on I will take my clothes into the bathroom with me and get ready before I come out." I touched his arm.

He sat up on one elbow and looked down at me. "I was so brazenly affectionate with you from the moment I realised I had feelings for you, to test myself, to see if I could control myself. I wanted your blood so badly, but I also wanted you so badly and I thought if I faced it head on and didn't kill you then I knew without any doubt I could always remain controlled around you, and you would be safe. But this is a bit different than that, and I don't think the head on approach is the best course of action because there's only so much control I have, and sometimes there are going to be moments that require a great deal of effort on my part to be strong." He reached over and ran his fingers down my cheek in the familiar way I was becoming used to.

"Well, we'll work it out, I promise; and it won't be forever, someday soon we'll both decide the time is right and the moment is right, and it'll just happen." I moved closer to him, and he put his arms around me so my head was on his chest.

"It is alien to me to feel so out of control with my feelings, yet have to keep so much control," he said evenly, he wasn't complaining, simply making an observation.

"Control over not killing me or not making love to me?" I asked.

"Both my darling, both." He sighed and dropped a kiss on my head.

We were silent after that, each lost in our own thoughts, knowing we can never be always anything but completely honest with each other; it was too dangerous to be anything other than that.

After a while, Michael got up and lifted me to my feet. "Come on you have to eat Angel, I won't have you losing weight and being all skin and bone, I've never considered skinny females attractive, and I have no desire to see you lose your gorgeous hourglass figure," he told me, running his hands up my sides.

I shivered at his touch and at his words; it was stupid, but I hadn't been sure before if vampires thought about things like that, what with them being so perfect in form and not usually dating mortals that it didn't occur to me they had body type preferences.

We went downstairs and I ordered pizza for everyone's dinner, well everyone except Michael.

I worried what Michael was going to say about why he wasn't eating, but when the pizzas came, he ate two slices for appearances sake as I stared at him in disbelief.

Dylan was chewing Michael's ear off about his Lamborghini, asking him many inane questions.

Kennedy just sat and stared at him in awe.

He took the car keys out of his pocket and tossed them to Dylan and told him to take it out tonight because he wouldn't be using it until the morning.

Dylan was ecstatic and looked at Michael with hero worship, he phoned his friend and told him he would come and pick him up in 'the coolest car ever' and ran out the door.

I got up and cleared away the pizza boxes, still wondering how Michael was able to eat the pizza and couldn't wait to ask him.

Kennedy was yammering on about school, basically talking about anything so she could sit and stare at Michael a while longer, I knew exactly what she was doing, and it amused me.

Her friend Lindsay came in, giggled, and blushed when Michael said hello to her, and it didn't escape my attention the looks she and Kennedy were shooting each other about him. I was chuckling to myself as I came back to sit at the table.

Michael pulled me into his lap and kissed me lightly in an easy display of open affection and sat tickling my arm gently as we talked to the girls, who could not have been more jealous.

Eventually they left to go and study, and we were alone again; Michael moved my hair around and softly kissed my neck.

"Is that all you've got vampire boy?" I asked mockingly.

Quick as a flash I found myself staring at the ceiling as he grabbed me and pulled my whole body backwards, so my hair was trailing on the floor and he kissed my neck hard, grazing it with his teeth as he moved his lips to my pulse.

My heart began to hammer in my chest, adrenaline flowing through me as I realised how utterly helpless, I was at his hands, how at any moment I could be just seconds from death if he ever decided to kill me. It was the darker side of lust, and I couldn't get enough of it.

I moved my head up and my lips found his hungrily, I kissed him hard and before I knew it, we were lying on the kitchen floor and my arms were pinned above my head as he crushed his lips to mine intensely.

I couldn't move under his vice like grip, so I surrendered to his will, with dizzy delight.

Kennedy and Lindsay came into the kitchen and stopped dead, staring at us lying on the kitchen floor all over each other.

"Geez, Angel, you have a bed you know," Kennedy said in disgust mixed with envy.

I broke up laughing and so did Michael and we got up off the floor and ran upstairs; when we were out of the sight of the girls, Michael picked me up and sped me to my room, everything went weird for a second then I was on my bed stunned.

I sat for a few minutes while my organs caught up with the rest of my body and waited for the woozy feeling to pass.

"That was insane, I have never felt anything like that," I told him, rapidly shaking my head from side to side to try and clear it.

He laughed at the state I was in. "Dear Angel, you have gone as white as me, and that's saying something! Don't worry you will get used to it."

"Used to that? I don't think so," I said. "How fast were we going?"

"We have varying degrees of speed with which we can move; we start with our terribly slow human movements, right up to the speed of light. What we did there was known as blurring and that's somewhere in between the two." He was still laughing.

"If that wasn't the fastest you can move, then please don't ever show me what is," I said, starting to feel a little better.

"Oh, come on, show some spine, I thought you were fearless," he said with a smirk on his flawless face.

"This isn't about being fearless, it's about my organs being in a different postcode to my body." I laughed.

"OK, it's your turn, let's see what you've got."

I took a hold of him and transported us both outside for a few seconds and then back into my room.

"Pretty impressive, how far can you do that?" he asked.

"As far as I need to go, across the room, country or world," I told him.

"That is amazing," he told me. "OK, show me your other powers."

"Right, but we should go outside for this," I told him, transporting us both outside quickly before he did the blurring thing again.

We had an old practice field situated far behind the house that was filled with targets and bins and other objects to practice with.

I handed him a clay plate and told him to throw it up in the air whenever he felt like it, he waited a minute then tossed it in the air where I quickly blasted it and held all the pieces in mid-air for a minute then let it go so all the pieces fell to the ground.

"Wow that just may be the most impressive thing I have ever seen, Angel," he said sincerely.

"Thank you but I'm not done yet," I told him. "Watch that back fence."

I blasted the whole fence to smithereens and threw a destruction ball at a bin and a light bolt at another one in quick succession, using both hands.

Then I used my telekinesis to load up the moving target rail with clay plates and blasted them one after the other as they moved rapidly past me.

He stood there utterly speechless, staring at me with wonder and respect.

"That is some serious fire power indeed. You have unbelievable control over it too. I am utterly amazed," he said, his lilac eyes shining with pride in me.

I took a bow, absurdly pleased at his reaction and the fact that I had impressed him so much. I was more than sure that there wasn't a lot that would impress an immortal, especially not *my* immortal who was so bright, brilliant, beautiful, and powerful beyond measure; at least my own powerful gifts levelled the playing field a little.

We spent a while playing at 'blow stuff up' since he was having so much fun watching me do it. I produced a ball of destruction and handed it to him to throw;

he threw it up the field and it landed with a crazy bang, blasting half the ground away because of his super strength. The ground looked like a meteor had hit it.

"Now that is what you call destruction," I said, my turn to be impressed. We both used our telekinesis to fill in the massive hole because I didn't fancy having to explain its existence.

We eventually went back inside and up to my room, deciding to watch movies in bed.

I got a pair of cotton bottoms and matching top out to sleep in and went into the bathroom to change and when I came out Michael had changed into a long-sleeved cotton top and bottoms and was looking at movies.

He looked so human standing there in sleepwear and picking out something to watch. "It's hard to remember sometimes that you are a dangerous vampire Michael, in moments like this when you look so unthreatening," I said watching him.

He turned swiftly around. "Never forget, Angel, never forget that I am a vampire and never ever forget how dangerous I am." His satin voice was low, calm and deadly.

I felt a prickle of fear go up my spine as I imagined just how deadly he could be. We looked at each other in silence.

for a minute then he was across the room and kissing me, lifting me off my toes a little and crushing me to him tightly, one hand in my hair holding the back of my head and the other around my back.

The moment took my heart away and stopped my breath; I was lost in the power of his kiss, the strength of his body and the sheer exhilaration of never being more completely alive.

I wished I could spend every minute of every day for the rest of my life doing nothing but kissing him.

But I can't.

We went over the Netflix and Amazon choices picked out titanic to watch and settled under the covers, cuddled up together.

"Now that's two people that get it, get the total love some people can have for each other; the whole 'if you jump, I jump' thing is a love like ours, that is so all consuming and powerful that they are willing to die together rather than be apart," he said about Jack and Rose.

"Yeah, but at the end after all that, when he dies and she doesn't always frustrate me, especially now that I'm with you; I don't understand it even more because I could never go on living without you. If I were Rose, I would have died with him in that water," I said seriously.

"But he didn't want her to die with him and I wouldn't want you to die with me either if you had any other choice," he told me animatedly. "It upsets me to think you would die because I was dead, I want you to go on living."

"There is no living without you, Michael," I said simply.

"Angel, there is going to come a time when I will have to choose between being with you and saving you and I will choose to save you. I will do whatever I have to in order to save you, and if that means my dying to do it, then that's what I'll do," he said looking at me with those molten amethyst eyes that made me lost.

"Well, let's just hope that day never comes, besides you're immortal so there's not a big chance of you dying," I said trying to lighten the mood.

We both decided to drop it and watched the end of the movie where I cried like I always did, Michael thought I was cute and ruffled my hair.

"I have to admit, now that I have you and feel the way I do about you, I sympathise much more with Jack and Rose than I did before; I used to think it was all a little silly but now I get it, I really get it," he said running his pale hands through his perfect hair.

"Our story is much more romantic," I whispered, half sitting up to look at him.

"Oh yes, once upon a time the vampire fell in love with the good witch. What a sick fairy tale I'm giving you; a lifetime filled with midnights monsters and your anti-hero is the world's greatest nightmare, the deadliest predator that ever existed and no knight on a white horse able to rescue you," he said this with an ironic tone to his voice.

"I don't want a knight on a white horse, I want a vampire in a black Lamborghini," I said flippantly. "Besides, you're forgetting one thing about fairy tales."

"And what would that be?" he asked, waiting for whatever my logic would be now.

"They all have happy endings."

"And that's a bad thing?" he asked incredulously.

"Compared with our fairy tale it is; you see our love won't have a happy ending because our love won't have an ending," I finished with a smile.

106

He laughed and shook his head. "Oddly, that makes some sense." He smiled at me with a sad look. "You won't ever get to ride off into the sunset with your royal prince and live happily ever after though."

"No, you're right, I won't; I'm much luckier than that because I'll get to drive off into midnight with my vampire prince and live forever," I said seriously, looking into his eyes.

"You really are a nutcase; do you know that?" he asked me laughing.

"Yup, I know that," I said happily.

"Why am I the only one to understand that you are wishing to give up your life to be with me?" he asked.

"Because you see it differently from me, Michael, I finally have something wonderful and magical that's mine, just mine and all mine and the bloody greater good has nothing to do with it. And I don't believe having a mortal life is the be all and end all; in fact, it's rather overrated and without you intolerable," I answered him desperate to make him get it, to accept that someday he was going to have to turn me.

He closed his eyes and put his head back, he shook his head, pain crossing his beautiful face. "I can't do it, Angel, I can't end your life, I cannot stand there while your heart stops beating and know I'm responsible for it, for turning you into something you were not supposed to be, can't you understand that?" he asked me sadly.

"All I want is to be with you forever and that won't ever change. My Wiccan life won't end, in fact I'll be even more powerful and I'm not exactly human anyway," I said leaning into his chest.

He wrapped his arms around me. "What a beautiful mess," he sighed.

I held onto him, knowing that no one in the history of the world had ever loved anyone the way I loved him, knowing if he ever left me, if I survived, that I would never ever love like this again.

I switched the light off and we cuddled up beneath the duvet, the long sleeves he wore a sufficient barrier against his cool skin from making me cold.

"This is heaven, to be with you all night, to not be alone in my bed wishing I were with you and only sleeping to dream of you. Angel you are my every day, my every night and my every dream and I'm not ashamed to admit it," he said holding me tighter.

"I love you, Michael, and it's the simplest thing in the whole world, I could never love you enough to satisfy me," I said sleepily.

I was so comfortable in his arms, I felt so safe and protected and loved; I never wanted to be without the shelter of his arms, the magic of his lips and the wonder of his lilac eyes.

We both fell asleep, and we stayed wrapped in each other's arms like that all night and it was the best night's sleep I had ever had.

I couldn't believe how right it was, that something so forbidden could ever be this right.

I was happier right then than I had ever been in my life.

Chapter Ten

Questions

I woke up, slowly coming into consciousness and being aware of Michael holding me close and I felt fantastic.

I couldn't believe I was waking up with him and lay luxuriating in the wonder of it, wondering if I would ever bother with sleep again because dreams were a waste of time when I had the real thing next to me; dreams were pathetic in comparison to the very real miracle that was holding me.

After all the nights I had ached, yearned and died for him, he was finally here with me, and it was better than I ever imagined.

I was watching Michael sleep and his flawless face was so peaceful and relaxed, all trace of tension, frustration and pain gone.

He looked so normal and so un-vampire-like just now, even with his perfectly pale features as a reminder of what he was.

Michael woke up then and his vivid eyes brightened when he saw me watching him, a slow smile spread across red lips. "Good morning, my Angel, how unbelievably wonderful is to wake up and see you next to me."

He pulled me in closer and we lay touching foreheads and staring into each other's eyes until it was time to get up.

I had my shower and got ready but when I came out of the bathroom, he wasn't there.

I went downstairs and found him in the kitchen making breakfast; he made toast and bacon and eggs and put the plates down for my siblings and myself.

I was looking at him in amazement, wondering where on earth he learned to cook; he never ceased to surprise me.

He put glasses with orange juice down for us, gave me quick kiss and said he was going to get showered and ready.

"He is the perfect guy." Kennedy sighed watching him walk out.

"He is the coolest guy," Dylan corrected her.

I didn't answer them because he was both; he was my cool, perfect vampire and a lot more besides.

I sat pondering great lovers, Romeo and Juliet, Sid and Nancy, Kurt and Courtney, Anthony and Cleopatra, Jack and Rose, Elizabeth Taylor and Richard Burton.

The fact that all the world's greatest loves mostly ended in tragedy was beside the point; the point was that none of them could touch us.

Marc Anthony and Cleopatra, in my opinion was the only one that came close and even then, it wasn't that close.

All great loves involved obstacles and huge things to overcome; always fighting against the outside resistances and influences of others trying to stop the relationship.

Our love had all that and more; we also had magic interfering and a love so forbidden there wasn't even a precedent for it.

I wondered just how much trouble we were going to have coming our way.

Not just from my side, but what would vampires think of one of their own being in love with a good witch?

I had a feeling they wouldn't exactly be thrilled about it, but the book did say it wasn't forbidden for them to fall for a mortal if they were willing to turn them.

A good witch however wasn't exactly a human, and I was sure they would not want a vampire of royal blood to be with one.

I was under no illusions that things will get messy, even dangerous.

I knew Michael would protect me from any vampires that might want to take matters into their own hands and eliminate the threat I posed, but the thought of that happening still scared me a bit.

They would have to be some suicidal vampires though to take on Michael; the book said he was the most powerful of their kind and I was fairly sure you didn't get many suicidal vampires so it might be OK.

I wondered how long we could keep who we were secret from the other side; I wasn't ready to deal with the repercussions yet.

Michael's family must know something though because if it was a vampire, he was going out with they would have met her by now. They maybe thought it was a human he was seeing because I'm guessing they had no idea it was actually a witch, Michael would have told me if they knew.

Everything had happened so fast between us; we hadn't even talked about when we were going to come out, and what the hell we were going to say.

We were still getting used to everything ourselves never mind trying to explain it to others. How do you explain the unexplainable?

I was totally lost in these thoughts when Michael came back down and stood studying me from the doorway.

"Things are going to get bad, Angel," he said coming towards me.

I looked up stunned, how had he known what I was thinking?

His lips lifted slightly at the corners in a half smile with no teeth showing.

His silky voice was even and completely normal. "I think I may be starting to read you very well, either that or my power of telepathy and the bond we have formed is somehow allowing me to read your mind occasionally."

I looked up at him. "How bad do you think it could get, Michael?"

"I really have no idea; it depends on how many rules we have broken. I do know this though, fate I may not be able to fight, but everything else I can; and I *will* keep you safe make no mistake about it, anyone who tries to hurt you will not live long; I swear that to you." His voice was like ice, cold calm ice that I could have skated across.

I looked into his eyes, instead of the lovely molten amethyst they usually were, they were like cold, hard stone. Unyielding and determined.

I felt the icy hand of fear grip my heart at the thought of him putting himself at risk to defend me.

As I looked at him, he had never looked more like a vampire than he did at this moment; his powerful body tense under his black leather jacket and his expression was truly frightening; everything about him radiated danger.

He was awe-inspiring.

I couldn't make myself look away from him, couldn't tear my eyes from this inhuman, glorious creature that would ruthlessly kill without mercy to ensure my safety.

I stood up and put my arms around his neck, still not looking away from his face, mesmerised by his beauty.

He kissed me then, an urgent, hungry kiss like he was afraid it would be the last time he ever kissed me, and I surrendered to it willingly, gripping his hair tightly as he held me in a vice and kissed me over and over.

Bullets had left guns slower than my heart was beating.

Sometimes the intensity between us was so strong it was almost more than I could handle, a normal person may have died from it. It was like my mind was trying to dilute it to protect me from how strong it was. Not that I wanted protection from it, I didn't want any of what he made me feel to be diluted in any way.

We left for uni, taking his car and since I had no afternoon classes on a Monday, he was skipping his afternoon lectures.

We drove into the car park and got out, running late because of our conversation this morning.

I sat in class and barley paid attention, my mind was still on what we talked about.

I knew I had to put it out of my mind, there was no point speculating about what could happen because we won't know until it does, and I wasn't going to let it dampen my happiness.

We would deal with it when we had to.

We got handed a new essay assignment; three thousand words on Wuthering Heights, easy. I had read the book lots of times and I had the movie, the one that starred Laurence Olivier, which was, in my opinion the best version by far.

Classes passed slowly as I waited impatiently to be with Michael again until finally it was one o'clock and I went quickly out of the class, Sally trailing behind me so she could fish for what was going on.

I looked up the corridor and he was there waiting for me, dark and intimidating looking, oozing mystery, and causing girls to bang into each other as they craned their necks to stare at him.

He was completely unaware of the effect he had on people, his eyes focused on me only and he didn't so much as sideways glance at any of the pretty girls desperate to get his attention.

Pride swelled up in me that he was all mine and totally disinterested in anyone other than me.

I ran into his arms, having missed him like mad all morning, crashing against him, he didn't even slightly stumble; he just gathered me up in a massive hug.

Sally and Liam were staring gobsmacked at the unattainable, cool and aloof Michael De Marco being so openly affectionate; they were too scared to even talk to him let alone throw themselves into his arms like I did, and they couldn't believe his response to me.

Sometimes I could not believe his response to me, especially since I knew what he really was.

We went to the car and decided to go shopping so Michael took me to the Italian centre.

We went in and had a look around; everything was lovely, there wasn't a bad thing in the whole shop.

This was a classy designer, and it did not surprise me in the least that he was Michael's favourite.

He tried on a classic black suit, and it was to die for gorgeous on him; I just sat gaping at how amazing he looked in it.

Michael was so dazzling he would look great in a bin liner, but he did look particularly spectacular in that suit.

He had a serious preference for dark clothes, with most of his wardrobe being black, with the occasional and grey thrown in, and sometimes red.

We had that in common I preferred black clothes too.

I tried on a little black dress, which was cut in such a way that made your figure look amazing, I loved it and so did Michael judging by his look when I came out the changing room.

"Well, I simply must buy you that dress Angel, you look devastating in it." A slow smile forming on his red lips as his eyes travelled over me.

I could feel the electric current blast through me as it did every time he looked at me like that, that seductive, smouldering gaze that held the promise of wonders to come and instantly made my knees go weak.

My heart went into overdrive and hearing how fast it was beating, He smiled knowingly at me.

I turned away from his dizzying stare and looked in the mirror at the dress; it did look good on me, a dress this well-made would look good on anyone.

He came up behind me and put his arms around my waist, catching eyes with me in the mirror and dazing me again.

The sales assistant came over gaping at Michael with open-mouthed admiration and offered us champagne that we declined; nothing could give me a bigger buzz than Michael.

I went back to the changing room and got out of the dress and back into my regular clothes.

Michael was trying on a black leather jacket that came down to his mid-thigh and it looked incredibly sexy on him; I loved him in leather, it somehow added to his dangerous appeal.

"OK, I will take the suit, a couple of shirts, the leather jacket, the dress and whatever shoes and bag the lady decides that goes with the dress," he told the happy salesclerk.

"Michael, that is too much, I really don't need the dress and matching stuff."

"I want you to have them, besides it's not just for you; I get the pleasure of seeing you in them," he answered, touching my face with his thumb.

"In that case, thank you very much, I love them." I gave him a quick kiss on the lips.

The salesclerk rang up the purchases, staring at me with envy, and gave him the total; it was thousands, Michael didn't even blink as he handed him his card.

We left the shop, headed down to Argyll Street, and went into a music shop.

We spent ages looking at music and discussing bands and I discovered Michael was as passionate as me about music.

"Well, when you've lived for over a thousand years and can live forever you really have to find something you will never get sick of and for me that's music and literature because both are so subjective you find new meanings in them all the time." He shrugged. "I like all musical genres, but I do have the most love for rock n roll." He was gesturing to the many rock vinyl in front of us as he said that.

"Yeah, me too, I admire anyone with musical talent but it's rock music that is in my love. But I have always said a good song is a god song, despite whether you like the artist or genre, so I have a very varied and eclectic musical collection."

"Something tells me you wanted to be a rock star," he said.

"I did, so much, but I wasn't allowed." I shook my head sadly. "Wiccan duties, greater good and all that." I shrugged.

"That *is* a shame, to have your dreams shattered before you can really dream them." He swept my hair from my face.

"No dream compares to you." I tilted my head to his hand that was still at my hair.

He kissed me then, right there in the rock section while people browsed the music and didn't even notice the world had stopped spinning for a minute.

On the way back to the car we were carrying on, flicking each other and running away laughing; he always caught me though, even without making his lightning-fast reflexes obvious.

We stopped at a fast-food restaurant and got burger meals for the gruesome twosome, as I referred affectionately to Dylan and Kennedy.

I was hungry and ate mine on the way home, just finishing as we pulled up at the house.

We went inside and I shouted there was a food here for any interested parties.

My brother was first down, grabbing the bag and going into the kitchen.

Michael and I went upstairs, and I was reminded of him eating pizza last night. "How did you manage to eat food last night? I thought vampires couldn't eat real food," I asked him, really interested in the explanation.

"It's not that we can't eat human food, it's just not very appealing to us, nor is it tasty and it wouldn't keep us strong if that's all we ate, even if we were inclined to do so. We need blood to survive but on occasion we are forced to eat your food to protect our secret," he said simply.

"What does human food taste like to you?" I asked him.

"I can't really describe it, I imagine it tastes to us what eating paper would taste like to you, although never having ate paper or been human I can't really compare the two."

"How often do you need to eat food to keep up appearances?"

"Not often, we tend to avoid situations that require us to do so, and we don't generally mix closely enough with humans for it to be a regular occurrence."

I was quiet for a minute contemplating.

"What?"

"Well, I was just wondering how you… erm… digest the food you eat?"

He laughed. "We don't digest it, it dissipates in our bodies."

"That is fascinating, I had no idea," I told him wide-eyed.

"Your magical book didn't say that then?"

"The book, as powerful as it is, doesn't have everything because my ancestors could only write what they know and if they didn't know any vampires personally then it wouldn't be in there."

"Are you going to add it in?" he asked looking at me closely, and I wondered what he thought about us having so much information on vampires, with all their secrecy.

"I hadn't thought about it but no, I won't use anything you tell me as fodder for a magical book; what you tell me is personal, between us and nothing to do with anyone else," I replied honestly.

It wouldn't make much difference to what was already in the book anyway; you can't kill a vampire so writing in that they can eat food if they must is informative, but not that helpful.

"I really don't mind if you put it in, Angel."

"Thanks for the offer but it would raise eyebrows how I came across this information."

"Can I see your book sometime?"

"Sure, why not, you won't actually be able to touch it because it will shield itself, but you can read it next to me while I hold it."

The thought that, like the entire underworld, he could have been after our book was so absurd that it didn't even enter my head; he didn't need our book to kill anyone, including me.

"It will be interesting for me to look in your book, I've never seen inside a real book of witchcraft before," he said, lying back on the bed and pulling me gently with him.

My mind wandered from the book to the song he played in the park, and I realised I had meant to ask him about it before.

"That first song you had playing in the park, what was it because it was so beautiful?"

"I have already put it onto your Michael playlist," he answered. "Somehow I just knew you would love it and want it."

I was mortified he saw I had a playlist dedicated to him and felt my cheeks burn red, I didn't even ask him how he managed to put it onto my phone without me noticing, I just accepted the fact that he could do anything.

He threw his head back laughing so hard at my embarrassment at being caught like a schoolgirl. "Angel, I have a playlist dedicated to you too so no need for you to feel disconcerted."

"You do? Why?" I was perplexed, I thought only girls done things like that.

"Because I love you and when I am not with you, I listen to it to make me feel closer to you." He laughed again. "Not that your cheeks going red wasn't both amusing and adorable."

Overcome with emotion I turned away and reached over and pressed play, knowing that song would be the first one to come on. It was.

We lay there just chilling out and listened to it, looking at each other.

Every moment passed in much the same wonderful way, we woke up together, went to Uni and spent our nights lying in bed talking, kissing and staring at each other.

The only time we were separated was in class and even that was torture; I never wanted to be apart from him.

Dallas came over on Wednesday for dinner and Michael had to eat food that night because as much as I trusted Dallas, I didn't quite know how to tell her Michael was a vampire. It's not something you can drop casually into a conversation or just blurt out... 'hey my boyfriend is a vampire who kills people and drinks their blood'; besides I was pretty sure I wasn't allowed to tell her and I wouldn't put her at risk like that, besides, it wasn't my secret to tell.

We had a fun night playing games and Michael beat us both without trouble at trivial pursuit and who wants to be a millionaire.

Dallas just thought he had a genius level of intelligence, not that the fact he had lived for over a millennium and a photographic vampire memory that made him so knowledgeable.

Michael played computer games with Dylan so I could have some time with Dallas, and I showed her my emerald and my new designer dress and filled her in on every detail of the date.

She was blown away by the whole romance of everything and by Michael himself, she said she had never met someone so impressive.

I could not agree more, he *was* impressive, very impressive and not just his looks but also everything about him.

"He's really in love with you Angel, it's written all over his face every time he looks at you, and he's so protective over you, he's so aware of your every move like he's ready to fight lions to save you."

She had no idea just how right she was, only it was much more than lions, he was ready to fight anything to save me.

"Yes, he's definitely a fighter." I smiled at the understatement of that.

After Dallas left, I was lying on the floor staring at the ceiling, thinking how I had never believed in love at first sight before, but I definitely believed what I felt the first time I looked in his eyes, that very first second and I had never doubted it.

I guess love teaches more than logic, our love did anyway because there was nothing logical about any of it, yet I was more enlightened than I had ever been.

He was suddenly standing over me, smiling. "What are you doing on the floor?"

"I don't know, I just felt like it I guess." I laughed.

He lay down next to me and took my hand.

"Can I ask you some questions?" I asked him.

"Angel, my love, you can ask me anything you want, anything at all."

"I was just wondering about your childhood and what it was like to be born a vampire," I said looking sideways at him.

"Well, growing up was pretty normal, both my parents were once human, so we always had plenty of toys and love, we always had decorations and gifts at Christmas, still do, and I believed in Santa Claus. We also have birthdays every year, most vampires don't you see because they weren't born vampires, but we do and that's pretty special, the others still celebrate the day they were born too."

"Wow, it's so human to have birthdays and Christmases, I wouldn't have imagined you do."

"My parents never lost that part of their humanity and never allowed us to. Some vampires struggle with what they are at some point, my parents included, but Ava and I were born to it, so we've never had to battle the humanity within versus killing for food, we have never known what it feels like to be mortal, so our parents made sure we had an idea by keeping human rituals and celebrations. It stops us seeing people as just food."

"So, you never struggle with what you are?"

"No, because I've never known any different, this is who I am, how I was born and I accept that, but I do see the vast struggle others have with it, which would make me reluctant to turn anyone, unless they had no other choice. I was born immortal, but humans aren't, they are born, they live and they die and that's their natural way so by turning them I would essentially be interfering with the natural order of things by having them live forever," he said simply.

"That makes sense, but if a person is making an informed choice to become immortal then you aren't condemning them, you're freeing them from the restraints and chains of humanity, from something they no longer want to be. If you've never struggled with it, people who ask for immortality may not either."

"The only time I have ever struggled is when I saw you, your strong magical blood was so appealing to me, and I would have killed you and not thought twice about it. But, when you looked up into my eyes you stirred something in me that I could not logically explain, not just your great beauty but something else and it was the most bizarre feeling I have had in over one thousand years. I was curious about you because of that. You were everything I never knew I wanted." He was looking at me openly, molten amethyst eyes reading my soul.

"So, I was the first mortal you would have felt bad about killing?"

"In a way. I wanted your blood but the first instant I heard your heart beating and you looked into my eyes, I wanted *you* more, I will always want you more than I want your blood, but never forget I want your blood too," he said seriously.

He sat up on one elbow and leaned his head to my chest very slowly and lay listening to my heart beating; I put my arms around him and forced my breathing to slow down.

We lay like that for a while; he was as still as a statue, not moving one single muscle, and I figured that must be a vampire trait, being able to keep so still like that, because a human could never do it.

"Your beating heart soothes me; I love to listen to it. Perhaps because I've never been so close to someone that had one."

I stroked his hair; I had no idea that someone listening to my heart could be so intense, but then again, I had only ever had the doctor listen to it with his cold stethoscope when I was ill.

On Thursday at lunch, we were sitting in the café studiously ignoring the stares of interest we were still receiving.

"I shall have to take you somewhere nice this weekend my love, give you a chance to wear your new dress," Michael said suddenly.

"Great, where are we going?" I asked excited.

"I'm not sure yet, I will have a think about it." He smiled warmly at me and I knew he wouldn't tell me where he was taking me.

We sat holding hands and looking at each other, grinning stupidly.

We were so caught up in each other we may well have been in an empty room for all the attention we paid to everyone surrounding us.

"Would you like to see the book tonight, Michael?"

"Yes, but only if you're sure you want to show it to me," he answered searching my face for any hidden doubts.

There was none. "I want to show it to you, it's my magical inheritance and I think you'll find it interesting." I smiled at him reassuringly, letting him know I wasn't just offering to show it to him out of a sense of obligation because he had asked.

"Then I would enjoy seeing it very much." He leaned over and kissed me as we got up to go to our classes.

Classes dragged by it was so tedious; all I wanted was to be with him, if it wasn't for the nights we got to spend together, I may not have survived it at all.

I had no idea what we were going to do once my parents came home all I knew was we couldn't be apart.

It wasn't as simple as just moving out of our family homes and moving in together; I had my Wiccan duties I couldn't escape from, and Michael had had his Lamia Regius lineage to contend with. Plus, I guess the De Marco family were stronger and more intimidating together.

When we got home, Michael gave Dylan and Kennedy money to go the movies and sealed the deal by giving Dylan his keys to his car.

After they left, Michael said, "I thought you would prefer them not to be home when you showed me the book; after all, as far as they are concerned, I am a mortal who has no idea of your family secret."

"Good thinking, babe, there would be no way to explain why I was showing you the book other than to confess you know we're witches."

We climbed the stairs to the loft moving through general family heirlooms you would find in most people's ancestral home until we came to the end, I moved the hidden wall and put my thumbprint on the security pad and the thick steel door swung open.

Michael was staring silently at all the witchcraft paraphernalia up there.

He was looking at all the potion ingredients with interest, picking jars up and reading what they were. "I have never even heard of half of this stuff."

"That's because most of it is only used for witchcraft, most people would have no idea what it can actually do," I said standing next to him. "This one, for example, Corridalius, is capable of blowing up a small country if mixed wrongly with this one, habivelous so we have to be careful when we're making them," I told him, showing him the jars.

"A new education finally, I really had no idea anything except explosives could blow things up until I met you and seen what you able to do it with just a hand gesture and now with all this." He gestured around the room staring wide eyed at the innocent looking jars.

"This is much more lethal than my blasting ability, that's why we have to be really careful mixing it, so we don't accidently blow up the house or anything," I said smiling.

He spent a while looking around and eventually came to the alter; it was rather dramatic looking when he did because the sunlight coming through the window shone a ray of light straight onto the book; it made it look quite mystical and I started to laugh.

"What are you laughing at?" he asked me, confused.

"The sun hitting the book like that and making it look way more dramatic than this moment calls for, all that's missing is some weird fog," I told him, still laughing.

He laughed too. "We do seem to have dramatic moments follow us around, don't we?"

I picked the book off the stand and took it to the couch. "Let's sit here, there's more room."

He sat down and looked at the front of the big heavy black book at the spindly writing that read... Niveus Veneficus 9-66 in dark red. "It's so old and mysterious looking; good thing not a lot of people speak Latin these days, if they stumbled across this, they wouldn't be able to translate what it says."

"No one is likely to stumble across it, we keep the loft door locked with a magical ward around it and the false security door does the rest, plus we don't get many non-magical visitors anyway. Besides most of what's inside is written in an ancient Wicca language," I told him.

I opened the book, flipped to the vampire section said a quick spell to translate into English for him, and let him read what it had to say.

"That is incredibly accurate, one of your ancestors must have known a vampire rather well at some point, otherwise they would *never* have known most of this stuff," he told me.

Interesting, so someone else in my family had been involved with a vampire, well well; it seems I'm not the only one to fall from grace.

I wished I could find out who it had been, they must never have been caught otherwise it would be in the book.

If I knew who it was, I could summon them and ask their advice. It was strangely comforting to know that some long ago relative was like me.

"I had no idea that dagger really existed," he said frowning. "Is there any way to find out who has it?"

"I'm not sure because if it doesn't say it in the book then the hunters name must not have been known. I could try and find out for you though."

"No, the book said they aren't really magical so if he attempted to kill a vampire with it, he would undoubtedly die within seconds of trying. It would be me he would come after since I'm the most powerful," he said.

"He would need a very powerful witch to bless the thing and there are none more powerful than us so whoever he is, he would probably come to us to do it and I would take it from him." I smiled at him.

We flicked through the book for a while longer and Michael was impressed with the wealth of magical knowledge it held.

I turned the page, and it was the section on Diabolus, ruler of the underworld.

Michael grunted when he saw it. "Diabolus, he came to my parents and wanted them to sign a treaty swearing we would never try to take over the underworld, they sent him packing, even though we have no desire to take over his domain they refused to bow down to such a vile creature," he said this with a look of disdain on his gorgeous face.

"Wow, they did? And what did he do?"

"What could he do? He left."

"That demon is the reason we get attacked, he doesn't attack us himself, not yet anyway, but every demon looking to impress him thinks killing us will move them up the food chain," I told him.

He looked at me, fury in his eyes. "Really? Well, I think I shall be having a little chat with Diabolus and inform him if he wishes to live much longer his minions better not lay a finger on you."

"You can't do that, Michael, it would expose our relationship, and besides, we can more than handle his minions."

"His minions yes, but what if he decides to come after you himself, he is well able to kill you, Angel."

"If that ever happens then you can get involved but not before then. How do you know he would listen to you anyway?"

He gave a humourless laugh. "Because he knows I can kill him, he fears my kind, and me especially. The last thing he wants is a pissed off upper echelon vampire finding him because he knows how it will end."

"Now it's my turn to be impressed," I said, looking at him with wonder.

We put the book back and went downstairs.

I had something to eat before my siblings got home so Michael wouldn't have to go through another uncomfortable scene eating food.

We went to my room, deciding to watch the music channels; turns out Michael loved watching music videos as much as I did.

I was heading into the bathroom to change for bed when I glanced at Michael and stopped dead.

He had taken off his jumper leaving only his t-shirt, which was lifted at the front, and his hands were on his belt, ready to undo it. He truly was carved by angels, every contour and muscle chipped perfectly.

I couldn't take my eyes off his pale hands on that belt; he saw me looking and stopped moving, a slight smile playing on his flawless lips then he walked slowly towards me.

My heart was hammering so hard even I could hear it and I found myself unable to swallow as my gaze went from his eyes to his belt and back again and wishing his t-shirt was off so I could see his bare chest.

I knew the imaginings I had of his body would be like a faded old black and white '50s' television next to a high-definition surround sound; in other words, not even close.

"Naughty naughty, Miss Angel, lusting after a vampire."

I couldn't speak yet, I didn't have to, my desire for him was in my expression and in my racing heart that I knew he could hear.

He was next to me then, his eyes burning into mine and the power of that look almost knocked me off my feet, I felt my knees tremble as he put his hand on the back of my neck and pulled my head to his and kissed me roughly.

I pushed against him, feeling his desire as his arms held me tightly to his body.

My hands took on a life of their own and grabbed his belt buckle, undoing it with force as he kissed me even harder.

All thoughts of right times and perfect moments gone as I got swept up in the passion and scorching heat of this moment.

He lifted me up and my legs were around his waist, not breaking the kiss he carried me to the bed and ripped my shirt open with one easy flick of his wrist. Oh, wow this was really happening. I was on fire as the passion for him ran through my entire body.

Then my door opened, and Kennedy came barging in. "Shit," I said.

She took in the scene on my bed with wide eyes, she bent and picked up a button from my blouse off the floor and stuttered out a sorry and went running back out the room.

Michael had moved off me, his hands were running through his hair as he sat up.

I just lay there dazed, trying to catch my breath. "Shit," I said again.

Michael stood up and fastened his belt and zip; he looked down at me and smiled. "We would have regretted that baby, the first time it happens for us it will be somewhere special, romantic and I will caress every inch of your body slowly." His silky voice was low and caressing.

"You're probably right." I sighed.

"I usually am," he said smiling slightly and averting his gaze from my torn blouse.

I got up from the bed and went to the bathroom to get changed, I looked at the state my torn shirt was in and how flushed I was and cursed Kennedy once again.

If that was a hint of things to come between us, it was going to be amazing, not that I thought for a second it wouldn't be; not with Michael's sexy smouldering looks and dangerous edge, and a thousand years of sexual experience.

I had a cold shower and had a hold of myself by the time I came out, ready for bed.

Neither of us spoke much; both of us were a bit shook up and not wanting to discuss it. Mainly because we couldn't trust ourselves to.

Chapter Eleven

Demon Slaughter

Finally, it was Saturday and Michael was taking me out tonight, I wondered where we would be going.

Michael got showered and went out to let me get ready and I put on music; happily, dancing around my room and feeling like my heart would explode with love.

At seven thirty Michael came in to change into his suit, I was in the bathroom pinning my hair up; I figured if I were wearing such a classy dress, then I would have a classy up-do to match.

I came out of the bathroom and my heart just stopped; Michael was standing there looking totally devastating in his new suit and holding a bouquet of long-stemmed red roses.

I tried to exhale but the sight of him had completely taken my breath away.

He was so dashingly handsome, much better than any leading man in any movie ever made, when you describe him as movie star handsome it was doing him a great disservice; he was so much better.

He handed me the roses and surveyed my look in appreciation, letting out a long whistle.

He twirled me around very slowly; taking in every inch of me. "You look so beautiful, Angel, legs for days."

He leant into my exposed neck and kissed the back of it gently, sending shivers down my spine.

"I love your hair up like that, I like to see your tempting neck," he said with a wicked glint in his bright amethyst eyes, and I laughed.

"And you, my dashing vampire, look more gorgeous than anyone has a right to look."

I put my roses in a vase with some water; I would sort them properly tomorrow.

"Thank you for the roses, I love them; they're so romantic." I smiled at him.

"OK, my fallen Angel, are you ready to go?"

"Yes; I am your prisoner, take me where you will my romantic immortal prince."

He took my hand, and we went downstairs and out to the newly polished Lamborghini.

We drove into Glasgow singing along to Mr Brightside, both of us feeling so free, alive, and happy.

He stopped the car at an in shot of the river Clyde in the city centre and I wondered if we were taking a water taxi to somewhere upriver.

Once we got out of the car and walked to the river edge however, I knew it wasn't a water taxi, I was looking at a beautiful white boat, lit up in the faded daylight by romantic lamps draped around the sides and across the top and a red carpet leading to the gangway.

I was once again taken aback by his sense of romance and imagination; I felt like I was living in some long-forgotten age where men knew how to woo women and treated them with respect and consideration.

An olden day king could not have courted his future queen better than Michael was with me.

When we got on the deck of the boat, I saw a table filled with candles and set for eating; there was champagne cooling in an ice bucket and love songs playing in the background.

It was perfection.

He took my hand as we set sail and twirled me around the deck to the music.

I looked up into his irresistible amethyst eyes; he had the softest expression on his translucent face as he whispered, "I love you."

I melted, my whole body sagged against him, and I could not look away from his glorious face. I would never forget how he was looking at me right now; it was imprinted on my soul forever.

I didn't know how many more overpowering surges of love for him my heart could take before it gave out and I just died right there in his strong arms.

As he spun me around with our gazes locked, I wanted to consume him wholly and be consumed by him; I would never regret becoming a fallen angel for my vampire, besides, I knew he would always catch me.

He sat me down and a waiter came out and opened the champagne, pouring us both a glass.

Michael held up his glass and said a toast, "I have seen snow fall in July, heat waves in December, I have seen many things you can only imagine but I never truly saw *anything* until I saw you. You are the light in my darkness and every moment I am blessed to spend with you I have the chance to love, to learn and to become something more than I ever imagined and if I were to lose you, I would be losing my whole world."

He was looking at me with so much emotion I felt my eyes well up a bit and I was speechless for a few minutes.

When I did speak, my voice was not quite steady. "Michael, I have spent my life in a state of numbness, broken dreams and duty, and then I met you and now I know what it's like to feel; I can feel the whole universe and everything it and if the world is still spinning and I am still feeling alive it's only because I am with you."

He leaned across the table and kissed me, and then we clinked glasses.

We drank some champagne, and the waiter came out with food, it was a sharing platter of Spanish tapas.

Michael picked up a fork and began feeding me bits from each dish; with the passing city lights as a beautiful backdrop and the tender look in his eyes, it was an amazingly romantic scene, and he took my heart away all over again.

After I was so full, I couldn't take another bite he put some creamy sauce on his finger and smudged it on the end of my nose.

"How cute you look," he said laughing.

"Very mature, Michael." I put some on his nose. "And how cute you look too," I said giggling.

We laughed and laughed, it really wasn't warranted, but we had just totally hit the giggles.

I picked up a sliced mushroom and stuck it to his forehead and nearly fell off my chair with laughter, he then put some tomato sauce on my chin. We looked ridiculous; and when the waiter came out to clear the table, he just looked at us, sitting there with sauce and mushrooms on our faces, with disapproval.

We laughed even harder at the waiter's face; he was obviously one of those snippy types who took himself far too seriously.

When we eventually stopped laughing, we cleaned each other's faces.

"There is chocolate cake for dessert but perhaps I should tell him to skip it, think of the massacre," Michael said starting to laugh again.

"No tell him to bring it out, I have plans for it," I said with a glint in my eye.

He just looked at me with narrowed eyes but signalled the waiter to bring it out.

When the cake was in front of me and the waiter left, I got up and sat on Michael's knee; I dipped my finger in the cake and then ran it along his lips. He sat very still, eyeing me speculatively until I put my mouth to his and slowly licked the chocolate from each lip. "Hmmm now that is what I call delicious," I said repeating my actions and licking his lips again.

"For that I would take up eating chocolate cake." He sighed in pleasure.

I put some on his throat and made a trail up to his lips and slowly ran my tongue along it, licking it all off gently.

I could feel him shiver. "Who knew food could be so nice," he said.

I looked at his chest and wanted to open his shirt and smear cake all over it and spend a long time licking it off.

He must have caught that thought and said, "That would only lead to us getting arrested, not that it wouldn't be worth it." He smiled that polar ice cap melting smile.

"Yeah, you're right, snippy waiter boy would take great pleasure in getting us arrested for indecent conduct."

I looked deeply into his beautiful eyes, yearning for him, knowing I could never get enough of him, not even if I lived a hundred thousand years.

He stood us up and we walked over to the railing, he was behind me with his arms wrapped around my waist and we stood watching the glimmering lights of the city pass by. It was a nice night, not too cold for October and no rain in sight.

"I love you, Michael," I said leaning further back into him.

"Oh, my Angel, I love you too, more than anything, more than I could ever have imagined in a thousand years."

I turned around and put my arms around his neck. "Dance with me, Michael," I whispered.

He held me tight, and I put my head on his chest as we swayed to the music.

I don't know how long we stayed like that; I didn't even notice the boat turn around and go back the way we came.

Eventually the boat came to a stop and Michael gave me a kiss before we disembarked.

In the car going home I was so serene and happy; I kept picking up his hand to kiss it.

"Why was there no one else on that boat except the staff?" I asked him.

"Because I hired it just for us, I didn't want people around us tonight."

"It was perfect, Michael, thank you," I said touching his face.

"You are welcome, my Angel; nothing is too good for you; you are betting everything you have on me, so I have to make it worth it," he said seriously.

"Every time I look at you, I know it will always be worth it Michael," I said just as seriously.

It was one am when we got home, Dylan was out with his friends and Kennedy was staying at Lindsay's house; we walked through the foyer, and I stopped him at the staircase. "Listen."

"To what?" he asked.

"The silence, it's nice to have the house to ourselves."

"Yes, it is but can we be trusted to be so alone? Knowing no one can walk in and interrupt us?" he asked looking at me.

I knew he was referring to the other day when we got carried away until Kennedy's barging in had forced us to stop.

"Mumm, I think we can handle it, I will put on the least sexy pj's I can find and we can bring the cats into bed with us."

He listened for a second. "One of the cats are in your room just now," he told me.

We had three black cats, Salem, Shadow and Sunset.

"That is utterly amazing how you can hear that. Doesn't it get distracting though being able to hear everything?"

"No, I learned at a young age how to tune sounds out and separate them from the things I wanted to hear; like your heart beat, for example, I purposely listened to it from the first moment I saw you."

We walked upstairs to my room, and I looked out my fleece pyjamas that had Donald duck on the front of them.

I stood looking with disgust in the mirror I couldn't believe I was about to show myself to him in these things, had it really come to this?

I came out the bathroom mortified at him seeing me like this, he was in bed, and burst out laughing. "Aww you look so cute."

I didn't want to look cute; cute did not go with demi-god.

I shot him a look of disgust and got into bed; he pulled me over to him, kissed my head, and ruffled my hair.

I slapped his hand away from my hair. "This is so humiliating," I grumbled.

"You look like you should be working in the Disney store, but I like it." He laughed.

"Yeah, yeah you're just so funny," I said sarcastically.

I put the light out to avoid further embarrassment and turned over onto my side; he cuddled into my back and kissed my neck.

"You still look sexy," he lied.

"Goodnight, Michael," I said.

He laughed. "Goodnight, baby."

I woke up first on Sunday and got up and got out of the offending duck pyjamas.

I decided to have a workout and get some sexual frustration out of my body so I changed into exercise clothes and went down stairs to our gym to do some kickboxing.

I was about half an hour into kicking the crap out of the martial arts dummy when Michael appeared.

He stood in the doorway, silently watching me until I was done.

I sat on the floor and was doing my stretches when he came over and sat next to me; he was looking at me in amusement so I shot him a look. "If you even think about mentioning the ridiculous pyjamas, I *will* find a way to kill you!"

He started to laugh, putting his palms out. "OK, OK, I won't mention it again I swear."

He stopped and looked at me the laughter leaving his eyes, replaced with desire as he lay me on my back and held me there.

"You don't want touch me Michael I'm all gross and sweaty from the workout, I need a shower," I told him trying to shove him off. A futile exercise.

He hit me with those eyes... *that* look. "You feel great," he said, then he put his head down and licked across my stomach. "And you taste great," he said huskily.

I felt my head explode and my heart start to race at the feel of his cool tongue across my stomach; it was pure electric, and my skin was suddenly feeling extra sensitive.

I gasped. "Are you trying to kill me? Because there's easier ways for you to do that," I said tightly, trying to stay uninvolved, to not get carried away.

He laughed. "I just like the way you taste, it's amazing to me; besides, I believe you started it with the cake last night," he said flipping me over and running his tongue slowly up my back and around my neck, making my whole body tremble.

I lay still, not able to move even if I wanted to and tried to remember how to breathe; inhale-exhale, inhale-exhale; I said to myself over and over like a mantra.

The feel of his tongue on my skin was making me lose concentration, it was excruciating pleasure.

"OK, you really need to stop now Michael," I managed to croak.

He flipped me back over and was up and out the room before I even realised, I was looking back at the ceiling.

I lay there for a while trying to recover; waiting for my body to stop shaking so I could get up.

We couldn't go on much longer like this, the attraction and chemistry between us was too great; we were so hyper aware of each other all the time that the slightest thing set us off.

A heard glass smashing, and a deep voice shout "witch" and I went running, shouting for Michael to stay where he was and not get involved.

I had just been thinking during my work out that it had been quiet on the demon front.

I came into the hall blasting, taking out two burly demons with bulging eyes and gnarly claws, but there was more.

My siblings weren't home; the demons must have sensed I was alone.

Just as I was deciding which one was the bigger threat and should be taken out first, they all came at me fast from opposite directions; two of them came charging at me while the third threw a massive blade at my head.

Before I even had a chance to react, a pale hand, quick as lightning reached in front of me and caught it.

The demons froze in utter fear, staring at the dangerous vampire behind me.

Michael's face was like ice, his expression pure murderous rage as he looked at the demons that wanted me dead.

He moved so fast none of us even seen it until he was ripping the six demons apart with his bare hands, literally tearing them limb from limb.

I stood motionless, watching him, his human façade completely gone, replaced by his full vampire nature as the body parts piled up.

I had never seen him less human or more dangerous as he brutally massacred the all of them, yet I could not make myself be afraid of him; it was respect I felt, not fear.

A head came rolling past me and I kicked it over to the pile of limbs, then I went upstairs and got a potion bottle and brought it back down to where Michael now stood quietly.

I walked over to the pile that was formerly six huge demons and looked around. I noticed an arm hanging from one of the chandeliers and waved it down to the pile. I threw the potion bottle (a concoction we called demon clean up) into it and the leftovers evaporated into thin air leaving only the shiny white marble floor.

I turned to Michael, and he was standing still as a statue watching me carefully, trying to gage my reaction. "I don't want you to be afraid," he said slowly.

I looked back at him calmly, still devoid of any kind of normal fear response and walked towards him. "I'm not afraid," I said.

He watched me wearily and noted there was no hesitation in my movements as I approached him and his face relaxed.

I put my arms around his neck and looked into his eyes. "Thank you for not listening to me, that was getting a bit dicey till you showed up," I said quietly.

I couldn't believe how much I loved him; every time I looked at him, I loved him even more.

"I couldn't just sit there while demons tried to kill you Angel, my instinct is to protect you at all costs, and I will not apologise for that." His silky voice was impassioned, and his hands were gripping the sides of my face.

"I know," I whispered, kissing him.

"It's just I keep thinking there will be some vampire thing that will freak you out and you'll leave me," he said sadly, putting his head down and not looking at me.

I lifted his chin. "Look at me, Michael." I put my hands on his heartbreakingly beautiful face. "Nothing, and I repeat, nothing will ever freak me out about you. There isn't anything in this whole universe that will ever make me leave you, I love you and I want to be with you forever."

He was staring into my eyes. "How did I ever get this lucky? You have been worth the thousand-year wait. You truly are my angel and I love you more than words could ever convey." His melodic voice was silky soft once more.

We went upstairs and decided to spend the whole day and night in bed; since my parents would be home next weekend this would be our last Sunday together.

I had a shower and changed into lounge around clothes and when I came out the bathroom Michael was laying stretched diagonally across the bed with his arms above his head.

Without looking around at me, he said, "And here I was hoping you would put on the hot fluffy Donald duck pyjamas again." He chuckled.

"Oh, so what, vampires are funny now?" I asked him, walking over to the bed.

"I wish I had taken a photo of you looking like a Disney girl." He was grinning up at me now.

"That's it, you'll be sorry now," I said and jumped on him, sitting on top of him and holding his arms in place above his head.

"I could easily get out of this but fortunately for you I have no desire to," he said laughing.

"You think so huh?" I said. "Well, come on then."

"I know so, and I am perfectly comfortable with you sitting on me. I'm really enjoying my view," he said not attempting to move.

"What if I took my top off, would you be so comfortable then?" I asked him grinning.

"It certainly wouldn't hurt my view but we both know you won't do it because you want the perfect night as much as I do my love. if you start stripping off on top of me… well there's only so much self-control I am capable of, and you would get carried away right along with me." He gave me a cheeky grin.

"Really? I am perfectly able to resist you. In fact, resisting you is bloody easy," I said looking at him smugly.

"Why don't you go ahead and take your top off then Miss Angel." He hit me with those eyes and his voice dropped to a seductive satin tone. "Or would you like me to take it off for you?"

I gulped remembering the other day. "No, that's OK, I would feel like I was taking liberties since its barley even a challenge to resist you," I said full of false bravado.

"I see and you don't want me to be at a disadvantage, is that it?" he asked playing along.

"That's exactly it." I smiled.

He lazily stretched his arms further up above him and said huskily, "In that case why don't you unbutton my shirt, then I won't be at a disadvantage. Go ahead… but do it very very slowly."

My heart went into overdrive as I imagined doing just that.

"Your heart is answering for you, my Angel," he said calmly.

"You don't play fair, listening to my heart is cheating!" I said and hit his chest in mock anger.

He laughed and pulled me down and cuddled me, I tipped his head back and bit his neck.

"What on earth are you biting my neck for crazy girl?" he asked laughing.

"Well, I figure nobody ever bites a vampire so I thought I would be the first," I answered him. "How did it feel?"

"It felt nice actually," he said touching the spot I'd bitten.

"Would it feel nice if you were to bite my neck?" I asked him, sensing an opportunity and sitting back up.

"Yes, we would exchange full blood from each other, and the vampire blood would make you feel wonderful even as the life drained from you," he said honestly.

"It would also be very intense though because it would be the moment you would make me immortal as bonds between two people go it doesn't get much more powerful than that," I said looking at him and touching his teeth.

He closed his eyes and pain flashed across his face and when he opened his eyes, he looked tortured. "We're not having this discussion again Angel, I will not condemn your higher purpose I love you too much."

"If you love me too much, then you would do it, Michael," I said sadly.

"Angel, you can have anything you want, anything your heart desires I will give you; but not that… never that."

"That's all I want," I whispered.

"Please… please don't ask me to do that," his satin voice was strained.

"I'm not asking you to do it right now, but you will have to do it eventually otherwise we can't be together forever; we couldn't even be together for my brief lifetime because once I start to age, we will have to split up," I told him, my voice rising; desperate to make him understand.

"No, we won't, we can be together till the end of your life." His tone was gentle.

"Don't you see we can't Michael? I would be an old woman and you would still be youthful; it wouldn't work."

"We would make it work, Angel."

"OK, let me put it to you this way, once I start to look a lot older than you, I will end our relationship; it will kill me, but I *will* do it."

He didn't answer he just pulled me down onto his chest; I lifted my legs so I was lying flat on him and we didn't move, both lost in our own thoughts.

I didn't understand his complete refusal to even think about changing me, he didn't struggle with what he was so how could he really believe he would be condemning me. He put too high a worth on being mortal.

I knew we would have to lighten the mood, so I got up and switched on a music channel and said, "Come on, let's laugh at those lame pop bands that think they're rockers."

He smiled at me. "OK, sounds like fun."

The mood had visibly shifted as we lay bantering about boy bands who thought they were cool and watching some of their cringe worthy videos.

No one bothered us and it was utter bliss to just lie together in bed uninterrupted, having a laugh and just revelling in being together, because we both knew once my parents came back, we wouldn't be together all the time.

I didn't want to think about that yet, we would come up with some solution I was sure we would, we had to, it was that simple; there was no way we could be parted now.

As I drifted off to sleep in his arms, I wondered what we would be like after we made love; if this was what our bond was like now how much stronger would it be after we slept together? With the added emotional attachments of sex with someone you love so deeply already.

I didn't know if we could bear the brunt of even more intense emotional feelings without exploding into little pieces. People just weren't built to experience this rainbow of never-ending powerful feelings. But then our love wasn't of this world, it was from somewhere else, another time and place that was eternal.

Maybe we have been lovers in all our past lives, and this is us just now able to stay together forever because Michael was now immortal. Our reward for our souls always finding each other because true love never dies. No matter what physical form you take or what other plane of existence you find yourself in. even death can't kill it.

Chapter Twelve

A Drop of Blood

Monday dawned dull, cold and wet and I could hear the rain beating on my window but waking up with Michael meant no weather conditions could put a dampener on my day.

We lay cuddled up together for a while and I felt myself drift back to sleep.

I was particularly tired this morning and I just really didn't want to get up for a few reasons, not the least of which was laying here holding me tightly.

He kissed my neck and made me shiver. "Come on, sleepy girl, time to get up."

He had been up and showered while I was still asleep, me being unconscious while he showered was a good thing because I usually sat and tortured myself with images of what he looked like with water running down his perfect hard body.

"Mmmm, five more minutes," I said sleepily, gripping his arms to me.

"Angel you are making it unbelievably difficult for me to get up," he said kissing my neck again. Only this time he wasn't messing about, he lifted my hair and kissed all around the back of my neck and across my shoulders and down my spine.

I was certainly awake now as his lips trailing kisses across my skin made my heart began to crack like thunder.

He laughed as he heard my heart. "I think you're awake now."

"Yes, I certainly am you evil kisser," I said sitting up. "That's better than a caffeine IV." I was fully alert.

He handed me a tray with fresh orange juice, scrambled eggs on toast and a single red rose. "Breakfast is served, my Angel."

"You made me breakfast in bed?" I asked, touched by this latest romantic gesture. "I can't believe you did this."

"Well, you deserve to be spoiled but I must admit to cheating with the rose, I took it from your bouquet," he said smiling at me.

"Wow could you be any more perfect?" I asked shaking my head and eating some eggs.

"I'm hardly perfect, Angel, I am in fact incredibly flawed you just can't see it," he said curtly.

I ignored that comment and ate my toast hungrily resolving to discuss it with him later. He had no flaws so it would be interesting to find out what he considered his flaws at a time when I could grill him properly.

He was dead wrong when he said I couldn't see it, I had never seen anything as clearly as I see him, I was more than aware of everything about him. Like his movements, his body language, the different means of looks he gives, changes imperceptible no one but I would notice.

My morning classes didn't go very well, I had not prepared for any of them and found myself having to just throw in random comments and hope they made sense.

At lunchtime I hurried to meet Michael, he had two afternoon classes on a Monday which he skipped for me last week so I told him I would wait for him today and go to the library and make a start on my Wuthering Heights paper.

Sally invited us both to her Halloween party on Saturday night; she lived in a three-bedroom student flat she shared with Liam and a girl I didn't know.

The flat was a mess, which made it perfect for throwing wild parties, and since all their neighbours were also students there were never any noise complaints. I told her we would come along because it did sound like fun.

Michael said he would walk me to the library, and we said our goodbyes to Sally and Liam and left the café.

Michael was quiet as we walked out, thinking about something; after a few minutes, he said, "Liam has a crush on you."

"No, he doesn't, don't be silly."

"Trust me he does. I caught his reaction when Sally asked us both to her party," he said easily.

"What reaction? He looked normal to me," I said laughing.

"That's because you see him through different eyes, I see him with my vampire eyes and a facial shift, even a tiny one, is as good as hearing words and he wasn't happy that I was invited along with you," he explained.

"Wait a minute you can detect slight facial flickers that I can't?" I asked him, shocked at this latest revelation.

"Yes, Angel, I can, all of my kind can read everyone like a book. You, however, are the exception to that rule; I find you awfully hard to read sometimes and I think it is because you're not human, or your magical shield, I am not entirely sure." He stopped and looked into my eyes.

"Hmm interesting. Does it bother you that you can't always read me?"

"Very much so. It is incredibly frustrating not to be able to pick up on your feelings when I can do it with everyone else," he answered still looking in my eyes.

"It's not like you don't know how I feel about you though, Michael. That is so clear it may as well be written across the sky in pink neon," I told him earnestly.

"It's not that, it's all the other little things I'm used to being able to pick up on. If you were human, I would know every little thing you were feeling about a situation, a conversation, a place or a person," he said releasing me from his gaze and beginning to walk again.

"Well, now you know how normal people feel," I said as he took my hand. "Does it bother you if Liam has a crush on me?" I asked as an afterthought.

"No. Why would it? Some insignificant little boy is no threat to me, if you were going to leave me it would be for a much bigger reason than some guy," he said shrugging his shoulders.

We were at the library now and I turned to him and put my hand on his cheek. "I love you, Michael," I told him simply.

"I know you do darling, and I love you too, much more than I could ever properly articulate," he said pulling me close and kissing me gently.

As he turned to leave, I noticed a girl walking along staring at him, she didn't take her eyes off him for a second and she walked right into a pole. That had to hurt. Seeing Michael was probably an extraordinary experience for most Humans, and they couldn't really be blamed for reactions like that one.

I actually got some studying done in the library I was surprised to be caught up in another romance other than my own, but I had always loved the story of Catherine and Heathcliff.

I realised it was ten past four and I gathered up my things and rushed out to meet Michael, I couldn't believe I was late.

As I rushed outside, I stopped in surprise because he was there waiting for me, looking dark and dangerous leaning against the Lambo in his leather coat. Once again, he took my breath away as I felt the complete body blitz hit me that always accompanied the unexpected situations involving him.

I let the feelings rush over me as I walked towards him, suddenly feeling like I was floating, and my crashing heart was the waves in which I sailed.

His lips turned up slightly and I knew he could hear my hearts erratic behaviour. He reached for me and swept me towards him so quickly I didn't even feel myself moving, and then I was in his arms in a strong embrace as he watched me with a mixture of amusement and passion.

On the drive home, I asked him how he knew to come and get me in the library.

"I knew you were going to be starting your Wuthering Heights essay and I knew you were going to get caught up in Heathcliff and Catherine's world, hence I knew I better come and get you, although I did think I would have to actually come in and get you," he said smiling at me.

"How did you know that I would be caught up in the story?" I asked him, astonished he knew that without me telling him.

"Because I know you love the book, I have seen the well-worn copy of it in your room." His observation of things like that was astounding.

"And what else have you concluded about it?" I asked genuinely fascinated with his opinion.

"Well, I know you have a masochistic need to believe Heathcliff's cruelty and violence is a tortured expression of his frustrated love of Catherine, and as such you see him as a romantic hero."

"And you disagree with that?" I asked him.

"Yes, I do, I think Heathcliff is the most frustrating character. He refuses to fight for his love, and instead has a chip on his shoulder so runs away to make a fortune and come back only for revenge and proceeds to spend the rest of his life being cruel and angry and making everyone, including himself, utterly miserable when it was his own choices that caused his situation." He shook his head.

"Cathy frustrates me to no end; I mean she supposedly had this powerful love that transcends social and moral norms; even going so far as to claim they are the same person yet she ups and marries someone else. I will never understand that. If you genuinely loved like that, nothing would make you marry someone else so I can see why it destroyed Heathcliff," I told him seriously.

"So, you condone his utter cruelty because it was done in the name of love?" he asked with interest.

"I don't condone it, but I guess I understand it to some degree."

"Well, that's the angle you should use on your essay," he said evenly, not the least bit surprised that I saw Heathcliff as a romantic hero.

I pondered that for a while. "Why are you not surprised at my view of Heathcliff?" I asked him, noticing we were at my house now.

He stopped the car and looked at me sighing. "Because you view me with the same blind romantic notions. You see the tortured Vampire in love with you and willing to do anything for you while completely overlooking my flaws." His silky voice was low and smooth.

"I do not overlook anything about you, Michael. What exactly is it you think I'm failing to see?" I asked him abruptly.

"You fail to see my utter selfishness at allowing you to become involved with me in the first place. You do not see how my love for you blinds me of all reason, and, that every minute you spend with me you are in danger from something or other and I'm allowing it because I simply do not have the strength to leave you or to turn you," he said slowly.

"I don't view that as flaws, Michael, the cards had already been dealt, and you and I are both just playing the hand we have because we can't not. We didn't set out to fall in love with each other but here we are and I for one am not sorry about it, nor would I do anything differently even if I could go back and start again," I said with my hands on his arms.

"I am not sorry about it, Angel, but I am sorry for how much more difficult it will make your life."

"Well, I'm not. You need to stop thinking that you are ruining my life because you're not; you are the reason for my life. You are my truth in a world full of lies," I said strongly.

"Oh, my Angel, every time I doubt true purity really exists all I have to do is look into your eyes. You are everything good in my life, you are everything I'm not and I cherish you and I will go on cherishing you for all of eternity." His eyes had softened, and his satin voice seemed to stroke my ears.

The rain was coming down hard now and beating a rhythmic drum on the car window as we sat staring at each other.

"Fancy that kiss in the rain now?" he asked his lips lifting in a smile that momentarily stunned me.

"Absolutely," I said laughing.

He leapt out of the car, and with one fluid movement had me out of the car and into his arms in the rain, kissing me and taking my breath away.

I held on to him tightly, the heat from the kiss overriding the cold rain as we got utterly soaked. We stayed kissing like that for a long time, neither one of us willing to be sensible and forsake the romance of the moment by going inside where it was dry.

Eventually we stopped kissing and stood looking at each other in wonder as the rain lashed down around us and the sky darkened, and our wet clothes clung to us like a second skin.

He looked unbelievable with the rain running off his hair and down his perfect face and his wet clothes defining every muscle in his chest. I trailed a finger across every defined bump utterly mesmerised at his exceptional beauty.

He stood very still as he watched me carefully, studying the expression on my face as I touched his chest over his wet clothes.

I looked up into his intense eyes and knew I should stop now but I could not seem to force myself to pull the hand back that was touching him.

He did it for me, moving so suddenly I jumped. He laughed and pulled me inside and out of the rain.

I had a warm shower to heat up then I made dinner for everyone. I made pasta with chicken and a cheese sauce and made pretence of asking Michael if he was hungry yet after the three cheeseburgers he ate at lunch. He laughed hard at my fabrications and said no he wasn't hungry yet, he would have something later and he wandered out of the kitchen.

We finished eating and I told my siblings to do the dishes since I had cooked and then I went off in search of Michael.

He wasn't in my room, so I went back downstairs and wandered from room to room looking for him.

I finally found him in the music room playing the piano. He was playing the most beautiful tune, so I picked up an acoustic guitar and joined in. the result was the loveliest sound and Michael wrote the notes down for the piano and the chords for the guitar.

We played it for a while both lost in the beauty of the music and Michael wrote down any changes we made.

"Now all we need is lyrics and we've got ourselves a hit," I said jokingly.

"Yes, I can see it now, vampire and witch record love song." He laughed.

We spent the rest of the night playing our song and perfecting it.

I was amazed at how naturally we played together and how the melody just seemed to come together so easily as we both played so uninhibitedly.

"Everlasting," he said suddenly.

"Everlasting what?"

"That's what we should name our song," he said. "The ballad everlasting."

"I love it," I told him.

We smiled at each other warmly both enjoying the musical talent of the other as we played our ballad again from the top.

We both went to bed that night humming the tune. I couldn't think of anything more romantic than composing a song together to express our love for one another.

The next day I was awake first, so I had my shower and got ready then went down to get some breakfast. He came into the kitchen just as I was pouring some milk into my bowl of cereal.

I looked into his eyes as he bent over to kiss me and noticed they were tired. He would need to feed in a soon. "Your eyes are tired," I told him.

"I need sustenance, my Angel?" he said. It was a rhetorical question.

I ate my cereal as he watched me silently, perhaps wondering, as I was, how much more difficult it was going to be for him to be around me all the time when he needed food.

I didn't want to make things harder for him, but I also selfishly didn't want him to go leave to go hunting. And he thought he was selfish? I was breaking new records in selfish just now.

The day passed without event, and I spent the morning listening to Sally's endless chatter about what she was going to wear on Saturday. She asked me what I was planning on wearing and I told her truthfully that I hadn't thought about it, and I would decide on Saturday.

She looked at me like I was lying and just not wanting to tell her what I was wearing. What was that about? Sometimes she bugged me no end. This was why she was just a university friend and not a real one, well that along with her nosiness and compulsive gossiping behind everyone's backs.

I noticed Michael's eyes even more by the end of the day and he looked in pain as my scent enveloped him.

I reached over and ran a finger over one of his eyes. "When are you going hunting?"

142

He closed his eyes briefly. "Tomorrow night."

"Is there anything I can do?" I asked him quietly.

"No, just don't fall over and cut yourself or anything and we should be OK." He smiled at me.

"Well lucky for you I'm very sure footed and well balanced so I don't fall over much," I said laughing a little.

"Yes, lucky me." He laughed too, a genuine laugh at the madness of this conversation. A conversation neither of us ever thought we would be having with someone. *Try not to bleed in case I kill you.* I knew some people would think me insane to be with someone who had to restrain himself from drinking my blood, but those people would never know a love like this. It was so powerful it overcame vampiric bloodlust.

He pulled the car up to my house and we got out. Michael told me he was just going straight up to my room because he wasn't much in the mood for pretending to eat, understandable when I could see how thirsty he was getting by the hour.

I walked into the kitchen and saw my siblings making dinner; I was relieved because I didn't feel like cooking tonight.

The kitchen was a riot though with pots and dishes on every surface and food all over the island in the middle.

"A bit overkill guys, you're only feeding three," I said looking around.

"We've got some friends coming over so we're having a dinner party," Dylan told me as he mixed mayonnaise into a bowl of tuna pasta.

"Oh right, well do you want me to help?" I asked.

"Nope, we've got it under control, help yourself to whatever you want to eat," Kennedy said.

"OK, I'll just have some of that tuna pasta Dylan then I'll get out of your way," I said picking up a plate and giving it to Dylan to fill.

I sat at the breakfast bar and ate my pasta in silence just watching them making even more mess. Knowing them they will say a spell to clean up instead of doing it themselves.

"Is Michael's Lamborghini Elemento parked out front?" Dylan asked me.

"Yes, why? Do you want him to move it into the garage?" I asked getting up.

"No no no I want it parked out there; it's such a cool car. I want all my mates to see it and drool," Dylan said seriously.

I looked at him and laughed, shaking my head. "OK then."

I walked to the door then turned around. "No one touches it, Dylan, I'm serious; if there is so much as a dirty mark or a scratch on that car, I will be blaming you and I'll let Michael kick your arse. Understand?"

"Yeah, sis, I get it," he grumbled as I walked out.

I went upstairs to my room and Michael was lying on the bed listening to music. I noticed I hadn't sorted my bouquet of roses properly and they were all still bunched up in the vase, so I took the vase into my bathroom and poured out the water and put in fresh water.

I came back into the room and began arranging the flowers, so they were spread out and telling Michael about Dylan wanting all his mates to drool over his car and he was laughing.

There was one rose tangled in another, so I pulled them apart and a thorn sliced down my middle finger. The blood poured out of the cut quickly and I froze.

Michael was staring at me in horror his eyes were wide and dark, and his body was tense. I could not move my legs.

He walked over to me as I stared fixatedly at his face. He lifted my hand up and looked at it for a second then he brought my bleeding finger to his mouth and sucked the blood from it in a strangely erotic manner.

I was hypnotised watching him drink my blood so sensuously and so naturally, and to be honest it felt quite nice. The pain from the cut was no longer there.

I couldn't move even if I wanted to as he gripped my arm tighter and began to suck my finger harder, his eyes were flaming now. Was he about to lose it? I didn't know, all I could do was hope he could control himself, but I realised that might be asking too much even from him.

"Michael," I said softly. "Michael, you're starting to hurt me."

He looked into my eyes, the pain and torture in his eyes was evident; he was conflicted by his love for me and the taste of my blood making him want more.

I could have transported out but we both needed to know he would stop, and besides, I would rather die by his hand than live without him, so I stayed put and just looked deep into his eyes.

He squeezed his eyes shut and tore my finger from his mouth. "Get away from me, Angel, you're not safe," he shouted desperately.

"It's OK, Michael, it's OK." I walked slowly closer to him. "You've controlled it." But I noticed his fangs had extended as he backed away from me and still, I couldn't make myself be afraid of him. I just gazed at his animalistic beauty in wonder.

"You are standing in the face of ultimate danger and hoping for miracles, Angel," he said tightly.

"I'm not hoping for miracles, Michael, I'm banking on you."

He looked at me as if I were insane as his fangs retracted and I saw the control sweep back over him.

We stood staring at each other, eyes locked and neither of us moving, not even blinking. The whole world stood still waiting to see what would happen.

He shook his head angrily and moved so fast I couldn't really see him. Then he was gone, and my curtains blew in with the wind telling me he had gone out the window.

I stood for a minute wondering if he would come back, if I would ever see him again and I began to shake, and my chest tightened at the thought I might not.

I walked over to my bed and fell on top of it where he had lain only a while before, and silent tears fell from my eyes. Tears of sorrow and regret that one careless act might cost me Michael's love forever.

How could I be so stupid? The one thing he asked me not to do was cut myself and that's exactly what I did; in a moment of unthinking stupidity, I cut my finger on a rose thorn. I wasn't even being careful, not aware that I could cut myself, but I should have been. I should have been a lot more vigilant. I knew he was thirsty and needed to hunt.

This was what he had been afraid of all along that I would become too complacent in his company and do something stupid, and now it had happened. He had been trying to drum into my thick head how dangerous he could be, how much danger I could be in with him, and I didn't listen.

I was a first-class idiot. I was selfish and thoughtless and if I lost him, I would only have myself to blame.

I lay on my bed and cried hopeless tears, wishing he had killed me if he was going to leave me.

I wasn't ashamed in the least of my desperate need for him; I was well past the point of pretending I didn't need him for me to live.

I felt like I had been kicked black and blue, my whole body ached badly. I needed him to come back. We had to fix this.

I refused to give up, I couldn't concede it was over; not like this, not with the all the love we have for each other. I refused to fall apart when there was still some hope he would come back.

I lay on my side, pulled my legs up, and held them in place with my arms, somehow forcing myself to keep it together by this one act; that if I could somehow hold my body physically together then I would stay emotionally stable too. I lay like this for a long time, unaware of time passing. I didn't even hear the party going on downstairs, I heard nothing but my own voice calling Michael's name every now and then.

I fell asleep like this and when I woke up my music was still playing but it was light outside and there was no sign of Michael, but his car was still where it had been the night before. I rolled onto my back and lay staring at the ceiling, willing myself not to fall apart.

I couldn't even phone Dallas because then I would have to tell her what Michael really was in order to get across how bad this was, and I couldn't just tell her we had an argument because she would think I was completely overreacting. There was no one I could talk to and the one person that could make it better didn't come back.

I got up and had a shower in a trance because I figured I should just go into Uni to take my mind off of it for a while, it had to beat just lying here like a half-shut knife.

I drove to Uni by myself for the first time in weeks and I felt the sharp pain of his absence hit me all over again. I didn't dare put on any music in case a song came on that would make me cry. A guy cut me off on the road and normally that kind of thing would make me angry, but I didn't even react today. I was drained of my emotions, unable to use any of them in case it opened a gate.

I pulled up to the car park and stopped my car but as I turned to get out, I just couldn't do it; I couldn't face people and I certainly couldn't face gossiping Sally studying the state I was in and grill me about what happened. No, that wasn't going to happen.

I put my seatbelt back on and turned my keys in the ignition and drove out of there like a maniac. It was already lunchtime anyway, so I had missed my morning classes, not that I particularly cared about missing them.

I spent the rest of the day just driving around trying not to let the empty feeling engulf me.

It was dark by the time I got home, I had no plans to eat so I just dragged myself upstairs and lay staring at the ceiling again.

About an hour later Kennedy knocked on my door and said there was someone to see me that it was a girl who looked like Michael. She looked at me and knew there was something wrong, but I just ignored her and told her to send Ava up.

Ava came into the room as quietly as Michael always moved. "Oh, Angel, are you alright?" she asked in her silky voice that was a lot like his.

"Not really, Ava. I don't know where he is or what he's thinking and it's making me crazy," I said sadly.

"He told me what happened when he came home last night, he was broken up about it. He loves you so much, Angel, and he's hating himself a whole lot right now," she said sitting down next to me.

"He has no reason to hate himself it was my entire stupid fault; I knew he was thirsty and yet I made no attempt to be careful. Do you think he'll come back?"

"Honestly, I don't know, Angel, he loves you to the point of irrationality and if he really thinks he could put you in danger like that again then he'll stay away from you to protect you, even if it kills him," she said slowly like she was thinking aloud.

"If he doesn't come back, he may as well have killed me than let me die this slow painful death without him," I said with tears in my eyes.

"Listen, Angel, I know my brother and he's prone to over analysing situations, but he'll see he wouldn't have killed you and his love for you will bring him back. I'm sure of it," she told me, wiping away a tear that was threatening to engulf me.

"I don't know, you didn't see his face, the way he looked at me when he left. It was fury and hatred in his expression."

"He was angry at himself, Angel, not you, although I know he was angry you didn't leave the room when he told you to, but it's not you he hates it's himself. He'll get over it once he knows you're safe with him."

"So, in the meantime I just have to lie here and try not to give up?" I asked her quietly, so quiet a human wouldn't have heard me.

"Yes, sweet Angel, you can't give up because it's not over. That much I am sure of," she said in a low serious voice.

"What made you come here tonight, Ava?" I asked, suddenly curious about why she would bother.

She sighed. "Because I know how much you and my stupid brother love each other, and after I saw you drive up to uni today then lose your courage to actually get out of the car, I knew I had to try to comfort you."

"That is so nice of you to care, thank-you for being so kind," I said touching her cool white hand.

"Well, I have a feeling you're going to be part of our family soon and I had to try to help you. Michael told me you know we're vampires, and how it doesn't bother you in the least, and he told me who you were. What a situation," she said gently.

"I know it's a mess, but we'll sort it out. Well, if he ever comes back." I gave her a slight smile.

She leaned over and put her cool cheek to mine and gave me a hug. "It'll be OK, Angel; my brother can't stay away from you; I think he's proven that time and again so keep your chin up."

I felt a bit better after Ava's visit and decided to have a hot bath and listen to some music. No matter how hot my bath was though I still couldn't get rid of the icy hand of fear that gripped me every time I thought about him, and my fragile heart was on the verge of shattering like glass. I wasn't used to feeling vulnerable.

I came out the bath and got dried and crawled under my covers. I could smell his lovely scent off my sheets and pillows, and it nearly knocked me over the edge. I hugged the blanket around me inhaling deeply.

Was this all I had left of him? His smell on my bed and some clothes in my wardrobe? No, I had to believe he would come back, I just had to.

I fell into a fitful sleep tossing and turning all night and dreaming of him.

I didn't even bother to get out of bed the next day. Who was I kidding that I was going to go to uni? It wasn't going to happen so I just put the duvet over my head and closed my eyes, hoping I would have the great oblivion of sleep again.

Hours passed and I wasn't even aware of it, I was just lying hidden beneath my duvet in a kind of limbo. Someone knocked on my door and I shouted at them to leave me alone. I really couldn't deal with questions and making up lies just now.

I wasn't interested in eating either I just wanted to be left alone to stay under my covers until I felt equipped to deal with the real world again.

I must have eventually fallen back asleep because when I opened my eyes again my room was in darkness and the whole house was silent.

I had no idea what time it was, and I couldn't have cared less I just wanted to sleep so I closed my eyes again knowing the relief of sleep was just minutes away.

I must have been dreaming again because I felt his body slide into bed next to me and his strong arms wrap around me. I could smell his comforting scent and feel his breath on my cheek and my heart constricted in yearning for him. Not wanting to wake up from this dream, I burrowed deeper into my covers. If I could only have him in my dreams, then asleep is where I'll stay.

"Angel!" His beautiful satin voice seemed so real. "Angel, you're awake."

I felt my body tense. I was awake? He was here. "Tell me when I switch the lamp on you won't disappear," I said desperately.

"I won't disappear I promise you," his silky voice said in my ear as he stroked my hair.

I put my arm out without moving from him and turned the lamp on. Light flooded the room, and he was still there, lying in my bed with his arms still around me and looking heart-breaking.

I turned to face him and threw myself into his embrace, burrowing into his neck and crying. "I didn't know where you were or if I would ever see you again and I missed you so much. I died and died for you in this bed, trying to keep believing you would come back so my heart didn't break and shatter into a million tiny pieces." I was rambling as I cried into him.

He held me tighter. "I'm so sorry to put you through that baby. I was dying too. I love you so much." His voice was thick with emotion.

I looked up into his beautiful face, his eyes were the lovely soft lilac again, and there were tears in them as he gazed at me. "I could never leave you, not really my Angel. I talked myself into never coming back but I couldn't do it, I finally realised a couple of hours ago if I'm not loving you everything else is a waste of time," he said as a tear fell from his eyes.

I wiped his cheeks. "I was never really in danger, Michael; I knew you wouldn't kill me I believed that with everything in me but you had to know it too. You gained control, you found some superhuman strength somewhere inside you and you controlled it even though you were tasting my blood and it should have been impossible for you to stop, but you did. That should tell you I will never be anything but safe with you no matter what."

"I should never have put you in that position, Angel, where it might cross your mind that I might actually kill you because I'm drinking your blood. I should have left the room till you healed the cut, but I couldn't stop myself when I saw you bleed," he said pain shooting across his face.

"I would give you my blood, Michael; I would give you the final beat of my heart if I could die in your arms because I don't want to... no... I *can't* live without you, I just can't. I would rather have you kill me than leave me," I said fiercely, gripping his face.

"I'm not going to do either, Angel; I won't kill you or leave you... I can't, it's that simple, I can't." His voice was flat. "For better or worse, I'm afraid you're stuck with me." He smiled then and his eyes softened as he watched me.

"At least you know you can even drink my blood and not kill me, that's got to be a relief," I said jokingly.

"I'm not sure we're ready to joke about it just yet, it's still a bit too fresh," he said seriously but a slight smile pulled at his lips.

He pulled me down and kissed me and I held onto him like I was afraid he would disappear again.

"Look at the state of us, we are absolutely useless without each other," he said laughing.

"I know, it's pathetic how much we need each other." I laughed. "I mean what kind of vampire are you that you can't even kill me?"

He shook his head. "More jokes? Really?"

"No that was the last one, you're right it's not very funny. I'm just so relieved to have you back," I said and kissed him.

We spent the whole night just lying kissing each other. I had no interest in sleeping now I just wanted to savour every second of being with him again, knowing that everything was going to be alright.

I think we finally fell asleep around sunrise.

Chapter Thirteen

Favourite Decade

I woke up first, Michael must have been exhausted it's not like he got as much sleep as I had yesterday. I stole a glance at the clock it was 12:30 pm. I knew we wouldn't be going into uni today so there was no sense waking him up. I just lay and gazed at him instead.

The overpowering feeling of love for him washed over me as I watched him sleep. He looked so carefree in his sleep, no sign of anxiety anywhere on his stunning face.

I took a deep breath and exhaled slowly relief flooding my body that we were together again and knowing there was nowhere else in the world I would rather be and no one else in the world I would rather be with.

Dylan came running in suddenly, not even stopping to knock first and looking freaked out. I sat bolt upright wondering what was wrong and asked him why his eyes were so wide.

"Angel, Mum and Dad just got back," he practically shouted it.

"Shit, I forgot they were home today," I practically shouted too as panic set in.

Michael woke up then and sat up when he saw my face. "What's going on?" he asked looking worried.

"Mum and Dad are back, and they saw your car parked outside," Dylan told Michael.

"What did you tell them?" he asked Dylan, rubbing his eyes.

"I just said you came by about an hour ago to see, Angel, but you two better get up and dressed fast in case Mum comes up to say hello," Dylan was practically shouting again.

"Yeah, you're right we better get dressed quickly. Dylan, go and stall them, tell them I'll be down soon," I said jumping out of bed and running into my bathroom.

Michael still had on his clothes from last night, so I quickly got showered and dressed and ran a brush through my hair, and then I put on a bit of make-up.

This was a nightmare I had completely forgotten it was Friday, how could I forget that? I was so stupid sometimes.

While I was getting ready Michael had made the bed and put all his stuff that was lying around in a bag and hid it in my wardrobe under a pile of clothes. Not that my mum would go trolling through my wardrobe, but it was best to be cautious just in case.

"OK, do I look flustered?" I asked him.

"A little. Just calm down and take a deep breath. It's not strange that your boyfriend would come by to spend time with you, but they may wonder why neither of us are in uni today," he said calmly.

"What am I going to say to that?" I asked, staring at him in disbelief of his total calm demeanour.

I started wracking my brain for excuses. This was ridiculous, I wasn't a child ditching school, I was a university student who knew which classes I could and could not afford to miss. It's not like they minded me missing classes when it was something Wiccan involved.

"Just tell them we're heading in now, we skipped morning classes so you could finish a paper that's due in today and I was helping you," he said reasonably.

"Yeah, that sounds fair enough. Plus, if I say we're going in now it means we don't have to hang around and get asked any questions." I grabbed my bag. "OK, let go."

We went downstairs. I found them all in the sitting room and I went in and gave my parents a hug and told them we were heading into uni to drop my essay off.

"Hello, Michael, nice to see you again," my mum said.

"Hello again, lovely to see you. You both look well," Michael said, then he walked right up to my father. "Hello, Mr Phoenix, my name is Michael De Marco, it's a pleasure to meet you." He was utterly charming and totally at ease and I looked at him in wonder.

"Hi, Michael, nice to finally meet you. I was beginning to think Angel was keeping you hidden," my dad said smiling.

"No, sir, I think we just kept missing each other," Michael said laughing lightly. "If you'll excuse us, I'm about to take your lovely daughter to hand in her assignment at university."

"Certainly, Michael. Will you be joining us for dinner?" my dad asked him.

"I would love to, sir, thank you. I shall look forward to hearing about your holiday." Michael was so cool and collected.

"Great, we'll leave at seven," my dad said clearly impressed by him.

We walked out the room in silence and we heard my dad tell everyone what a refreshing change to meet such a well-mannered young man. Michael's lips turned up at the edges in a half smile.

In the car I was still amazed at his charm and eloquence to my parents, especially since I had worked myself up into a bit of a state.

"You were so calm and articulate, and you certainly impressed my father," I told him.

"It's not difficult to be well mannered and polite besides, I had to do something as you were on the verge of cracking and shouting Michael's been staying here," he said raising his eyebrows at me.

"I was not, I was perfectly calm I'll have you know," I lied.

"Really? So, your hand in mine was perspiring for no reason?"

"It was warm." Standing my ground.

"I see." He was laughing now.

"OK, maybe I was a bit nervous, but I wouldn't have blurted anything out about you staying with me," I said, pushing his left arm.

"Nevertheless, I thought it best I step in just to be on the safe side. Besides, I had to introduce myself to your father, it would have been rude not to," he said with an amused tone still in his silky voice.

"Well, now you've gone and roped yourself into eating tonight in your efforts not to be rude." I pointed out smugly.

"That wasn't to be polite, my Angel, that was a necessity, otherwise I wouldn't get to see you tonight."

Damn him could I never win an argument? He had an answer for everything, and he was always right.

"Hmmphh, I suppose you have a point but you don't need to look so pleased about it," I grumbled.

He laughed. "You look so cute when you're sullen."

I hit his arm again. Bloody know it all vampire. If I were over a thousand years old, I would know a lot about everything too.

"Where are we going anyway?" I asked him.

"Nowhere in particular, I thought we could just drive around for a while then I will take you home and come back to collect you at seven."

"Sounds good. Hey, I have an idea where we can go just now," I said perking up.

"And where would that be?" interest on his face.

"Well, if I can drive your car, I can take us there."

"You can drive my car any time you like my love," he said, pulling over and getting out.

I was impressed, most guys wouldn't even let a girl so much as sit in the driver's seat of their car if it were as special as this one. He really was unique. I slid over to the driving seat smiling happily.

He got in the passenger side and looked at me questioningly. "Why are you so happy all of a sudden?"

"I was just thinking how most guys wouldn't let their girlfriends near a car like this, hell most guys wouldn't even let them near a car that's nowhere near the quality of this one." I looked at him from the driver seat, I could get used to this.

"You are much more important that any hunk of metal. I have driven top of the range cars since they were invented, what I haven't had my whole life is you. This is just a car, you on the other hand are my life," he said it so matter of fact that it was so beautifully simple in its truth.

I just stared at him dazed by his eloquence again, at how naturally he tells me I am his life; without a flutter of doubt, stammering or embarrassment. It was like telling someone the sky is blue.

"What?" he asked tilting his head.

"Nothing you just stun me sometimes with how truly amazing you are," I answered softly gazing at his incredible face.

I dragged my eyes away and started the car, the powerful engine roared to life like thunder in hurricane and I moved away from the kerb gaining speed with ease. I looked at the speedometer and saw it could do over 210mph, wow. This car was a dream to drive; it was so smooth and responded to the slightest command.

"You look so sexy controlling this car," he said, putting his hand on my thigh and running it up and back down.

"Do I?" The rushes I was getting were no longer due to driving the car.

"Yes, you really do, I can't seem to take my eyes off of you."

I turned up the road that led to the Cathkin Braes and went zooming up the hill.

The Braes was a series of hills set high above the city of Glasgow and the views were immense. In my opinion there were no better city views than the ones you got from here except in a plane.

I stopped the car at a lay-by, and we got out, coming around to the front and stopping to take in the breath-taking views.

Michael walked forward onto the grass. "Good choice, my love, this is spectacular." He was looking out across the horizon. The whole city spread before him. "It would be even more spectacular at night."

"It's not as good as my view of you but it's a pretty close second," flirting now, leaning on the bonnet of the Lamborghini and looking at his back.

He turned around and leisurely came toward me, a slow seductive smile spreading on his perfect red lips. "Is that so?" he asked lazily with a glint in his lilac eyes.

My heart went into overdrive as I caught that look again and I stopped breathing as I watched him approach me like a captivating predator circling its prey.

"The way you handled my car was incredibly sexy, do you think you can handle me?" His lilac eyes flashing brightly, standing before me now and looking down into my eyes. He was utterly seductive oozing with sex appeal and pure danger.

I was awestruck by his sheer magnetism and couldn't form any words in order to reply so I just nodded yes slowly, not breaking the eye lock.

His lips came onto mine in a kiss so divine it was almost a religious experience and my heart just stopped.

I wound my arms around his neck, and he used his body to push me back onto the car bonnet; his hands took mine and he lifted my arms above my head, holding them in place with one hand while the other unzipped my leather jacket.

The kiss became more insistent, and both his hands came sweeping down my sides, came around my waist and ran up the whole front of my body and back up to my raised hands. His breathing was laboured as his hands roamed over me and he kissed me even harder, I thought I was going to faint as the sensations from his touch made me dizzy and my head started to spin wildly. I wanted him to touch me like this for eternity it was agonising pleasure.

I tried to free my hands but he held them firmly in place and began to slow the kiss down.

When he finally stopped kissing me, he just lay his head in my neck as we both caught our breaths.

"Your self-control really knows no bounds," I observed after a while.

"That was incredibly erotic I will definitely be bringing you back here when we can see it through," he said pulling his head out of my neck and looking at me.

"Yes, I would like that… a lot." I couldn't even imagine it… "How did you manage to be so strong there and gain control like that?" I asked.

He looked at me incredulously. "You are just asking me this now? Of all the things I must control around you, you are picking this one instance?" His voice was also incredulous.

"Well, no, I guess I mean how do you always manage to be strong?" I corrected my wording.

"Let's just say I'm getting plenty of practice. On the job training if you will. I had no idea just how strong I could be." He got up from the car bonnet and winked at me. "Come now, I shall take you home minx."

I wondered how he always seemed to know the time when he didn't ever look at his watch. I was beginning to think there wasn't anything he couldn't do or anything he didn't know? He really was brilliant.

When he dropped me off, I went to my room to get ready. I put on music and cranked the volume, hoping it would take my mind from the night ahead. I was incredibly uncomfortable with the idea of my vampire boyfriend sitting across the table from my parents in a restaurant. In what world would that ever be, OK? It was a bloody insane thing to do, and it was all Michael's fault.

I was drying my hair and jumping around to Kickstart my heart. I put my make-up on and went into my wardrobe to decide what to wear and picked out a black halter neck playsuit with a red belt and high red stiletto heels. I had put my hair into big Bardot waves, so the playsuit finished my '50s' look. I surveyed myself in the mirror and thought I looked different, not bad different, just not the way I usually looked with my straight hair.

I went downstairs at seven and went into the entertainment room, which had the bar. The whole room was more like a club; as well as the bar it had tables and stools, a dance floor, flat screens and DJ decks with lighting systems. Patio doors opened it to the outside for whenever there was a big party. Not that we had many big parties.

The first thing I noticed when I walked in was Michael standing there. He looked elegant and classy in another custom-made black suit. Tonight, he wore an open collar violet shirt under his jacket, and it looked unbelievable with his eyes, it really made them stand out even more than they already did if that was possible.

I was struck by his beauty all over again and caught my breath as I stood there stupidly gaping at him. His face lit up when he looked at me and his eyes seemed to somehow brighten. Everyone in that room must have felt the spark between us.

He gave me that captivating smile as he approached me. "You look amazing, my beautiful Angel," he said, taking my arm and walking me over to the bar and handing me a glass of white wine, all without taking his eyes off me. I knew my family were staring at us, but I couldn't break that stare yet.

"Thank you," I said taking the glass from him and drinking half the glass to calm my nerves.

My mum took a photo of us, which broke the stare between us after the first flash. I was excited, I knew that would be a magic picture if it captured us locking eyes and looking at each other the way we do.

We spent ten minutes taking pictures then my dad said we should go because we had reservations for eight thirty; obviously he had no idea how fast Michael drove, we would be at the restaurant long before them.

In the car, Michael's eyes slid over me seductively and he reached his elegant hand out and lifted my hair up. "I love your hair like this it's so soft looking, and that playsuit looks unbelievable on your gorgeous body. It was almost the death of me when you walked into that room," he murmured huskily.

"That's so sweet, thank you," I said feeling a bit self-conscious at the way he was looking at me, I didn't really know how else to respond.

He laughed. "Sweet certainly wasn't the thoughts I was having about you."

I looked at him and burst out laughing. "Oh, the mighty vampire loses his cool."

"Yes, I'm afraid I have. I try so hard to keep it together and then in you walk looking like a '50s' screen goddess and blow it for me." He smiled at me and touched my cheek.

"Did you like the '50s?"

"I did, yes, it was a very glamorous era for movies that really appealed to me."

"What has been your favourite decade in the last hundred years?" I had been wanting to ask him that for a while but always seemed to get side-tracked when I thought to ask him. Although I knew a lot of history, a conversation about over one thousand years is mind boggling and really for another time.

"Mm, well I liked the '20s a lot because there was so much change happening, and I loved the '60s for the same reason, but mostly because of the music. The crazy '80s were so delightfully tacky. However, the '80s along with the '60s was the dawn of some of the best rock bands in history, so I guess they were my favourite decades."

He looked thoughtful for a few seconds before continuing, "I also think of the '80s as the last decade of technological innocence, a time before everyone had mobiles and the internet. People had to talk to each other, and meet up instead of texting, facetiming, e-mailing, and commenting on social groups. As much as I like computers and understand the convenience of Google and mobile phones there's something which saddens me about it too. The '80s was the last decade before the burst of this kind of technology, so it makes it a bit special for me." He shrugged. "The best year of my entire life though is this one, because I met you." He gave me the softest smile when that melted my heart.

We were at the restaurant now so Michael gave the keys to the awestruck valet parker who couldn't take his eyes off the car. We went inside and got seated at our table to wait for the others.

"You look so perfect tonight I cannot seem to take my eyes off you." His eyes travelling over my face.

"I don't ever want you to stop looking at me like that," I whispered, taking his hand and holding it tightly.

"I would not, could not, not ever. I promise you that," he whispered back.

I put my head into his neck, and he kissed my head. Sometimes I was just so overcome that he was mine, that this godlike creature loved me and belonged to me. It was unreal.

A while later my family arrived my dad asked if we had been here long, and we lied and said no. We didn't need to inform him how fast Michael drove he would only worry.

The waiter took the drink orders and gave us all menus. I looked at Michael behind my menu wondering what the hell he was going to order; this was a disaster waiting to happen.

"So how was your holiday?" I asked my parents.

"Great, it was so relaxing, and the hotel is looking fantastic," my mum said.

"Was the opening good?" I asked.

"Yes, it was pretty fabulous and most of Marbella turned up," my dad said.

They spent a while telling us about the hotel and how it looked in decoration and how the staff were all excellent.

"I'm a bit lost so I apologise for interrupting but is this hotel owned by someone you know?" Michael asked.

"You mean Angel hasn't told you it's our hotel?" my mum asked him.

"No, she hasn't mentioned it… wait a minute the Phoenix Glasgow, London and New York are your hotels?" He seemed impressed.

"Yes, and that was the Phoenix Marbella that just opened there," my dad said.

"I have stayed at the Phoenix London, and it was very luxurious, a really lovely hotel, one of the best I have stayed in actually. I can't believe I didn't make the connection," Michael said.

"I'm surprised Angel hasn't told you," my mum said, raising her eyebrows.

"It just didn't come up, Mum," I mumbled. I had no idea why I didn't tell him, it just didn't seem relevant, not compared to the whole forbidden love thing anyway.

"What do your parents do Michael?" my dad inquired.

"My father is a pilot and my mother buys and sells property," he told them.

The waiter came and took everyone's orders; my dad was the only one to want a starter so at least Michael would only need to choke a main meal down. He had barley glanced at the menu and ordered the first thing he saw since all human food tasted the same to him it didn't matter what he got.

"A pilot, that's impressive," my dad said.

"Yes, he's incredibly good. He used to fly Concorde for British Airways," Michael told him.

"Wow, Concorde, that's amazing. What does he fly now that Concorde is no longer in operation?" my mum asked.

"He still flies just not Concorde," Michael told them. "He bought a fleet of aircraft and opened his own airline company DM Elite."

They were both enthralled in this and went on a while about how good his father's airline was and I knew they could spend all night quizzing Michael, a thought I didn't relish since we had too much to hide.

"Your last name is Italian, does your father come from Italy?" my mum asked him.

"No, my father was born here but his father was Italian and came to Scotland to study medicine in his twenties. He met my grandmother, so he decided to stay, and they got married and had my father."

I kicked Dylan under the table and made eyes at him. He got the hint probably just thinking I wanted him to interrupt, because it was embarrassing for me to have my parents quiz my super cool boyfriend.

He started talking about everything he had been doing since they were away, going on for ages. Even telling them what he ate for breakfast every day. I had to hide my smile and stop myself from laughing at him. He was good. My parents looked like they wanted to go to sleep but plastered interested smiles on their faces as they listened to him.

"Shut up, Dylan. What the hell is wrong with you?" Kennedy said, looking at him like he'd gone mad.

It was ten o'clock by now so we could make our escape, having stayed a respectable hour and a half eating.

"We're going to go now anyway, we're going out tonight to the club," I told everyone.

"Thank you for a lovely meal and a very pleasant evening. It was nice to get to know you both a bit better," Michael said. He was just naturally charming; he didn't have to work at it.

"Same for us, Michael. We know you are important to Angel so we're glad to know a bit about you," my dad said.

"Your daughter is the most important thing in my life sir and rest assured I will look after her," Michael said shaking my dad's hand as we got up.

"Good to know, Michael. You two have a good time tonight," my dad said.

Outside the valet driver brought the car around and reluctantly handed the keys back over to Michael, who tipped him generously.

We drove up to the Pub and Michael parked right outside which caused a lot of attention as everyone was staring at his car, then at us when we got out. This must be kind of like what famous people go through minus the autograph hunters.

We went inside and to the bar and Michael ordered me a vodka and coke and a soft drink for himself, which he obviously wasn't going to drink but it would look a bit strange if he were standing in a bar without a drink in his hand.

Some guy came up and asked Michael if that was his car and went on about how cool it was, and I thought he was never going to leave but eventually he did after about half an hour.

"I was on the verge of giving him the car just to get rid of him," he said to me pulling me into his arms and holding me close.

"I was on the verge of running him over with it," I said only half joking.

He laughed. "You are incorrigible, Miss Angel. Remind me never to get on your bad side."

Michael went to the bar to get me another drink and two drunk guys came up and began hassling me, asking for kisses and trying to grab me.

"Get your bloody hands off me," I said angrily, swiping at hands.

"Oh, she's a feisty one, mate," one of them said to the other.

"Come on sexy you know you want to give us a kiss," the other one said.

"Nice legs," one said putting his hands on one of my legs. Before I could react, and kickbox them both, a cold voice was heard. Michael looked murderous.

"Put one more hand on her and I will rip your arms off." Michael was behind them. His voice was like ice.

They turned around to say something rude to him and stopped when they saw the dangerous expression on his face, his eyes were deadly as he looked at them. They muttered some apologies and backed quickly away. They had no idea he was a vampire but knew there was something about Michael you just didn't mess with if you wanted to live long.

"Are you alright," he asked me, still staring at the two idiots.

"Yes, I'm fine they were just a pair of drunken idiots thinking that's how to pull a female, I'm pretty sure it never works," I said evenly, putting my arm around him.

He still looked angry. "I'm sorry, Angel, but when it comes to you, I don't take anything lightly. I realise I am much too overprotective but no one touches

161

you or hassles you, I won't tolerate it," he said looking away from them and back at me.

"I know, baby, but people like those two really aren't worth getting upset over. It's a good thing you're immortal otherwise your stress levels would be through the roof, besides, I can handle myself," I said smiling at him at nodding where the two guys had gone. Both their drinks fell back onto them, staining their clothes.

He smiled at me. "And that is merely a blip on your powers. I can't really blame them for wanting to touch you, but you are mine and nobody but me gets to do that."

I kissed him then, deliriously happy that he said I was his, I already knew it but to hear him say it was simply amazing somehow.

We left and went to the Club for an hour, but it wasn't good, there was a lot of guys who had too much to drink, and I didn't want another one pissing Michael off. The next one might be more aggressive, and Michael would lose it, either that or the guy would end up his next meal. It wouldn't be too hard for Michael to find him when he had his scent.

We drove home and I was wondering how we were going to spend our nights together now. I couldn't be parted from him for long, I couldn't stand it.

"Michael, what are we going to do about our nights now?" I asked him.

"I was thinking I will drop you off like the perfect gentleman then take my car home and fly back. If you leave your bedroom window open, I can just come in undetected," he said it like it was the most normal thing to fly through a window. Like people done that all the time.

"That's a great idea and I will just make sure to keep my bedroom door locked so no one can come in suddenly." I was so relieved we had a solution. "How long will it take you to take your car home and fly back?"

"Not long, it'll take me about forty minutes to drive home and only minutes to fly to your house," he said stroking my face.

He dropped me off and we kissed at the door like we were saying goodnight and then he went away. I went upstairs and opened my window for him then got changed and got into bed and put some music on while I waited for him.

After what seemed like a million years but was actually very little over forty minutes he was standing in front of my bed. I didn't even see him come through the window and I was watching out for him.

"Angel," he said, pulling my attention from the window.

"*How* do you do that? I was looking right at the window," I said in amazement.

"It's a vampire thing," he said looking at me and taking off his suit jacket.

I could feel the familiar heat course through my body as I watched him, I wanted to leap up and rip that shirt violently off his body.

"Oh no, not again… go into the wardrobe and get changed. My sanity can't take another beating today," I said pointing to the wardrobe and wrenching my eyes away from him.

He laughed, I loved the sound of his laughter it was like music. "Well, well, look who's being strong now."

"Yes, only because you weren't touching me, kissing me or giving me that look," I grumbled.

"What look?"

"That way you have of looking at me that makes me forget anything else in the world exists as I get totally lost in it. The one that causes my limbs to stop working and a near coronary," I said. He knew fine well what look I was referring to.

He laughed. "Oh, *that* look."

He went into my wardrobe and got changed and I made sure my door was locked.

Chapter Fourteen

Hellhounds

The next morning, we were lying in bed having a sleepy cuddle when Michael looked towards the door. "Someone's coming."

"Who? Are they coming here?"

"I don't know who but yes they are coming here." He slid out of bed and into the wardrobe soundlessly just as the knock on the door came.

"Hang on," I shouted, getting out of bed and padding across the room to open the door.

It was my mum. "I thought I would bring you up some breakfast, sweetie."

My mum never woke me up on a Saturday so I could only assume she wanted to talk about Michael.

"Why are you waking me up, Mum?" I asked her, rubbing my eyes like I was just out of a sleep and getting back into bed.

She handed me my toast and sat down. "I just thought you might be hungry."

Yeah right! I took a bite from my toast and waited for her to speak. I didn't have to wait long.

"So, Michael seems nice, he's very polite and charming."

"Yes, he is, Mum, and he's gorgeous on the inside and out."

"That he is dear almost inhumanly so." She was scrutinising my face.

I didn't so much as flicker an eyelash. "He's the love of my life, Mum."

"I think you are the love of his life too Angel but there's something about him… not quite right. Not demonic but not human either. Did you look in the book?"

I sighed. I would have to pick my words carefully. "Yes, Mum, and he's not evil."

"OK, so he's not evil but what is he?" she asked knowing I knew.

"He's just a guy madly in love with your daughter, a guy who would throw himself in front of a speeding train or a bomb to save her. Isn't that enough for you?"

She looked at me with narrowed eyes. "Enough for now, Angel, but you are going to have to tell us eventually. A secret like that affects us all."

"I know, Mum, but for now please leave it alone. For me," I asked her.

She knew then that she wasn't going to like it, but she knew I was safe with him and that's all that mattered for now.

"OK, Angel, I won't bring it up again. Just keep your eyes wide open."

When she left, Michael came back out, he had gotten changed. "Well, that was a bit surprising, I didn't think she would back off so easily."

"Yeah, you and me both. She knows you love me though so I'm guessing that's what swung it. Why are you dressed?"

"I thought I would fly home, get changed and drive back. Are we going to this Halloween party tonight?"

"Well, it's too late to hire anything but I have an old cat woman costume somewhere so if you have something lying around, we could go."

"I don't have any Halloween costumes, but I could borrow one of my father's pilot uniforms."

"A pilot uniform… you in a pilot uniform… I may have a stroke."

He laughed, throwing his head back and running his hands through his hair. "You are incorrigible."

I smiled up at him. "Only when it comes to you."

"Alright then, here's the plan I will go home and come back tonight to take you to the party."

"Tonight? Why not today? You could bring your costume with you and get ready here."

"I think it would look strange if I came to get ready with you, we're not gal pals, I'm your boyfriend taking you out on a date." He was laughing hard, and I joined in.

"Yes, of course, you're right, I hadn't thought about it like that. OK I'll see you tonight about eight o'clock."

He bent down and kissed me lightly. "I'll miss you, Angel."

"I'll miss you too, but we'll see each other in nine hours," I said sweeping my hands through his hair.

After he left, I looked out my cat woman costume and tried it on thinking that this was going to be a long day without him. It's amazing how used to having someone around you get and when they're not with you time drags. I couldn't really remember how I passed time before. It was like my whole past was a blur and everything only came into focus when I met Michael.

"Angel… Angel, come quickly, there's Pixie's downstairs that need our help." Dylan had burst into my room shouting excitedly and then ran back out.

What was he on about? I knew I would have to go downstairs to get a full answer, so I walked out of my room and downstairs, not rushing because Dylan tended to exaggerate things.

What confronted me was not Dylan's imagination but a house full of Pixies. The Fairy-like creatures were *everywhere*.

"They have come to us for protection. Hellhounds are killing them and stealing their protection powder," my dad told me.

"What do Hellhounds want with pixie powder?" I asked.

"Hellhounds guard Diablo and his domain so I think it's safe to assume he could be looking to power up and make some sort of move. He would need a lot of it to keep protected which means the Hellhounds have probably been ordered to kill all Pixies," my dad said looking at the book.

"OK, so how do we get them to stop? I'm assuming only Diablo can call off his dogs."

"Yes, that's true so we have to kill them with some heavy-duty potion and a spell."

"How many of them are attacking you?" I asked some Pixies.

"Around six, they got twelve of us before we could all flee here." One little female Pixie told me. She was about ten inches in height and wore a little green outfit with the hat cut out around her pointed ears.

"OK, six isn't too bad, he has a lot more than six though so let's get organised with making this potion. Do we have all the ingredients?" I asked my dad who was still looking at the book.

"I think so, but we'll have to go up to the loft and check. Kennedy, Dylan you two stay here and look after the Pixies in case the Hellhounds come here. I don't think they will, I've not has any visions of that but we can't leave them unprotected just in case," my dad said.

I went up to the loft with my parents and we began looking out potion ingredients, some of them were obscure and it took my mum a while to find them. It's not like lion's mane hair clippings and toad's nails were ingredients we used all the time. Where did we even get them in the first place? Some of this stuff must be centuries old and very well preserved.

The potion took a while to make, and I wrote out the spell from the book.

Hounds of hell can no longer dwell,
In this night leave my sight
You are banished with this spell,
Cast with all my might.

With the spell done and the potion almost ready, we were preparing for battle. I was a tad apprehensive in going after Diablo's dogs as I wasn't sure this would be easy; they didn't guard the leader of evil for nothing so they must be powerful.

The book said they were extremely vicious and deadly but not very bright, making them unable to plan attacks themselves just follow orders. That would explain why they didn't attack here; they wouldn't have the initiative to do that. They will just lie in wait in the pixie realm for them all to come back.

My dad called my siblings upstairs and told them to stay with the pixies in case there was a surprise attack on them. Diablo would figure us all to go after the hellhounds, leaving the pixies vulnerable to any other creature he sent up. If we could round them all up in one place, we could surround the room in a protection blanket using our own made light dust to make an impenetrable pentagram symbol.

We decided to do that, and my siblings went downstairs to get all the pixies to the loft. I looked out the light dust and began to shake it onto the ground in the form of a giant pentagram where the points reached the four walls of the room for maximum protected space. No evil could pass through this barrier once it was blessed. I blessed it by cutting my finger and placing a drop of blood onto each point of the pentagram.

This ritual was not to be taken lightly and we couldn't use it daily to keep evil from our home. It was only to be used in the protection of weaker creatures whose existence are threatened or in dire emergencies.

The pixies were pouring into the room, and I told them all they must not cross the boundary of light because they wouldn't be protected if they did.

Once they were all settled, we left to kill the hellhounds. I put up my invisibility shield and my father took my mother under his so we could transport in undetected and check out where the dogs were.

We arrived at the pixie realm invisible and had a walk around. I wished we were telepathic like Michael and Ava because it would mean we could attack in sync with the potions before chanting the spell.

The hounds were patrolling the grounds in two groups of three. I had never seen a hellhound in person before and they were grotesque horrible looking creatures. They were massively built standing around twelve feet with huge shoulders and back, and legs like tree trunks. Their paws were bigger than my head and their claws were exceptionally long and sharp. They had short black fur and bulging bright red eyes. Their muzzles were huge with big razor-sharp yellow teeth, with green ooze dripping from them. They were pacing around salivating and growling, sometimes pawing the ground in the same way bulls do before they attack.

If this didn't work, we were puppy chow. We walked around a bit more studying the best angles to take them. My mum would have to stay with my dad behind his protection shield, which meant I would have to take the other three on my own.

"OK, let's do this," I whispered and got into position near my three.

I dropped my invisibility shield and lifted my protection shield. "Woof woof," I said loudly, and the hounds burled towards me with a roar. I threw my arm up, palm outwards as they bounded towards me, using telekinesis to halt them and hold them in place. It took a lot of concentration to pull this off, but I held them with my left hand, arm shaking to keep them in place, and used my right to launch the potions and hit all three at the same time accurately. When the potions hit their mark, I shouted the spell three times, once for each of the hounds and they exploded in a loud bang.

I stood for a few minutes with my left arm still out before dropping it exhausted. That was a lot of telekinesis to hold those three massive things, it had drained my mind and I felt so tired. I turned to see my parent's high fiving at the death of their hounds. Mission accomplished all six were a goner.

We transported home to the loft and my siblings had killed three demons that arrived after we left. Diablo had covered his bases, sending in hellhounds and demons. He really must want that pixie powder badly. Too bad for him all his creatures had died in their mission. He must have at the very least been half expecting that.

I collapsed onto the couch amid hundreds of thanks from the pixies as they left, trickling out groups at a time. I think I managed to say a few you're welcome before falling fast asleep.

I awoke at seven, the loft was in darkness, and it took me a few minutes to orient myself. I looked at my watch and jumped up, running downstairs to my room and jumping in the shower. Michael would be here in less than an hour and I hadn't even begun to get ready. Good thing I looked out my costume earlier. I still felt tired as I dried my hair and done my make up.

I would have to practice using multiple telekinetic abilities at once to avoid the brain drain it caused with creatures as strong as they were. It was something I should have well had control over but kept putting off the intense practice it would require.

I put my costume on and arranged my hair under the cat ears and put on high stiletto heels to finish it off. It looked good despite my tired expression. It was ten to eight, I had gotten ready with time to spare so I lay down on my bed and waited for Michael. I couldn't wait to see him. I closed my eyes and must have fallen back asleep because the next thing I knew Michael was sitting on the bed next to me and stroking my hair.

"Are you alright?" he asked when I opened my eyes.

"Yes, just really tired," I said sitting up and looking at him.

He looked heart stopping in the pilot's uniform and I just gaped at his beauty and sexiness, unable to believe just how unbelievable he looked in it. Just when I thought he couldn't get any better he did.

"Wow you look incredible," I said breathlessly.

"I was just about to say the same thing to you, Angel. That skin-tight lycra clinging to your body like a second skin may be more than I can take." His eyes travelled my body slowly as he spoke.

I felt my skin begin to tingle where his eyes roamed, and my heart began to race. The expression on his face was lustful and wanton and his iridescent eyes burned with desire for me. I had to look away in order to exhale because my breath just caught mid inhale.

He reached a pale cool hand out to my chin and brought my face back around to look at him. I was completely lost the instant my eyes met his and I felt like my entire body was falling into them, being sucked through a lilac whirlpool.

My lips trembled as he kissed me and I was his prisoner, I couldn't move a single muscle.

Suddenly he stopped. "Why are you so tired, Angel."

"We had to kill some hellhounds today because they were trying to wipe out pixies and steal their powder." I sat up with a sigh.

"*You what?* You could have been killed." His brows furrowed in annoyance.

"No, I couldn't have, we were well prepared. I'm just so tired because I had to use multiple telekinesis at once but I'm OK."

"Angel, I won't have you running off and risking your life to save some pixies. You should have called me, and I would have taken care of it for you."

"I didn't need you to take care of it for me Michael. This is who I am, and killing evil is what I do." I pulled my arm from his grip. Who did he think he was anyway?

"It may be what you do but I cannot bear the thought of you taking on vile underworld creatures without me there to protect you and I will not apologise for that Angel." His eyes were flashing in anger and he leapt from the bed in one fluid movement.

"Will you calm down? I'm not hurt or dying just a bit tired. Yes, sometimes I must take chances in battles, and I don't always know whether I will survive. I'm not like you, Michael, you are so sure of everything, so confidant and you have all of the answers all of the time."

He looked at me in disbelief. "You think I have all of the answers? I don't have any answers Angel, in my whole life I never imagined falling in love with a mortal. The very idea of it was so inconceivable it never even entered my head and for the first time I have begun to struggle with what I am, that I take mortal lives to survive. I never gave that a second thought before you. The only thing I am sure of anymore is my irrefutable love for you. And your safety is the most important thing to me, if anything were to happen to you, I would not survive it, nor would I want to. I would cease to exist. I know you are a powerful witch, but you are not indestructible."

"Then make me indestructible, Michael," I said quietly, all traces of anger evaporated by his words.

He sighed heavily and walked towards me. "Angel, most of my reasons for not turning you are purely selfish. I place a high value on your mortality even if you do not, and I am trying desperately to maintain some last vestige of honour and not rob you of it. There will come a day when you would question whether eternal life was worth what you had to give up in order to receive it. When that day comes, you will look at me in a certain way and part of you inside will begin to die and you will start to resent me, and I couldn't stand that."

I buried my face in his stomach. "I would never resent you. Never. It isn't indestructibility, never ageing and powerful sexual magnetism that makes me want to be immortal Michael, it is because I want to be with you for eternity."

He gently lifted my head from his stomach so he could look into my eyes. "My sweet Angel, how I love you. My resolve weakens each time you bring this up. You must understand everything you would be giving up. Not just your mortality and your beautiful beating heart, but you would also have to give up your magical destiny, the very thing that makes you who you are. If you were to become a vampire, you would have to kill in order to survive. You could no longer fulfil your Wiccan duties by fighting evil. You would, for all intents and purposes, be joining the dark side and I'm not sure you could live with that."

I grabbed his arms. "If I get to be with you, I can live with anything. I know all being a vampire entails and I still want to become one. I want to be like you and be with you forever."

"Don't you get it, Angel? You fight evil to preserve life. If I were to turn you, you would have to take lives and it would tear you apart."

"Losing you would be the only thing that would tear me apart." My voice was low now, sad.

He ran his hand through his hair and turned away from me, walking over to the window. He was like a beautiful statue, standing there so completely still as he watched the rain beat down heavily outside.

The only sound in the room was the rain hitting the glass and my heart beating just a little too fast. I knew neither one of us could resolve this tonight.

We didn't go to the Halloween party.

The next month passed quickly, we spent all our free time together with Michael sneaking into my room at night and flying home in the morning. We went out every weekend except when Michael had to hunt. We went to the movies, and out for dinner, and on Fridays and on Saturdays we went clubbing then spent Sundays lazing around in bed reading to each other from our favourite books, going for drives and just savouring every moment we spent together.

One Friday I dragged him to a vampire movie that he enjoyed in an ironic way. I was expecting him to scorn it as nonsense, but he didn't.

Dallas came with us and after we were seated in the restaurant, we started to discuss the movie.

Dallas loved the lead vampire and went on for ages about the romance of it. "Can you imagine falling for a vampire? That would be amazing. I *wish* my boyfriend was a vampire." She sighed.

"Why?" Michael asked her curiously.

"I guess because it's just so romantic, the obstacles to overcome just to be together because that kind of love is so blinding and all-consuming. The whole being together forever in a literal sense and not a human lifetime sense, well, it can't be denied. Plus, vampires are so sexy, every one of them are gorgeous, not just in that movie but every movie." Her eyes were dreamy.

"So, you believe vampires exist?" he asked her.

"Yes, I do. Don't you?"

He smiled at her easily. "Yes, I do too."

(What on earth was he doing?)

She looked at him seriously. "You could be a vampire you know; you have the same physical traits as them; the unusual eyes, pale skin, gorgeous looks, and your mannerisms and presence are like theirs."

He sat back in his chair and studied her a second. "You think I'm a vampire?" His tone was bemused.

She laughed. "I would have suspected it but you're eating food and go out in sunlight so you can't be."

Michael gave a wry smile. "What if that was a myth? There are many myths about vampires."

She thought about it for a second, chewing her steak. "Then it's not impossible that you are one."

This conversation was making me uncomfortable; it was a little too close to the truth and Dallas wasn't allowed to know the truth, so I changed the subject.

Whose stupid idea was it to go to a vampire movie with a fucking vampire... oh, yes, that would be mine.

It was December before I knew it and uni was finishing up next week. I started my Christmas shopping and managed to get gifts for my parents, my siblings and Dallas. All that was left was Michael.

It was his birthday on New Year's Eve too, but I had already gotten him a first edition of his favourite book. It was exceedingly difficult to track down and cost a lot of money, but I knew he would love it. I had no idea what to get him for Christmas though and agonised over it for days. What do you get someone who had lived for over a Millennium and had everything? I considered a watch but discarded that idea since he never looked at any he wore. I googled unique gift ideas and found platinum cufflinks with hidden messages inside. I loved that idea, so I ordered them and sat and wrote things to put inside them. I decided on two…

In a world of lies you are my truth.

You are my every day, my every night and my every dream.

He always wore cufflinks when he wore a suit so it was a practical gift but the hidden messages from me made it intensely personal.

With his main birthday and Christmas gifts bought, I went and got him some other things to open. I got him a couple of vinyl he had been talking about wanting, a Gucci wallet, the *Godfather* trilogy – because I remembered him saying his brother stood on his and broke it, and a lilac tie that matched his eyes perfectly.

I would give him the wallet and records for his Christmas and the DVDs and tie for his birthday. Although, you could stream every movie, and he did use that, he always said he like to have physical copies of books, movies and music. He's collected things his whole life to keep as part of history. I could not wait to see *that* collection. Thing's museums would kill for.

I thought about getting him aftershave and spent a while smelling different ones, none of which smelled halfway as good as his natural scent, so I decided against it. Besides, he never wore aftershave.

One day, a week before Christmas he arrived at my house. I had just finished wrapping everything and was putting my family's gifts under the Christmas tree in the living room when he came in and wrapped his arms around me from behind, surprising me. I leaned back into him, and he tipped my head back and kissed my pulse, letting his lips rest against it for a minute.

I stood lost in the sensations of his arms holding me tightly, the intoxicating scent of him and his lips on my neck. I shivered in pleasure, quite happy to stand like this all day.

He moved his lips off my neck and said nonchalantly. "I want you to meet my family."

My eyes widened. "When? What brought this on?"

He let me go and I turned to face him. He shrugged. "I've been thinking about it for a while, and they keep asking to meet you which is getting rather tiresome. So, I thought tomorrow is as good a day as any for you to face a group of vampires." He sat down and looked away bored.

"I would love to meet your family Michael," I said excitedly.

He looked back at me, his lilac eyes probing mine. "You would?"

"Yes. Why wouldn't I?" I asked confused.

"Because they're vampires, I should think that would have given you a little resistance to the idea."

I rolled my eyes at him. "Well, it doesn't. It's your family so I kind of guessed they were vampires." My tone was sarcastic.

He smiled slightly. "You do enjoy flirting with disaster my love."

I sat down next him. "Why? Are they looking to kill me?" I asked in the same sarcastic tone as before.

"Hardly, but you ought to not be so cavalier about it, they are still dangerous," he said curtly.

"OK, so they are dangerous, I get it. I do want to meet them though. They're part of you and I want to know everything about you."

He visibly relaxed. "OK, so tomorrow then?"

I smiled brightly at him, and his eyes softened. "Tomorrow is fine." I stiffened. "What should I wear?"

"Anything you feel comfortable in. they won't care what you wear." He laughed at my expression of alarm.

"Tell me about them, how they changed."

"Well, it was in the year 965 and my father was questioning the stars in the sky, taking notes of changes, kind of like an astronomer before there was such a thing, he and my mother took some likeminded people out to a park to do some stargazing and a few cubs got them. My parents and two of the students were the only ones to survive the attack and my father thinks it was because the cubs had already gorged themselves so fed them blood as they were taking theirs, or maybe it was deliberate who knows. When they woke, they were vampires."

"What did they do?"

"They didn't know what to do because usually when someone is turned the vampire who sires them looks after them and shows them the ropes, but since it was bloodthirsty cubs let loose, they had no one to teach them. They had to learn everything the hard way. They stuck together though and those two that survived are my siblings."

"That must have been terrifying for them to suddenly be vampires and no idea how to gain control."

"It was especially hard on my mother, having to kill to survive but eventually the beast won, and she had to accept it."

We sat in silence a while and I thought how awful that must have been for his family in the beginning.

We went up to my room and Michael sat and played the guitar as I trolled through my wardrobe trying to decide what is appropriate attire for meeting my boyfriend's vampire family. I was throwing clothes around, discarding everything I looked at.

"This is absurd, Angel; trust me they will not be studying your outfit," he shouted from the room.

"You only get one chance to make a first impression Michael so my outfit must be right," I shouted back from inside the wardrobe. No idea why I shouted back, he could have heard me whispering.

I looked up and he was leaning against the entrance smiling at me. He looked so dark and alluring standing in the shadow of the door wearing a black polo necked jumper that I forgot what I was doing and simply stared at him.

As he came into the light towards me his skin was even more translucent, sandwiched between the high neck of his black jumper and his jet-black hair. He was radiant and dangerous and sexy all at once. I wondered for the millionth time if I would I ever get used to his beauty.

He smiled lazily at my starry-eyed expression and kissed me gently on the lips. "Right, crazy lady, I think I shall leave you to your madness. I still have some Christmas shopping to do."

"OK, babe. What time will you pick me up tomorrow?"

"Noon. And please no freaking out over clothes, you look gorgeous Whatever you wear." He brushed my cheek with the back of his cool hand.

I snaked my arms around his neck and kissed him firmly, he responded by pulling my body into his so tightly I thought a bone might break.

After he left, I tried on several outfits, finally I settled on a black pencil skirt and a black satin halter neck top with a white jacket and black stilettos. It was smart but not overdressed.

Chapter Fifteen

Meet the Vampires

The next morning, I was a nervous wreck. What if they didn't like me? What if I didn't like them? How were they going to react to my being a witch? What were they like? What if they were horrible? Like horrible proper scary vampires, would I be scared? What if I was so nervous, I froze up and couldn't speak? What if they were annoyed it has taken so long to meet me? What the hell was I going to talk to them about? What if they thought I wasn't good enough?

My mind was firing questions faster that I could answer them, I had to get a grip of myself, or I would be heading for a panic attack.

I sat down and took deep slow breaths until I was under control again. I couldn't think like this; if they didn't like me, they didn't like me, there wasn't much I could do about it. Besides, it was Michael I was with not them.

The thought from the back of my head crept forward into my consciousness and I knew why I had been freaking out before.

If I were to become one of them someday, I would spend eternity as part of their family so them liking me was crucial, and vice versa. Damn I hate when I told myself the truth. Why couldn't I be great at self-denial like most people were?

I went down to the kitchen for breakfast and had some cereal. My mum came in and I told her I was going to meet the De Marcos today.

"Well, it's about time, Angel, they're probably wondering why they haven't met you yet when Michael comes here all the time," she admonished.

This was not making me feel better, so I hurriedly finished my cereal and went back to my room to do some more worrying alone.

I had my shower and took a long time getting ready just so I had something other than my neurosis to focus on.

I put on Bon Jovi. "Come on, Jon, soothe me," I said out loud. Great I was talking to myself now. Maybe I should answer myself in a different voice and be done with it, have my family cart me off to a mental institution where I could sit and sing cheesy show tunes all day to reaffirm my insanity and ensure they threw away the key. I didn't even know any show tunes.

I began to giggle uncontrollably and found I couldn't stop. It was like in school when someone would say something that wasn't really all that funny, but you would hit the giggles and the more you try to stop laughing the more you giggle. I always done this at inappropriate times and apparently, I still do. The things you learn about yourself when you weren't looking for any kind of self-discovery was annoying.

Finally, it was noon and I put my music off and made my way downstairs. I took it slowly because if I rushed, I would undoubtedly fall and break a tooth or something. What a great first impression that would be; Michael's toothless girlfriend. I felt the giggles rise again as I opened the front door but when I saw Michael they stopped dead, as did I.

He was so beautiful I thought I would burst into flames just from the heat of being near him. He was wearing his customary black.

Black trousers, a fitted black shirt with a black jacket that had a thick red band around the right arm that somehow made it unbelievably sexy. He was wearing dog tags over the shirt and a black fedora on his head. He looked like a cross between a model and a rock star. The combination was stunningly effective. The weak winter sun sparkled in his lilac eyes like diamonds when he lifted his head up. I caught my breath and couldn't remember how to move.

I pulled my phone out to capture the utter perfection of how he looked at this moment. His glittering eyes slowly followed down the length of my body and back up to my face and his lips turned up in a sexy smile.

We looked at each other for the longest minute until I pulled my eyes down, away from his electrical gaze and thus allowing myself to remember how to walk.

I went towards him, and his eyes never so much as flickered from me as I approached.

He reached his hand towards me. "You look so perfect today I can't seem to look away." His satin voice was even silkier than usual.

He ran his hands through my newly washed and straightened hair, lifting it up from my shoulders and dropping it back into place. The gesture was so natural it caught me off guard. It was one of those moments that it hit me again that this unbelievable guy was all mine. Sometimes it was hard to comprehend the fact we belonged to each other, that we belonged together.

"We should go your family will be expecting us."

We got into the car, and he took off. Neither of us spoke for about five minutes then he said, "So are you nervous?"

"Yes," I admitted sheepishly. "I'm scared they won't like me."

He shot me a look of open curiosity. "What makes you think they might not like you?"

I shrugged. "I don't know I'm just being paranoid and thinking the worst, that they'll hate me, throw me out and ban you from seeing me ever again."

He smiled. "What an absurd concept. They are going to love you, my Angel. And for the record they can't ban me from seeing you. I'm afraid my love for you is infinitely irreversible."

His words made me smile and I felt reassured. I lifted his hand and kissed it lightly.

"On an altogether separate note, I am more than a little pleased to see your gorgeous legs today." He reached his hand over and ran it down my thigh with gentle pressure. I shivered at his touch, wanting more. When he went to lift his hand, I put mine over it roughly to keep it there. We looked at each other and he had *that* look on his perfect face, the one that made me hyperventilate. My heart raced faster. I wanted him so much I wondered briefly if I could die from it.

He looked back at the road, his face tense. That simple leg stroke had affected me in an unexpected way, and I put my head back on the head rest, closed my eyes and took a deep breath. I removed my hand from on top of his and placed it at my side.

He left his hand on my thigh.

We were both so aware of his hand you could almost feel the heat in the car.

This was really getting to be too much; we were going to have to talk about it soon. I don't think either of us could go on like this much longer.

Before I knew it, we had turned onto a deserted road. Michael flipped a switch and two huge iron gates with a distinctive crest on them opened to let us through and we continued up a long winding hill. On either side, it was dense with thick trees, and I couldn't see much up ahead until we came around a bend and the castle came into view. You couldn't see it from the main road because of the forests surrounding it. They were even more vigilant about their privacy than we were it seemed. Two families with a huge secret.

"Is that your family crest on the gates?"

"Yes. It symbolises love, loyalty, and power."

The castle was getting clearer, and I was just gaping at it. He slowed the car as we approached, it was so intimidating looking. I had never known anyone that lived in an actual castle before, so this was all new to me.

We came to the drawbridge and Michael flicked another switch and drove downwards underneath the castle. I wasn't expecting that, I was expecting the massive doors to open, and we would drive through them.

"How is this possible?" I asked, completely bewildered.

He laughed lightly. "We demolished the old dungeons in the '40s and built a car park and created a hill to drive in and out of. It is rather more convenient than parking outside and hauling those doors open and closed."

It was well lit and painted white. Every car in there was outstanding, I counted ten in total.

We got out the car and I noticed not just stairs leading up but also a lift. They really had thought of everything.

"This is amazing," I told him a bit awestruck.

He took hold of my hand, and we went into the lift.

"Are you ready to meet my family," he asked kissing me lightly.

"Yes, let's do it," I said full of false bravado.

He pressed a button for floor one – there were five in total including basement and roof – and the lift began to rise. I was really feeling the nerves now. Would they be all waiting to greet us at the lift?

"They'll be in the main family room," he said amused, knowing how nervous I was.

"How did you know what I was thinking?"

"Sometimes, not always, I can read you like a book; like you've spoken aloud."

"Is that how your telepathy works?"

"Not exactly, it's more like hearing unspoken words and seeing images like mind reading. Ava, for instance, knows we're in the lift because I have alerted her, but I haven't alerted my parents," he explained.

"How can you just tell Ava and not your parents," I asked as we got out of the lift.

"Because we can put each other on mute, and we can block our thoughts; kind of like an imaginary wall going up. We all do that most of the time for privacy and when someone we have on mute is trying to tell us something it feels like a slight pressure in the middle of our brain, so we know to un-mute them."

"Wow, that's truly amazing," I said, extremely impressed at how this vampire power worked.

"Ava and I can hold entire conversations in our head without including our parents and they have no idea because they won't feel the pressure in their heads unless we're trying to talk to them."

"That is so interesting."

We had walked through a corridor and out into a giant hall. I could see a huge staircase up ahead and there were doors all around us.

The décor was nothing like I imagined, I had pictured it like ancient castles you see on TV, dark and gothic like the outside, but it was completely modernised except for a few suits of armour and some chandeliers I saw darted around. The walls and ceiling were cream in colour and the floors were a rich fawn stone.

We passed the staircase and he stopped outside huge double doors.

"OK, Angel, this is the room. Are you ready?"

I squared my shoulders and composed my face into a blank canvas, game face time. "Yes."

He opened the doors and we walked inside.

His family were sitting around four huge luxurious cream couches. The room was enormous with impossibly high ceilings. It was light and airy, not at all what anyone would expect inside a castle and there was some expensive looking art on the walls. A grand piano sat next to the furthest away window and there was a beautiful stone fireplace on the wall opposite.

I took all of this in, in the mere seconds it took to walk into the room.

I looked now at his family. They were the most glamorous and beautiful people I had ever seen. All of them were as elegant and classy as Michael.

I was completely intimidated and wanted to run from the room and hide.

"Welcome to our home, Angel. Michael has told us so many lovely things about you." A woman, I assumed to be Michael's mum, walked towards me gracefully. "My name is Lilly and I am utterly delighted to meet you." She surprised me by giving me a warm hug, with a happy smile on her face.

"It's lovely to meet you, Mrs De Marco." I liked the woman instantly.

"This is my husband, and Michael's dad, Alexander," she said turning me around gently.

"Hello, Angel, it is simply wonderful to meet the girl who has finally captured my son's heart, and I must say you do not disappoint. You are as beautiful as Michael said you were." He kissed my hand.

"Thank you, Mr De Marco. It is nice to meet you." I liked his dad too.

They were both warm and welcoming people, trying to put me at ease in what they must know was a nervous situation for me.

I noticed they had the same gorgeous iridescent lilac eyes as Michael and Ava and the same lovely jet-black hair and high cheekbones. They were beautiful and their children had both of their genetic markers.

His mum took my arm and walked me to the couch. "This is my other children. Ava, you know." She swept her hand towards two people as she introduced them. "This is Derek and Elizabeth."

"Nice to meet you," I said smiling.

His siblings didn't have the jet-black hair, but they did have the unusual lilac eyes and they were also incredibly beautiful.

"Come and sit down, Angel," his mother invited. "Tell us about yourself."

I sat down and Michael sat beside me and took my hand, giving it a reassuring squeeze.

"Please don't question her endlessly, Mum," he pleaded.

I noticed Ava looking at him and saw him move his head to one side then the other like an imperceptible gesture of no. I wondered if she had asked him a question.

"Michael tells us your parents own the Phoenix hotels. That's impressive."

"Thank you, yes, they do." I was uncomfortable being the centre of these beautiful people's attention.

"We have stayed in them a few times and were extremely impressed. The décor and the service are first class," his mum said.

"Any time you wish to stay in any of our hotels please let me know and I will arrange it for you," I told them sincerely. No way was Michael's family going to pay to stay in one of our hotels.

"Why thank you, Angel, that is ever so kind of you and we shall," his father said.

"Now Michael tells us you know what we are, and I have to say I am rather in awe of your courage at coming here today, most mortals would never have considered it," his mother said with curiosity tingeing her voice.

"Yes, but Michael also tells us courage is not something you lack," his father chimed in.

I looked from one to the other. "I didn't need courage to come here and meet you. I wasn't afraid in the least," I said easily.

They all looked at each other in surprise at how confident I seemed. Ava and Michael shared a look, no doubt having a secret conversation. I wished so much that I could talk to him in my head any time I wanted, so that even when we weren't together, he would always be with me.

His dad laughed easily. "Well, Michael, you certainly weren't exaggerating about her bravery."

Michael looked at his dad. "Nor her considerable disregard for fear."

His dad raised an eyebrow. "Not always a bad thing, son, if she scared easily, she wouldn't be sitting here now; in fact she wouldn't be with you at all. Isn't that correct, Angel?"

"That is completely correct, sir," I answered, shooting a triumphant look at Michael.

He sighed. "Still there are some things deserving of at least a little fear."

I didn't answer him.

His mum patted my arm. "Well, you have no need to fear us anyway, Angel, we would never hurt you. We may be vampires, but we certainly far from savages so you are welcome in our home anytime sweetheart."

"Thank you, that means a lot," I told her truthfully.

It did mean a lot to me to be accepted so easily by Michael's family. I was relieved.

We chatted for a while about university, and other normal topics. As they talked, I was looking at them all with wonder. I couldn't get over how stunning and unbelievable they all were.

At one point his mum left the room and came back with a cold can of juice for me, she told me Michael had mentioned it was my favourite. I was touched that she had gone out of her way to buy in something none of them would ever use, just because I liked it. Michael's family were every bit as thoughtful as he was.

"Now I see where Michael gets his incredible manners from," I told her.

"I am going to give Angel a tour of the house," Michael said, standing up and pulling me gently to my feet.

His brother sniggered. "Yes, I will just bet you are." Michael ignored him.

"Yes, I would love that. You have a beautiful home," I said.

"We'll be around if you need anything, Angel, and you're welcome to stay as long as you wish," his mum said, as we were walking out.

We left the room and Michael led me up the grand staircase. I kept pausing to admire paintings that were not reprints and look around me in amazement. In the first-floor hallway I noticed lovely sconces along one wall, a nod to olden times. I thought they looked like ones I had seen in IKEA, but I was pretty sure the De Marcos didn't shop there.

A few minutes later he stopped at another set of huge double doors and opened them silently.

"This is my room," he told me, leading me inside and dropping my hand so I could look around.

His room was massive, with the same high ceilings as downstairs. He also had a stone fireplace.

"Does it work?" I asked him, pointing to the fireplace and walking over to it.

"Yes, but it isn't on much, hardly ever actually. Why? Do you like it?"

I nodded. "I love fireplaces, they are so romantic. I always wanted to cosy up in front of one with someone I love on a cold winter night. Feeling safe and secure as the blisteringly cold wind howls outside and…" I trailed off.

He was watching my face closely. "And?"

I blushed slightly. "Nothing." Why was this so hard to bring up?

He was studying me for the longest moment, trying to figure out what I was going to add and why I had stopped.

He took both my hands and turned me to face him. "May I hazard a guess?"

I looked up and his eyes held me captive. I nodded.

"You were going to add that you wanted to make love all night in front of it."

I nodded again slowly as my heart raced faster than a speeding bullet. I wasn't sure if it raced so hard because he had guessed so right on the mark, or if it was hearing his satin voice caress me with the words.

"And you stopped because you were reluctant to voice the subject?"

Again, I nodded, still a silent captive to his lilac eyes that were shimmering with a multitude of emotions.

My head was hazy as I got utterly lost in his gaze, and the room, the castle and the whole world melted away until all I was aware of was him, and how he was looking at me right now. A look filled with so much love and wonder and pain it made my heart ache.

"You will have that, Angel; you will have everything your heart desires," he promised.

I couldn't speak or move all I could do was stay locked in his gaze. I knew I should say something but there didn't seem to be any words good enough to adequately express how I was feeling. Minutes passed.

He released me from the captivity of his eyes and turned away. He stood motionless staring into the unlit fireplace, with his hands on the ledge and his head bowed.

I walked over to him and pressed myself into his back, wrapping my arms tightly around his waist.

"I don't know why this is so difficult to talk about," I said bewildered.

"It's because we have been avoiding it for so long now for fear, we would get carried away just by saying the words out loud too often."

He turned around and gathered me into his arms, lifting me off my feet and burying his face in my neck and hair.

"I love you so much, Angel, I don't think you are aware of just how much. There isn't anything I cherish more than you. Nothing and no one shall ever come above you. I would kill to protect you and die to save you."

I held on tight to him. "Michael my love… my life, I feel the same way. Without you nothing else is worth it. You and I falling in love makes no sense… and yet it makes the most sense of everything in this forsaken world we live in." I wasn't sure I was articulating myself enough. He was the only thing in this chaotic world that made sense to me and my love for him was the only truly pure and real thing in it, the one and only thing I was sure of.

He set me on my feet and looked deep into my eyes. "Angel, there have been many moments that were right for us to make love in terms of setting and mood, but none that we were emotionally ready for. All this happened so fast, and it is *so* forbidden we had to deal with the torrent of emotions we were feeling before we were able to deal with the power of the physical side."

"Do you think we're there yet?" I asked him quietly.

His eyes locked with mine. "Yes, I do."

He ran his cool hand gently down my face; his eyes were the softest I had ever seen them, like lilac clouds. "Angel, I want to make love to you more than I have ever wanted anything in my life. I have yearned for you more than you could ever fully comprehend."

My heart betrayed me again by just stopping dead at his words. How I had longed to hear those words without even knowing it. I had craved so much to be as physically close to him as was truly possible, but I had no idea how much I needed to hear him reciprocate those feelings. For the second time since we met, he had saved my soul... saved me.

Relief washed over me in waves and the tension I never knew was there lifted and I felt light and free and alive. Michael wanted me... *Me*, not any other girl – of whom he could take his pick of – but me.

His lips turned up slightly as he heard my heart stop then thunder in my chest.

"Sometimes you have no need of words, my Angel, your heart speaks to me, and I love that."

I didn't answer him I just grabbed his shirt and kissed him, knocking his hat off and gripping his hair. He responded quickly and spun me around and against the wall. The kiss was violent, full of every pent-up physical emotion we had left unsaid all this time. I could feel the strength and power of his body as he let go for once and didn't handle me like glass. I loved it. It was the most passionate kiss we had ever had, and we had had a lot of them.

Was this about it? I didn't think so. We had waited painfully this long so I was sure we could wait a little longer till it was perfect.

We must have both been thinking the same thing because we stopped kissing each other at the same second. We were both breathing faster and as we looked at each other we started laughing hard, so hard I was doubled over, and he was holding onto the wall. I had no clue why this was so funny, but it was.

We settled down a bit and he sat on a chair. "Well, that was unexpected," he said catching his breath.

"It certainly was," I said still sniggering a bit.

"I would surmise it to be because we are both so relieved to have had the talk. We finally addressed the pink elephant in the room properly and it may have caused a small amount of hysteria." His eyes were bright and animated.

"I'm so glad we both agree the time has come." My breathing was evening out again.

He looked at me seriously. "Just a short while longer, Angel. I want to give you the greatest night of your life and I will, I promise you that. I just need time to plan it."

I sat on his knee. "I can be patient a while longer baby."

"Do you want to stay here tonight?" he asked as I cuddled up on his lap.

"I don't have any unsexy pyjamas to sleep in here," I said only half mockingly.

He smiled at me. "You have a point."

I got up and began to look around his room. I noticed it was black and white, the effect was very striking, and the black décor was very Michael.

He had a pin board on one wall filled with photos of his family from various locations. I studied them a while noting how close they all seemed.

"I don't have any photos of you to add on there, a fact I shall be remedying right now." He got up and headed across the room to a large desk, which housed his laptop, printer and other desk like things.

He opened a drawer and took out a digital camera. It looked to me like the same one a professional photographer would use.

There were framed photos around his room in black and white. They were pictures of undisclosed sights, but all were taken beautifully and were dramatic and artistic.

"I love these. Did you take them?" I asked amazed.

"Yes, its photos from places around the world from over the years, I like to document the changes over time. I always take my camera with me when I go away anywhere. I love photography." He held his camera up and began shooting pictures of me.

"No, please, don't I look a mess?" I pleaded.

"You do not look a mess you look dishevelled and sexy from our kiss."

I ignored him and continued to walk around his room to look at his pictures and he followed me continuing to snap away with his camera.

I stopped suddenly as I looked at a drawing of me in a frame. My eyes were wide open looking up at something and my lips were slightly parted, and my hair was falling around to one side. What the... He could draw *too*?

He had stopped taking my picture and was watching me. "Do you like it?" he asked unsurely as if he were afraid I wouldn't.

"Very much. When did you draw this?" I was touched.

It was an exact likeness of me; every detail was perfect like I had sat for it.

"After we met in the car park the first time. I memorised everything about your face as you looked up at me in surprise when I helped you, and then I came home and drew you."

I couldn't believe it. "Why?" I asked like a moron.

"Because I fell in love with you at that exact moment and I wanted to capture it. I knew I shouldn't have been trying to keep a memento of you since I knew I had to stay away from you, but I couldn't stop myself."

I felt like crying. I was in total disbelief that he had felt so strongly about me that he had to draw me.

At least I wasn't the only one acting erratically when we met. I remembered thinking he must have thought I was a lunatic with my irrational reaction to him.

"I was in pain with every line I drew... utterly tortured because I knew I had to leave you alone, my un-beating heart was breaking at knowing you could never be mine." His face was furrowed in pain at the memory.

"And now I am yours because it was destined to be. Did having the drawing make it harder for you?" I asked my heart breaking for him.

"Yes, but I couldn't bring myself to throw it out, if all I could ever have of you was that, then I couldn't destroy it, I knew I would keep it for all eternity."

He turned away and moved elegantly across the desk, before continuing, "I would be utterly resolved to stay away from you, to not ruin your life and then I would look at that drawing, and my will would crumble around me. I would sit and give myself a hundred justifications to go after you and a thousand to stay away." He shook his head. "I loathed myself for being so weak when I didn't stay away. It was indefensible and I knew it." His silky voice was ferocious.

I touched his cheek. "I'm not sorry in the least. I would have been inconsolable if you had stayed away from me. I was hopelessly in love with you."

"But you would have gotten over it. I was prepared to be miserable for the rest of eternity over you if I knew you would be happy, and I wasn't ruining your life but then... I saw something in your eyes in the lift that day... a sadness perhaps, that allowed me to justify being so utterly selfish and have you."

"So, the night you came to the club you knew I was there?"

"Yes, I knew. I followed your scent and completely disregarded all my thousand reasons to stay away and came to get you. I thought myself the most reprehensible creature in existence and felt incredibly guilty, so I tried to warn you to stay away from me, which was inexcusable and cowardly. I could not keep away from you so I hoped you would keep away from me."

"Michael, I could not have stayed away from you if my life depended on it. My life *did* depend on it; you could have killed me… and somewhere deep down I knew it, but death was better than living without you." I grabbed both sides of his face. "*You* are not to blame, and you must stop these thoughts right now. I would not want my life to have turned out any other way, because without you, it wasn't living it was just existing."

He looked into my eyes then and I watched the pain in them slowly lift. I felt exhausted; this had been an emotionally wrought day.

I was still in shock that he had been tortured so much over me, somehow, I always believed I loved him much more acutely than he loved me but now I knew that wasn't true at all and the knowledge hurt me to imagine him in so much pain, but at the same time equally pleased me.

"Does it scare you that my love for you has been so dark and obsessive from the second I looked into your bright green eyes?" he asked clinically.

I looked straight into his eyes, without hesitation. "No, it doesn't scare me one bit."

He laughed then. "You truly are one of a kind, Angel."

I hugged him tightly. "Michael?"

"Yes."

"I was completely obsessed with you from that first instant I looked up at you. There was no way you were ever getting rid of me."

He laughed again and looked at me with total pleasure across his gorgeous face.

"Now if you don't mind, I would like to go back to snooping around your room."

"Be my guest, my love, I certainly don't think I have anything to hide from you now."

I narrowed my eyes at him. "What about cheesy music hiding in your collection."

"Don't you know I'm much too cool for cheesy music?" he said laughing.

"Oh yeah, I forgot you were Mr suave vampire."

I began to look around again. "Where is your music and books?"

He picked up a remote control and a wall panel slid back and there behind it was a library of music and books.

"Wow!"

"We have a library here in the house with every book you could ever imagine, including scrolls from hundreds of years over the millennium, but this is my collection of my favourite books and music."

As I was looking through them, I noted he likes everything from Shakespeare to Stephen King. A varied reader like myself.

His music collection was huge. He had vinyl from throughout the decades and it was all organised by year. I could only imagine the music he had on his laptop.

After I had moseyed around his music for a while, I gave up on trying to find some hideous boy band, or one of top Broadway show tunes or anything equally as embarrassing to own. He obviously *was* just too cool.

I turned my attention to his bed and walked over to it while he took pictures. His bed was big enough to sleep ten people easy. I sat down on it, and it was the most comfortable, soft mattress imaginable. Amazing. His sheets were black satin, and I ran my hand slowly across its soft surface. If you could touch Michael's voice this is what it would feel like. I was mesmerised by it and lay down across it.

Michael reached down and fanned my hair around the sheet and lifted my top slightly to show my stomach and began snapping pictures.

"Turn and put your legs up against the wall crossing your ankles," he commanded.

I felt my heart race and did as he asked. I lay across the bed with my legs on the wall. My skirt had ridden up high on my thighs, but I wasn't indecent at least.

"Gorgeous. You look unbelievably sexy."

He stood on the bed to take some pictures from above me. He stopped suddenly, his expression changing, and he knelt beside me.

He ran his hand up the whole length of my leg slowly, his eyes carefully following his hand movements.

I stopped breathing and my heart crashed. I lay perfectly still as he reached the top where my skirt hem sat, and the room went hazy. I was in danger of needing a medical professional standing by.

His eyes met mine as he toyed with the hem of my skirt, and I could see the conflicting emotions in them. Desire then resolution and around again.

"Would you object if I were to tear that skirt from you?" His eyes going back and forth still.

I knew my answer here would be the decider for him and as much as I yearned for him to do it, I also knew he would be annoyed at himself tomorrow because he wanted so much to give me my perfect night. I considered any night with him to be special, but knowing how much he beat himself up when it comes to me, I wouldn't allow it.

I reluctantly took his hands off my skirt. I didn't say anything; I didn't need to. His closed lips turned up in a smile and his eyes softened with love instead of desire.

He lay down beside me and we just turned our heads and continued to stare at each other, holding hands. It was very intense.

I have no idea how long we stayed like that, but I eventually broke the stare because I needed the bathroom. I checked my watch when I got up and it was midnight. When I came back into the room he was standing at the window.

"Midnight... A vampire's favourite time. The in-between of night and day where anything is possible, and anything goes," he said without looking around. Sometimes I forgot how good his senses were.

How the hell did he know it was midnight? There wasn't a clock in the room. The mystery of how he told time intrigued me no end.

Maybe instinctively knowing it was midnight could be a vampire thing but that didn't explain how he always knew what time of day or night it was.

"Midnight is also a witch's favourite time. It's not known as the witching hour for nothing, it is when the veil between worlds is thinnest, and we are at our most powerful," I told him.

He didn't answer and continued to stare out of the window for five minutes. I just stood silently behind him wondering what he was thinking.

"I'll take you home, Angel."

His mood had shifted, and I had no idea why, but his body seemed tense.

"Are you alright?" I asked him slightly alarmed.

He turned from the window, and I wondered if his superior eyesight had seen something in the darkness.

"Yes, I'm fine." His tone invited no further discussion.

This was odd; I was only in the bathroom a few minutes. I noticed his eyes had hardened; all traces of softness gone from his face.

"I can just transport home if you want?"

He looked at me with controlled tenseness. "No, you are safer with me."

The car ride home was silent, but he kept my hand the whole way.

I was trying to think what could have changed his mood so quickly he had either seen something, heard something or Ava had told him something he didn't like.

When we got to my house, he opened my door for me looking around intently. Looking to see if we had been followed? I wasn't sure. When he was satisfied there was nothing there, he walked me to the door.

"Will you be coming back tonight?" I asked him.

"No, I have something I need to take care of so keep your window closed."

"Michael, you're freaking me out a bit will you just tell me what I should be looking out for?"

"It isn't anything for you to worry about I just want you to take a few extra precautions tonight."

"OK, I will, but are you going to be alright?"

He kissed me then. "I'll be fine I swear to you, it's just a minor annoyance."

I opened my front door and he kissed me again.

"I'll come around tomorrow afternoon." His voice was curt.

"OK. Please be careful, Michael," I pleaded.

"I will." He turned and went to his car, stopping before he went in. "Angel?"

"What?"

"Do you have any protection things for your entire house like a spell or a potion?"

"Yes. We don't use things like that often though."

"Use it tonight please. Everywhere."

And with that he was off and speeding away into the midnight.

Chapter Sixteen

Rome

I protected the house quickly and went to my room. I stood looking out my window to the pitch-black calm night. There were no high winds or heavy rain, nothing but still silence as far as the eye could see. I wondered what Michael had seen. This was really frustrating.

I got ready for bed I was so tired yet anxiousness was keeping me from falling asleep. I lay in the dark trying to clear my mind but sleep continued to elude me.

I tossed and turned all night managing only a broken sleep so I woke up grumpy and tired. I kept checking my phone all morning in case Michael had called or text and grew increasingly irritated that he hadn't.

At twelve o'clock he finally called to tell me he wouldn't be over till late tonight but wouldn't tell me why still. He just said he would tell me tonight so I snapped I would be sleeping when he came over since I had hardly slept last night and hung up the phone.

I really wanted to say don't bother coming over at all, but I wanted to see him, I needed to see him I was like a junkie needing my fix of him. I was pathetic really. He didn't call back to try to smooth things over like I expected and it made me slightly anxious.

I recalled how soft he had been last night, how his eyes were so warm and inviting when he was close to me. He was almost vulnerable at times, well as vulnerable as I imagined a vampire could get.

I spent the day searching Wiccan literature in the loft for any possible ways to make myself immortal, a spell, a potion, a ritual, anything.

Everything I read came back to the same thing; the only way to become immortal was to be turned by a vampire. The book had already told me that but I wanted to be thorough on the off chance the book had missed something. I was disappointed because I had hoped to have a back-up plan if he continued to refuse to turn me. There was an interesting page on sky guardians though, I pondered if I could speak to one?

That night I lay in a hot bath and attempted to relax and quiet my mind. I took a book in with me to escape into someone else's problems for a while.

When I got out, I made sure my window was open, then I switched out the light and lay in bed with music on. I must have fallen asleep because when I woke up it was morning.

I noticed three things, there was music playing in my ears because I had fallen asleep with my earphones on, my room was freezing because the window was still open and lastly, Michael was not here, and I had no idea why.

I closed the window and got ready and tried not to panic that something had happened to him or that he wasn't speaking to me for rudely hanging up on him yesterday.

I was in the kitchen with Dylan eating my breakfast when he arrived. Kennedy had opened the door to him and walked him through to the kitchen stammering out some incoherent sentences and blushing when he looked at her. He got that a lot from people when they spoke to him. His beauty and unbelievable confidence made most people nervous around him, not to mention his underlying danger.

He gave me a kiss and ruffled Dylan's hair. "Alright, kid?"

Dylan looked chuffed; he had some kind of hero worship for Michael going on.

"I love your jacket, Michael, it's so cool," Dylan said of Michaels leather jacket.

Michael took his jacket off and tossed it to Dylan. "You can have it. I'm not loving it much."

"Wow, thanks this is awesome," Dylan said jumping up and trying it on. It was a much too big for him but, the way he was growing he will soon somewhat fit it, plus his happy face said he didn't care.

I still hadn't spoken and took my time eating as Michael waited silently for me to finish. He was watching me carefully as Dylan and Kennedy left the kitchen, and once we were alone, he spoke.

"I'm sorry about last night, Angel, but I had to stay home."

"I was worried about you and when I woke up today and you weren't here, I started imagining all sorts. You could have phoned me or at least sent a text."

"I knew you were safe that's all that mattered to me."

"Are you going to tell me what it was all about?"

"We had some unexpected visitors. I sensed them nearby while you were in the bathroom. They were... *other* vampires, Angel, ones who wouldn't think twice about dining on your you. Not that I would allow that to happen but still I had to get you out of harm's way."

"So that's why you told me to protect the house?"

"Yes. I knew they would pick up your strong magical blood in my house, which is irresistible to most vampires, and I did not want to take any chances of them following it, so I stayed until they left this morning."

"What did they want from your family?" I was no longer angry; he had only been protecting me.

"Well, that's the peculiar part, they were travelling and heard rumours of a vampire hunter surfacing and stopped by our house to warn us since in all likelihood it will be me he will come after."

"Are the rumours true?"

"I'm not sure, it could just be talk but they wanted to warn us anyway since they are somewhat family friends."

"I'll keep my ears open for any talk though I am sure it will be us he comes to for the blessing of his dagger."

"I'm not overly worried, Angel. If he attacks, he will die before he gets the dagger from his hand." His voice was detached but his eyes flashed danger.

I shuddered; I wouldn't want to be that vampire hunter taking on Michael.

My family were spending Christmas in the new hotel and I opted to stay here and be with Michael. His family had invited me over for Christmas and I was going there on Christmas Eve after my family left.

We all opened our gifts for each other before they left in the afternoon and my mum made a delicious Christmas dinner.

She was disappointed I wasn't coming with them and tried to change my mind.

After they left, I called Michael. "Hey you, that's my family away so come over any time."

"I'm just turning into your driveway so I shall be there momentarily."

He wasn't kidding I had just put the phone down and he was coming through the door.

My heart skipped a beat when I saw him; no matter how much time we spent together my heart still jumped when I saw him again.

We went to my room and I packed an overnight bag. I had decided on a cream skirt and matching jacket for Christmas day with a red top underneath and matching shoes. Today I wore black trousers and a fluffy black jumper, it was more smart/casual.

Michael looked as delicious as usual in black trousers and a plain black jumper that fitted to his body in ways I couldn't allow myself to think about.

It was dark when we left; night was Michael's favourite time to drive because he could turn off his lights and floor the accelerator with little chance of detection. I stopped watching the speedometer after it moved up past 160.

When we got to Michael's house, everyone was gathered in the family room that I had met them in two weeks ago, so I guessed this was their favoured room considering how many there were.

They had a huge Christmas tree and decorations everywhere and I loved how festive it was. They were all relaxed and laughing and having fun as we walked in, and Ava was playing the Santa Claus is coming to town on the piano and singing along.

Even though Michael had told me they celebrated Christmas, I couldn't help but be a little surprised at how normal it all was.

Lilly handed me a glass of white wine and I noticed they were all drinking what appeared to be red wine. Michael caught my slight eye widen.

"It's blood with vodka in it."

I choked on my sip of wine in surprise. "What?"

He smiled. "Adding alcohol to blood is the only way vampires can enjoy the alcohol effects, well other than feeding on someone who is intoxicated. We don't do it very often just special occasions."

"Where do you get the blood from?"

"Derek knows someone who works in a blood bank."

"And what does this person think he wants the blood for?"

"He doesn't ask, Derek razzle dazzles him so he has to comply." The way he said this made me think, *I have no idea vampires could do that.*

"Oh" was all I could think of to say.

Everyone was really merry, and Michael was playing the piano while we all sang along to songs from the '60s. It was so much fun and I was in awe of Michael's talent all over again.

I was standing opposite him at the piano just watching him in pleasure. He began to play bed of roses and my heart just melted. He looked up at me as he played and I was swept away. I went around and sat beside him and we began to play our song we composed together.

When we went to Michael's room, I was very tipsy. I looked at Michael and the alcohol he had consumed did not show on him except a slight glint in his eyes.

I went into his bathroom and got changed. It had begun to snow earlier and Michael was watching it fall from the window. I stood next to him and put my head against him. "I love snow it's so pretty."

He put his arms around me. "Merry Christmas, my Angel." And he kissed me.

I knew if I looked at my watch, I would see it was midnight. He was doing it again, the unexplained time thing.

We watched the snow falling for a while. It was picturesque outside, it seemed to make the whole world feel like it was silent, and I was so happy to be here in this moment with Michael.

The next morning I woke to find Michael had made breakfast. The tray was at the bottom of the bed and he was standing watching me.

"I can't believe I have my very own Christmas Angel," he said handing me the tray.

"This is so sweet, thank you. Merry Christmas, baby." I gave him a kiss.

"Eat your breakfast and then you can open your presents," he said feeding me a strawberry.

I ate my food quickly excited to get to swapping gifts.

He opened his first and he loved his presents. He had a tear in his eye when he read the hidden messages in the cufflinks.

"What an amazing gift, Angel, thank you. I love you so very very much." He wrapped his arms around me and squeezed me tightly.

He handed me a small black velvet box. I opened it and saw an exquisite diamond eternity ring. I took it out and saw the diamonds continued all the way around. I gasped.

He took the ring from me. "I realise an eternity ring is traditionally bought after the engagement and wedding rings but I wanted to give you something to symbolise that my love for you is forever." He placed the ring on my right hand. "I would put it on your left hand but I'm saving that." He smiled.

"Oh, Michael, I love it, thank you. It is the most beautiful ring I have ever seen."

"You're welcome, my love. It looks beautiful on you."

I had tears in my eyes as I kissed him.

"You have another one to open," he said handing me an envelope.

"What is this?"

"Open it and see." He was grinning from ear to ear.

I opened the envelope and took out a sheet of paper. It was an e-mail from a five-star hotel in Rome confirming a booking for two for December 27.

My eyes shot open wide, and my heart began to race.

"Does this mean what I think it means?" I asked excitedly.

"It does," he said giving me the most beautiful smile that dazed me momentarily.

"Aghhh," I screamed happily throwing myself on him.

He gripped me tightly and kissed me hard, pulling me down on top of him.

"Hands down, best Christmas ever." I squealed.

"Agreed." He laughed.

"I have to go home and pack today. It will take me the next two days to decide what to take."

He sat up and ran his hands through his hair. "On that note I have another gift… well it's actually more for me but I got it for you."

He handed me an expensive wrapped box and I opened it quickly. Inside was sexy black lace underwear, fishnet silk stockings, garter the works. I took it out the box and held it up.

"So this is what you like? Nice," I said with raised eyebrows.

His head was down and he was looking up at me through thick black lashes. The look was both coy and sexy as he nodded. "I'll like it all the more when in taking it off of your gorgeous body."

I gulped and my heart accelerated faster than his sports car as I imagined him doing that.

"How did you know my bra size?"

He smiled. "Do you honestly think I haven't been paying attention?"

I laughed. "Naughty boy."

"You're about to find out." He was giving me *that* look.

I was on the verge of hyperventilating; that look was going to kill me one of these days. Maybe sooner than I thought once he gave me that look when it was leading to the real thing.

I went down and said goodbye to the De Marcos his mum hugged me and told me to have a wonderful time in Rome.

I could swear his brother was giving me knowing looks; he had a cheeky grin on his face when he told me I was in for a fantastic trip.

Ava's smile was a little too wide. "Have the best time, Angel." She leaned in and whispered, "I have a feeling you won't be seeing much of Rome." And she kissed my cheek and went flitting away.

OK, this was odd. I wasn't sure I was entirely comfortable with his whole family knowing we were consummating our relationship.

Michael caught my discomfort and swept me out of there quickly.

When we got to my house, we went to my room to pack and we ran upstairs in excitement.

Even Michael, who wasn't a fan of taking long to pick outfits, was sharing my enthusiasm.

I had never seen him act so boyishly cute; like a little child on Christmas morning running to see if Santa had been.

It was very endearing. The panther became the puppy.

At this moment the deadly killing machine only looked like he could lick someone to death.

"You can decide how you want to get there, Angel, we can either take the jet or you can transport us."

"I'm too eager to get there so we'll transport if that's OK?"

"Perfectly OK." He dazed me with his smile again and I had to shake my head to clear it.

I goggled the hotel we would be staying in so we could have a look at the inside.

It looked amazing and I noticed it was the best hotel in Rome; mainly because it said it was the best hotel in Rome. I did believe it because I knew Michael would have nothing less than the best.

I had a sneak scan of the rates and seen our room was around two thousand pounds a night to stay in. wow. Michael never did anything by half. He was definitely an all or nothing type.

The next two days dragged by, but finally, it was time.

Michael came over after dark with his suitcase. We both wanted to arrive at night for the sake of romance.

I had on the underwear he bought me underneath my skirt and top. I had never been more excited and more terrified about something in my life.

It wasn't as if I hadn't had sex before, I had, but I had never slept with someone I loved this way… this much… this intensely. Moreover, I was afraid of not impressing him. He literally has a millennium of experience on me, and the woman he had slept with have at least had hundreds of years too.

"Are you alright, Angel?"

"Depends on what second you ask me. I am filled with nerves."

"I know I can hear it in your heartbeat. Would you rather not do this yet?"

I looked at him incredulously. "Are you crazy? I want nothing more than this to happen. I'm just scared of living up to your expectations."

His eyebrows lifted. "Are you serious?"

"Yes," I admitted sheepishly.

"Angel, I have been having sex with vampires for a millennia but I have never been with anyone I have loved. It will be wonderful for me because I love you so much. I swear you have nothing to live up to."

"Really."

"Really." He stroked my face gently. "Now are we ready to go?"

"Yes, let's go." My stomach was churning with nervous excitement as I held him and transported us to Rome.

Michael walked to the reception desk to check us in. The two women behind the desk banged into each other because they were staring at him so hard.

I giggled at their reaction but Michael didn't even seem to notice and spoke to them in fluent Italian (which was sexy as hell) and signed for our room key.

The bellboy took our cases and we followed him to the presidential suite. Michael gave him a tip and said something in Italian and he left our cases at the door without opening it and went away.

Michael opened the door himself and held it for me to go inside. My heart was racing so fast. This was it…

The living room was spectacular; it was decorated in white and gold custom-made Italian design.

The entrance to the bedroom had white pillars and I gasped as I walked through.

There was a trail of red rose petals leading towards the bed, and red rose petals covering the whole top of the bed.

He was giving me a bed of roses.

My eyes filled with tears at what was the most romantic thing I had ever known.

Candles were lit all around the beautiful white room, hundreds of them flickering like magic.

Michael was standing at the doorway watching me and I turned slowly towards him in awe.

"This is incredible, Michael, it's like a dream."

He didn't say anything he just walked slowly towards me gazing into my eyes and capturing my soul.

With every step he took towards me, my heart faltered and raced in rapid succession.

He was removing his jacket without breaking the look and tossed it casually onto a nearby chair.

I was rooted to the spot utterly mesmerised by the slow seductive way he moved.

He stood before me and very slowly lifted his hands to my top. He began to undo the zip agonising slowly, never taking his eyes from mine he slid it from my shoulders.

His fingertips slowly caressed my waist as he reached behind me and unzipped my skirt and watched it drop to the floor.

As I stepped out the fallen skirt, his head travelled the length my body and as his eyes came back to mine, he had *that* look in them.

I was breathless with anticipation.

He pulled me in to his arms and kissed me slowly and deeply, running his hands through my hair. He was in no rush.

I removed his shirt with unsteady hands and I placed them on his chest. As I ran them down to his stomach, I became acutely aware of how smooth his skin was and I could feel every bump and ridge of his muscles beneath my fingertips.

I moved my hands down and undid his belt and as he watched this action closely, my heart thundered.

He tightened his hold on me and his bare chest rubbed against mine.

The feel of his skin on mine was like a bolt of lightning and as his hands roamed my body, removing my sexy underwear it felt like a million tiny shockwaves coursing all through me.

He dropped his head to my neck giving it feathery kisses and I wrapped my arms around his broad shoulders sighing in delight; my neck was a hot spot for me as he lifted me up. My legs wound tightly around his waist and he carried me to the bed.

Our eyes were completely locked together and he placed me gently amongst the rose petals.

Slowly and seductively, as I quivered under his touch, he picked up a rose petal and traced it leisurely over my long legs, stomach and breasts, causing my throat to constrict with desire.

My head was reeling and was about to burst.

I lost all sense of time with the unfathomable sensations tearing through me, and I gasped loudly as his tongue travelled over every contour and inch of my body with unrivalled expertise.

My whole body was trembling under his magic touch and I couldn't catch my breath. I never knew *anything* could feel so glorious.

I couldn't form any coherent thoughts as he expertly took me to heaven; and my whole body exploded in intense pleasure.

Our bodies were in perfect sync and our eyes were locked together as we made love all night.

The next day I woke up and felt like my body had every bit of tenseness hammered out of it. I felt sated, safe, and truly alive.

My happiness knew no bounds and I felt like I was about to burst with it.

Last night had been the greatest night of my life.

Michael was awake beside me. "Good morning, my Angel. How are you feeling today?" Was it my imagination or did he sound slightly unsure?

I sighed in contentment. "Absolutely wonderful. I have never felt better in all my life."

He smiled. "Good, that was my intention."

"Well, you certainly achieved it. How are you feeling?"

"Amazing. That was the most wonderfully intense experience I have ever had. I feel connected to you in ways I never believed possible."

I stretched languorously; every part of me was tingling.

He was watching me silently, a slight smile playing on his lovely lips.

"You're glowing, Angel, I am finding It difficult to tear my eyes from you."

"Who says you have to?"

He laughed. "You have to eat and I am going for a shower."

I realised I was famished. "I am so hungry. I don't think I've ever been this hungry."

His lips lifted knowingly and he leapt from the bed to answer the knock at the door. He threw on a bathrobe and let in room service.

"When did you order my food?"

"While you slept. I woke before you."

He brought the tray over to me and went into the shower.

I was still eating when he came out and I looked up at him.

The sight that greeted me made me drop my fork and lose my appetite.

He was wet from the shower with only a small a towel tied around his waist and there were rivulets of water dripping down his flawless alabaster chest, curving into every defined muscle and down his washboard stomach.

His arms were strong and his powerful legs were better than any football player.

His ebony hair was wet and pushed back by his hand, highlighting his impossibly high cheekbones. His piercing lilac eyes with his wet lashes glittered in the sun coming through the window.

Anyone seeing him like this would know instantly he was not human; his beauty was otherworldly; no human was this spectacular.

He was magnificent... utterly magnificent.

I couldn't tear my eyes off of him. I forgot how to breathe, how to move, I even forgot my own name.

He walked over to me and I pulled him back into bed.

Hours later it was dark again and I got up to have a shower. When I stood up, my legs were shaking like crazy.

Michael reached his hand over and touched my left leg. "You're trembling."

"You've made me tremble," I said breathlessly.

His expression was so soft and his eyes were so tender as he got up and carried me into the shower, and then jumped in with me.

He washed my hair and my body and made me tremble even more under the hot water raining down on us.

As I brushed my teeth, I noticed a bite mark on my neck. Not a love bite, a real one. I touched it hesitantly thinking it was going to hurt but it didn't.

"You bit me." I inspected it, it was kind of sexy.

"I got carried away."

He dipped his head and softly kissed the spot he had bitten.

We didn't leave the room for five days.

On New Year's Eve we celebrated his birthday, and saw the bells in on the terrace of our room overlooking the city lights and watched the fireworks go off at midnight, it was magical.

I gave him his gifts, which he loved. He adored the first edition of his favourite book and read to me from it a little every day.

On the fifth day, we were joking about how we really need to go outside and at least see a little of Rome.

"The hotel staff will be talking about us, the only person to see us since we arrived is the room service guy." He laughed.

So, we ventured out to see some sights. The weather was pleasant; warm but cool. We visited the coliseum, which was fascinating, and the Sistine chapel to see Michelangelo's painting which was truly a masterpiece.

We also visited the Spanish steps where Michael kissed me at the bottom and the top, taking selfies of out happiness. We went to palazzo Poli and made a wish in the Trevi Fountain. An older Italian woman told Michael that if you throw a coin into the water from over your left shoulder it means you will be sure to return to Rome, so we did that too.

Michael took his camera and we got lots of brilliant pictures. It was a great day. Rome was unbelievably romantic.

The Italian drivers were insane; it was like watching the whacky races.

"How incredibly silly of these humans to drive in such a manner," Michael commented idly, shaking his head.

The Italian people weren't very subtle about staring at Michael, in fact they were bordering on rude. Young men scowled at him when their girlfriends openly admired him and the wait staff in the restaurant were falling over themselves to serve him. Even the men.

The food was unbelievable; it was the best I had ever tasted. Proper authentic Italian food, that the restaurants – although great – could not compare to.

When we left the restaurant, it was dark and we strolled through the streets hand in hand watching the natives go about their night.

About an hour later I was realised I was incredibly thirsty, and Michael went into a shop to get me a bottle of water.

The street we were on was packed with people going in and out of bars and café's and no one was paying attention to anyone else.

Suddenly four men surrounded me, they all had a knife and forced me into a nearby dark alley.

I was highly trained in hand-to-hand combat with weapons, but I didn't need the attention it would cause a girl taking down four armed men, then the police would come and the whole thing would be a nightmare.

I couldn't use my powers in front of all these people, so I went along with them, knowing the alley was dead end. I was *beyond furious* and planned to disarm them and throw them against every wall in the alley with my telekinesis when we were out of sight.

I realised leaving four witnesses to my powers was risky, but I had no choice, unless I killed them, which throwing them hard against every was just might do. At the very least their weapon hands would be shattered for life.

I had never felt so savage in my life, and I kill demons.

Michael would be frantic when he noticed me missing and I wasn't sure he would be able to pick up my scent with so many humans in such proximity.

I was wrong.

As the four of them held knifes to my back and sides and roughly dragged me by the hair deeper into the alley, I just had to wait a few steps and could take them out.

I had *never* wanted to kill anything more than them.

Michael appeared from nowhere ahead of them looking like the Angel of death.

His expression was undisputedly deadly, and his lovely lilac eyes had darkened and flashed with layers of pure danger.

I knew how this was going to end.

One of the men threw me to the ground and I jumped using my martial arts training to get up quickly and tossed him had against a wall… hard with complete aggression.

I threw up a giant invisibility shield so that no one from the street could witness what was about to go down.

I couldn't stop Michael killing these rapists or even potential murderers even if I wanted to.

They looked unequivocally petrified and were desperately glancing around for an escape route.

Where were they going go, they couldn't outrun him, besides which both of us we supernatural.

Michael took slow step toward them.

His muscles were tensed to spring as he circled them slowly; it reminded me of a lion before it attacked its prey.

Then… fast as lightning, he snapped two of their necks simultaneously with a flick of his wrist and they dropped silently, dead before they hit the ground.

The last two men were terrified now and pleaded with Michael not to kill them. Both men were crowded into a corner, fighting each other who was in front.

Michael laughed humourlessly. "Now you know how your victims feel, you pieces of shit. Just be thankful I'm making it quick, well, not as quick as your buddies there, but I am hungry."

I knew from the book a vampire sucking your blood could be an almost orgasmic experience, or it could be incredibly painful, it was down to the vampire which one.

One of the men asked what this mythical creature was, "What the hell?"

Michael turned slowly icy voice. "Oh, I'm much worse than hell."

They were making the sign of the cross at him, and Michael laughed coldly. "Your God is not going to save either of you."

He turned to me; his eyes were blazing inhumanly. "Now you'll finally see for yourself what being a vampire is really all about."

I was rooted to the spot as I watched him move gracefully towards the man. His movements were hypnotically sensual as his fangs extended and he tipped the man's neck back and bit down on his carotid artery.

He drank the blood without spilling a single drop.

I stood mesmerised watching my vampire kill so easily.

Part of me was disturbed, but mostly I was impressed by his utter detachment and skilful elegant style. He was spellbinding with his finesse and grace.

When he was finished, he looked up at me and I noticed there wasn't so much as a smear of blood on his face.

"Are you afraid?" he asked quietly, not making a move towards me.

"No and stop asking me that every time you do something vampiric… it's annoying."

"Are you repulsed?"

"No, and again, the things I have seen and killed; nothing repulses me."

He was staring at me in disbelief. "That is not a normal reaction Angel."

I walked over to him and kissed him hard; I grabbed his hair crushing my lips onto his. He kissed me back for a minute before he pulled away.

"Have you taken leave of your senses? You just watched me kill four armed men and sucked the blood lives from two of them till death and your response is to kiss me."

I shrugged. "So?"

He ran his hand through his hair and laughed. "I honestly don't know whether to commend you or have you committed."

"Well while you're deciding I'm going to transport us back to the hotel. We don't want anyone seeing us leave this crime scene."

"Someone may have witnessed it when they walked past, Angel."

"I put an invisibility shield across the alley when I saw your face. I knew you were going to kill them."

We were back in our hotel room in less than a second and carried on our conversation.

"So this is what has become of you, Angel, protecting me while I kill. How can you be alright with that?"

"Michael, those men were the worst dregs of humanity, they would have killed me or left me for dead given half a chance. The fact that I have powers would have saved me but the next woman, and the ones after that would have no chance against them so in my eyes you did the female population of Rome a huge service tonight."

"That was not exactly my motives for doing it, however true that may be. No one will ever hurt you in any way and get to live Angel, if you get so much a scratch on your beautiful skin, I will kill whomever is responsible and I will not make excuses for that. However, *you* should have been horrified watching me do it. I played judge, jury and executioner and I murdered them in cold blood."

"I don't know what you want me to say, Michael. I wasn't horrified and I'm not insane. I love you and that's as simple as I can say it."

"There really is no deterring you from wanting to become a vampire is there? The only reason I let you watch was to put you off ever wanting to become one."

"Well, it didn't work."

"Come here, my crazy fallen Angel, what am I going to do with you?" He held his arms out to me.

I ran into them willingly and he kissed me with reverent passion as we went crashing down onto the floor.

We left Rome after that.

Chapter Seventeen

The Hunter

When we got back from Rome, I informed my parents that I wanted Michael to be able to stay over some nights. I was dreading this conversation but it had to be done. They were both just looking at me blankly when I gave them my request.

"What about demon attacks, Angel? If he's here a lot he will see that happen," my father inquired.

I took a deep breath. "He knows our secret; I told him what we were."

"You did what?" Oh, she was mad. "Angelica, it isn't just your secret to tell, it involves all of us and I think it was irresponsible of you to tell him without consulting us." My mum was *furious*.

"Why did you tell him?" My dad was not amused.

"I love him, and I want to be with him forever and I wanted him to know the real me. Is that so hard to understand?"

"Well, it's done now, I suppose. Fine he can stay over *but* not every night, Angel," my mum said.

"OK, thanks. We can spend a few nights at his house."

"Slow it down a bit, Angelica. Why do you have to spend every night together?" Her tone was snappish.

"Look, I couldn't explain it even if I tried to; so, to simplify it we want to be together, we… we just cannot be parted. I know it makes no logical sense and you can't or don't get it but that's how it is."

"How do his parents feel about this?" my dad asked.

"They're fine with it," I answered truthfully. After all, Michael *was* over a thousand years old.

"Fine, you're going to do what you want anyway, Angel, you don't need our approval," my mum said.

"You're right I don't but I would like your blessing."

"We'll see how it goes," my dad said.

I went to my room relieved *that* conversation was over. I knew they would never understand the love between Michael and I, hell I barley understood it and I was living it. I knew they were going freak out when they found out he was a vampire. What then? They would ask me to make a choice and I would choose him; I knew that, I did not even have to think about it. It was as sure as the air I had to breathe to in order to survive.

Then I had a thought, did they really need to know he was a vampire? Maybe one day, but not for a long time. Although I *knew* my mother would eventually check the book.

I pondered that one for a second. Even if she did, check the book, she didn't have much to go on. She knew he was very beautiful and pale, she knew he was charming and she knew he was polite, and she suspected he was strong. That didn't necessarily equate to vampire.

I decided to put it out of my mind. There was no sense worrying about it until I had to. Makes for less stress.

I phoned Michael and told him they agreed he could stay here if it wasn't every night, so he suggested we spend Friday, Saturday and Sundays at his house. Perfect.

We decided to bring clothes to keep at each other's houses no way were we going back and forth with bags all the time.

The months passed in a haze of complete happiness. He took me to Paris for valentines and it was incredibly romantic, it couldn't beat Rome though probably because that's where we first made love but it was a close second. Plus, no one got murdered in Paris… well, someone could have gotten murdered but it wasn't by us so that was a plus for Paris. We were so totally in love. I didn't think anyone had ever loved like this before, not this intensely.

The more time I spent with the De Marcos the more I just loved that family. They were all unique and talented in different ways and they were fun to be around.

Ava and I were forming a close friendship and I loved her.

I just kept waiting on the other shoe to drop…

I saw Dallas a lot too; we would double date once a week and we would go out alone together once a month, usually to a club.

Michael was a basket case when we went out alone because he constantly worried that something would happen to me.

He even admitted to keeping track of me with his sensing power in case I got into trouble *and* putting a tracker on phone. I hadn't even known he had a sensing power until he confessed to using it on me.

I wasn't angry about it because I knew he wasn't doing it to be a jealous boyfriend. After all, there wasn't anything on this planet or any other that he had to be jealous about. He was doing it out of concern for my safety.

What did irk me was he knew how powerful I was and still felt the need for this.

A little overboard...? Definitely. However, he did realise that. He wouldn't stop doing it, but he did own up to it.

I wondered what kind of state he would be in if I was a human with no powers.

Everything was quiet on the demon front too. We hadn't had any attacks in months.

We were almost like a normal couple, obviously that couldn't last.

One Monday night in May Michael told me he was staying late in the library to do research for an essay, so I told him to meet me at home and I transported to my room to finish typing up my own essay.

I was aware of some noises in the loft but I didn't think anything of it.

About two hours later Dylan transported into my room utterly panic-stricken.

"Angel, its Michael he's in serious trouble," he was screaming.

"What?" I couldn't figure out what kind of trouble Michael could be in or how Dylan knew about it.

"There's a vampire hunter after him right now and we gave him potions to help because we never knew Michael was a vampire and that it was him the hunter was after." His words were a jumble because he was freaking out. "I couldn't let it happen, Angel, I had to come and get you."

"You done the right thing, Dylan, thank you." I was trying to stay calm.

I was confused, with me being the most powerful, I thought I would have blessed the knife with my blood, but Dylan said both Mum and Dad sliced their palms open themselves and blessed it that way instead. Not the time to think of this.

"What potions?"

"A pausing potion, a paralysing potion and a disabling potion to throw together. Mum said it won't stop him but will weaken him enough for the hunter to stab his heart with the dagger, but it would only last five, tops six, minutes due to his strength."

"Take me to them, Dylan, now," I shouted.

We transported to the dark car park where Michael had left his car. They must have been waiting for him here. I couldn't see the rest of my family, but I could sense them there watching, so they must have their invisibility shield up. "COWARDS!" I screamed at them.

The hunter threw the potions just after I shouted at my family, and Michael fell to his knees.

The hunter moved towards him, the dagger lighting up the night like a beacon, it was a neon vivid blue with the power of my family blood which had blessed it.

I ran and threw myself between him and Michael. So much for my family never having to find out.

"Drop the dagger. Do not take one more step," I said angrily.

"Move aside, girlie, he's a vampire, the most powerful of his kind," the hunter said.

"I know who he is, and I'm warning you I won't let you kill him," I shouted.

He took another step forward and lifted the dagger.

"He's getting stronger by the second and then he'll kill you," I said evenly.

"Will you get out of my way I'm going to kill him while I still can."

I stole a quick glance at Michael to make sure he was OK. He was gaining strength but still looked a little disoriented. I couldn't chance him taking on this vampire hunter with a magical dagger in his current condition.

"Don't make me kill you," I begged him.

He ignored me and moved quickly towards Michael. He wasn't quick enough though and I threw him backwards with a tilt of my head.

"Are you insane, girl?" he asked as he got up, aimed the dagger at Michael, and ran to him at speed.

I was done messing about. Without the slightest hesitation, I used telekinesis to take the dagger from him, turning it quickly in mid-air, and sending it full force into his chest.

I closed my eyes for a second as the enormity of what I had done washed over me, and when I opened them, I knew my parents had left.

I was upset that it had come to having to kill the hunter, but I would never have let him try to harm Michael.

If it was choice between Michael and the hunter it was no choice at all.

I looked around and Michael was getting to his feet. He looked at me in despair and pulled me into his arms.

"I am so sorry you had to do that, Angel, I know how hard it must have been for you. Are you alright?"

"I'm OK, babe, are you alright?"

"Yes, my strength has returned. I sensed the hunter earlier and knew he was going to try this tonight. I wanted very much to keep you out of it, Angel, but I was not prepared for the potions."

"It was my family that gave them to him but when Dylan saw it was you, he came to get me."

Dylan checked the hunter and he was very dead so he pulled the now gold dagger from his chest and approached us, and handed the dagger to Michael.

"Thank you, Dylan," he said and shook his hand.

"The potions are designed to stop demons but because you're a vampire they only slowed you down for a couple of minutes. Even so, I couldn't let him try and kill you but my family would have stopped me from intervening so I had to get Angel."

"You did the right thing, buddy. Thank you. The family will be angry at you now though," I said ruffling his hair.

"I don't care, Angel, they can be angry. They should have stopped him when they saw it was Michael," he answered.

"Are you OK to drive?" I asked Michael.

He nodded. "Yes, I'm fine now."

"OK then, I am going to go home and deal with this tonight," I said.

"I'll come with you, Angel, you shouldn't have to face this wretched situation alone."

"No, Michael, I have to face them myself. It won't take long."

"I don't like this. I would much rather come with you."

"I'll be with her, Michael, it's OK," Dylan said.

We looked at each other for the longest minute, then he spoke again.

"Promise me you will phone me the second it's done."

"I promise."

I gave him a quick kiss and Dylan and I transported home.

My parents and my sister were sitting in silence when we arrived. No one spoke for a while.

My mum was the first to speak. "He's a vampire Angelica... A VAMPIRE. How can you defend him? Kill for him?"

"Because I love him, Mother."

"Do you have any idea what you have done? You are in a relationship with a vampire AND you have killed to protect him."

"I *am* aware of the facts."

"You will end this farce now, Angelica. You cannot be with a vampire," my dad said.

"I will not end it. We love each other," I said quietly.

"So you are willing to put us all at risk then?" Kennedy asked.

I shot her a look. "How are you at risk? He has been staying here four nights a week for the last three months and you haven't been in danger once."

"Be that as it may, you still have to end this relationship. It is forbidden in more ways than I can even count," my mum said.

"I'm not going to end it... I can't. I love him more than everything in the world combined and I won't give him up."

"So how is this going to turn out is he going to make you a vampire like he is and force you to give up your Wiccan destiny?" my dad asked angrily.

"He isn't forcing me to do anything and he doesn't want to turn me. We just want to be together," I said angrily.

"There are consequences for that. Do you really imagine the consul will just accept it? Or his leaders for that matter? You are inviting disaster and we will all be dragged into it," my dad said.

"You won't be dragged into it. Neither side has to find out and if they do, I will take full responsibility," I said.

"If you are going to continue this... this disgusting alliance he cannot stay here. We will not be party to this in any way," my mum said.

"Disgusting alliance? How dare you call our relationship disgusting, Mother. It is the purest most truthful thing I have ever known and I will not have you speak about it like that." I wasn't shouting but I was very angry.

Nobody spoke for five minutes until they got tore into Dylan for not only condoning it, but also helping me to save Michael. Dylan said he didn't care if Michael was a vampire because he loved him and he knew his love for me was special. My mum just shook her head at him.

Dylan had enough of their judgement and said, "Fuck you all," and gave him the finger.

We went up to my room and I phoned Michael. I told him what had been said and he informed me he had told his family too.

"Oh no. what did they say?" I asked.

"They weren't massively concerned but they were a little annoyed I hadn't told them before now," he said.

"So they're alright with it then?"

"Yes, they're fine with it. I'll be over in a minute."

I put the phone down and sat next to Dylan. Michael appeared and Dylan jumped.

"I guess I have to get used to you moving like a vampire in front of me now." He laughed.

The three of us sat around talking for a couple of hours and Dylan was quizzing Michael on vampire things like myths/truths, Michael told him they made a lot of the myths up to put witches of the truth and saying 'cool' a lot at his answers. He asked Michael if what was in the book was true and Michael told him the truth that fir the most part it was hence one of his ancestors had a relationship at some point in history with one, Dylan looked astounded. "Why would she put privileged information in the book."

"No idea, buddy, maybe he gave her permission, I gave Angel permission but she didn't take it."

Dylan nodded in approval.

After Dylan left, I locked my room door and we got into bed. Michael wrapped me in his arms and somehow nothing seemed quite as bad anymore.

The next morning we went to uni as normal and I was subjected to Sally's endless gossiping. Today she was slamming a girl for the clothes she wore to the union last night. I could not have been less interested and she got a bit huffy over it.

At lunchtime, we skipped the café and went to sit on the grass since it wasn't very cold outside and we wanted to be alone.

Michael was quiet and I wondered why as I watched him stare into the distance.

"What's wrong?" I finally asked.

"I have been debating on whether to tell you this so soon after last night, Angel, but I think you should know."

"Tell me what?"

"Last night someone else was there. Two of them actually."

"Who?"

"I don't know. My senses were a little off because of the potion but I know someone was there and one of them was a demon and I *think* the other was mortal."

"Does that mean I should expect the police soon?"

"That's the peculiar part. It wasn't a witness per se as much as someone in the know."

"Who the hell could it be?" I asked.

"I have no idea but I'm sure we'll know eventually, when whatever angle they are working from becomes apparent."

"Well that officially makes them a problem for another day." I sighed.

Michael lifted my chin and held me with his eyes.

"What do you say to checking into a hotel and escaping reality for a while?"

"I say what are we waiting for, let's do it."

He dazed me with his smile and lifted me to my feet and we took off in his car.

We decided against going to the Phoenix hotel even though it was the best in the city. We checked into the second best instead.

Uni classes were wrapping up for the Easter holidays anyway so we decided to stay insulated in the hotel for a while.

I text Dylan and asked him if anyone was home and he said no so I transported back to get some clothes and toiletries. I told Dylan where we would be and to not tell anyone else.

Michael was lying on the bed when I got back and staring at the ceiling. He looked up at me as I unpacked my bag.

"My beautiful Angel, how I long to see you smile again."

I looked at his flawless face. His unbelievable lilac eyes… his luscious lips… my heart melted.

"You are the only thing in this whole world I can smile for Michael. I don't feel good about my family right now but I'll get over it."

He stood up and walked towards me slowly, pulling his t-shirt over his head. I froze mid breath and watched him fixatedly. He was so glorious. The scorching heat between us made my senses reel.

"I'll make you feel good, Angel."

He lifted me up and we went spinning around the room kissing passionately. My heart thundered and my head exploded when he crashed me onto the bed. We frantically tore each other's clothes off and I grabbed his hair hard as we rolled around in a frenzy of utter need. He was right… he did make me feel good.

We spent the rest of the day in bed; I was curled up tight in his arms with my head on his chest. He stoked my hair and tickled my back. It was heaven and I wished we could stay like this forever.

The days passed blissfully, holed up together in that room with no one to bother us. We could almost pretend the outside world didn't exist.

However, it did, and all too soon we had to get back to reality. Michael had to hunt, his eyes were in pain, and he couldn't put it off any longer.

There was no one in when I went home, and I was relieved because I had no desire to slice through the atmosphere all the way to my room.

I closed my bedroom door with a sigh and switched on the light.

That's when I saw I wasn't alone.

And my sense I had worked on told me the visitor wasn't friendly either.

Chapter Eighteen

The Immortal Leaders

I dropped my bag with a start as the shadowy figure came into focus.

It was a vampire and not one of the De Marcos.

I was frightened. This vampire didn't have the lovely lilac eyes I was used to gazing into. His eyes were red and violent.

His lips twisted in a creepy smile as he came towards me. Chills went up my spine but I tried not to flinch or show any obvious signs of fear.

"You must be Angel, the little witch we've heard so much about?" His voice wasn't silky like Michael's.

I looked at him in the eye. "Yes, I am. And you are?"

"I work for the immortal leaders dear and I have been sent to deliver a message to you."

"Go on then, give me the message." My voice sounded braver than I felt.

"It has come to their attention by an interested party that one of our own is involved with you. It cannot be allowed to continue so you have a choice... you can either die for him or he dies for you."

"They can't kill him, he's Royalty," I said, aghast.

"Oh, but they can my dear and will. You see the minute he took up with a witch as powerful as yourself he became fair game. No vampire would object to his execution now, thus his birth right will not save him." He gave me that creepy grin again.

"You bastards." All fear was gone now replaced with a cold hard anger at this horrible being and the ones he represented.

"Regardless of your opinion of us, you have to make a choice, dear."

I sat down heavily and put my head in my hands. I had to fight the urge to cry, scream, and throw things at the unfairness of this situation. I told him I would be back in ten minutes because I had to sort my head out and get some air. He knew I wouldn't run, there wasn't anywhere to run to.

I transported outside and stood in the practice field blowing things up in rage and anguish. It started to rain and the tears that were streaming down my face went unnoticed.

There was no choice... I would die for him. I knew that the second the messenger gave me my options. I was just taking out my fury and pain before agreeing to it.

I pulled myself together as best as I could and transported back to my room to be sentenced.

"How do I know your bosses won't kill Michael as well?" I had to make sure we had a solid deal.

"They do not want to have to kill him dear and with your death as his punishment the matter will be closed. You have their word on that."

If he called me dear one more time, I was liable to try to gouge his eyes out.

"How do I know they will keep their word?"

"You don't, you just have to trust that they cannot justify killing him once they remove you from the picture."

"Fine, I will come tomorrow night." I sighed.

"Good girl. Are you sure you love him enough to sacrifice your life to save him?"

"What would you know about love? Just tell me where I need to go and then get the hell out of my sight."

He gave me his creepy grin again. "It is in New York." He tossed a business card at me. "When you arrive, tell the receptionist you have an appointment with Drake."

"OK, now get out," I shouted.

He disappeared faster than my eyes could track his movements.

I remembered every detail of Michael from this morning. I would hold onto that image... I would never see my immortal beloved again and that image was all I had left to cling to.

I sat and cried hopeless tears. There was no way out for us, I understood that now.

I could not bring myself to regret a moment of it, even knowing this outcome.

I got up and sat at my window looking out at the rain and I recalled every amazing second that I spent with Michael.

I knew I had been blessed to love him and to have him love me back. With him, I was alive.

My heart began to shatter… it was over and I never got to say goodbye.

I didn't sleep that night; I just sat at the window with only my memories and useless tears for company.

The next afternoon I transported to New York and checked into a hotel near Times Square. I requested a high floor so I could get lost in the view.

I decided to send Dylan an email to read to my family and Michael. I couldn't trust anyone else in my family to make sure Michael heard my last words to him and I knew Dylan would deliver it no matter what he had to do.

I put on the hotel computer and signed into my e-mail account. I knew this would take a while.

I put on music and began to type.

Dear Dylan,

Please make sure you read this email to the family and please make sure Michael gets to read it. I love you little brother you are my star.

I write this now so as not to have left you all in the dark about my whereabouts or actions. You will receive this email when it is too late to stop me.

I have spent my life sacrificing for the greater good, fighting evil and even resigning myself to marrying the correct magical being whom I did not love in order to preserve the family expectations of our evolution.

Then I met Michael… he is a vampire and I love him.

We have broken every rule by falling in love and most of our world and underworld is extremely unhappy about it, not to mention, you, my family.

As I write this, I am currently in America, in a hotel room looking out at a night time Manhattan. The rain is beating a steady drum against the window and the lights of the city are, as always, simply stunning.

This may be the last thing I ever say because I am presently about to be killed.

I have offered myself to the leaders of the Immortals in the understanding Michael will be allowed to live.

I wanted nothing more than to be with Michael forever; but as that is not an option for us. I have no will to live without him.

The Immortal leaders would have killed him had I not agreed to take his place, and a world where he does not exist, is not a world I have any desire to inhabit.

I love you all. I know you do not understand my love for a Vampire and will never understand my reasons for what I do now; but know this, to die in order to save someone you love is the greatest way I can ever imagine of ending any mortal life and I have no regrets.

I may have been selfish when I refused to give up my Vampire, but I see it as finally having a part of life for myself and not allowing my magical Inheritance to take it from me like it has everything else.

I am not sorry it happened; I would do it all again even knowing this outcome. Please take comfort from that fact. I HAVE NO REGRETS.

I am sure I will be seeing you all again, as we all know death is not always the end in our family. I am sure you will summon me from the beyond to yell at me for my decision.

Please do not blame Michael for this. He has no knowledge of what I am about to do and should he know, he would sacrifice himself to save me and I do not want that.

To Michael,

I have loved you in this mortal life; more than words could ever do justice to; and I will love you in whatever comes after that.

You are part of my soul, you inhabit my heart, and I will live on as part of you.

Please do not avenge me, this is my choice, and it is the better of the only two we had.

We always knew we were doomed; that we would never be allowed to be together and the consequences of breaking the rules would be great.

Michael my lover, my friend, and my soul mate; I have no regrets in loving you and I would not change it for anything.

I only truly came alive when your love brought me to life.

All that I am I owe to you, for you I was born, for you I live and for you I give my last breath.

It has been said many times; live the life you dream and I was loved by you; that was my only life dream ever worth having and you made it come true.

As I look back over my whole life, it is not how long I have lived or how many breaths I have taken that is important; it is how many moments that taken my breath away and there were thousands; and they were all with you.

Death cannot kill what is not measured by time.

Our love is immortal, it is transcendent, and it is stronger than death.

Do not let my death be in vain, be happy my immortal beloved.

My whole life was always about doing the right thing then I met you and it changed me. It altered me in ways I could never fully explain.

It may not have been the right thing in anyone else's eyes but for us nothing was ever more right.

Now I am doing the right thing…

I am not trying to be noble but I am dying for something.

Something far greater and more powerful than all of us.

I am not afraid. Dying is not hard and dying for someone I love is easy.

Take comfort from that.

I will see you in another place and time as I know this is not the end of our story, our love is epic.

Forever

Angel. xxxxxxxxx

That ought to do it. I have explained it as much as I can.

It was time to go now. No point putting off the inevitable.

I pressed send knowing my brother wouldn't check his emails until tomorrow morning.

I went outside and flagged a taxi. The rain was coming down heavily as if it was following my tears from Scotland to here.

I was staring out the window at the passing buildings and thinking of Michael kissing me in the rain. The memory was painfully sweet and my heart ached with joy, sorrow, and love. It was a love so big this world couldn't hold it. The taxi came to a stop outside the address I had given him; I paid him and got out the taxi. I stood a minute taking a deep breath to steady myself. I would not give the immortal leaders the pleasure of seeing me break.

It's funny I always thought of myself as fearless, but I wasn't. A person can't be fearless if they have nothing to lose. Before Michael, I never had anything to lose when I went into battle and after Michael, I had a lot. I wasn't afraid for my own life I was afraid of losing him.

I took the post-it note he had once written me from my pocket and studied it… remembering.

I took a final deep breath and went inside.

I walked to the reception desk and noticed it was a human. Did she know whom she worked for? I told her I had an appointment with Drake and she told me to take the lift to floor one hundred.

I went to the lift and pressed 100. The lift shot up and deposited me at the floor in seconds. It went up so fast my ears actually popped.

Another human who identified herself as Drake's assistant Sarah greeted me. I followed her into a huge bright room with breath-taking Manhattan views. She told me to take a seat and Drake would be in soon.

I stood looking out the window with my back to the door and tried to stay calm. Clearly, this was not the room I would die in.

"So you're the brave little witch willing to die for love?" a voice from behind me said lightly.

I turned around and saw a beautiful but somewhat scary red-eyed vampire. He was wearing a full-length red cloak that swished from side to side as he moved silently. His hair was white blonde and he was as flawless as the De Marcos.

"Drake, I presume?" I snapped.

He laughed a high musical laugh that did not match his ominous appearance at all. "Yes, Angel, I am Count Drake."

"Well, it's not a pleasure to meet you *Count Drake.*" My tone was rebellious.

"You are a brave one, aren't you?" he asked smiling.

I didn't answer him I just kept my head up and didn't look away from his examination of me.

"You must be something really special for Michael De Marco to risk everything for," he said as he placed his hand on my hair.

I was so angry, I blew up the back wall when I threw his hand off me. Good, I hope I had destroyed some expensive art.

"Well, you certainly are as powerful as I had heard."

I enjoyed the fact that he was slightly aggravated.

"Do you have anything you would like to say?" he asked.

I shook my head and he turned away as five other vampires entered the room. They had the same red eyes and red cloaks as Drake so I assumed they were the rest of the immortal leaders.

"So this is her," a beautiful blonde female vampire said, appraising me. "She certainly is a beauty for a mortal."

"I wouldn't recommend touching her, Adrianna, she gets a bit annoyed at that, as you can see," Drake said, gesturing to the back wall.

She laughed. "Her powers are impressive, but no matter she won't be blowing anything up soon enough."

I glared at her and wished I could blow her up. Bitch.

"Come now and we shall take you to the last room you will ever see," she said evilly. "I'm bored now and want to end this so I can go back to my lover."

I hoped her lover was a vampire and he ripped her bloody throat out.

They led me from that room to a black empty room where Drake pulled a false wall back to reveal a dark corridor.

We went into the corridor and I followed them through twists and turns until they stopped and Drake opened another wall.

This room was more like a death room, and I noticed some tin baths scattered around it with holes dug out underneath them.

I didn't have to wonder long what it was all about.

"We like to boil blood before we drink it, so someone will be along shortly to fill a bath and light the fire under it," Drake said, leaving.

"I will so enjoy your blood little witch, it is the sweetest I have smelled in a long time. Michael De Marco is a fool not to have killed you and feasted himself," Adrianna said as she swept from the room.

They were going to boil me alive before drinking my blood!

I was afraid of how much that was going to hurt. I wracked my brain for a spell that would kill my senses but I couldn't think of any. Damn, I should have thought of a painful death and brought a spell with me.

I sat down and pictured Michael in my mind. I concentrated on recreating every single detail about him.

I realised it didn't matter how painful my death would be, it was nothing compared to the excruciating loss of Michael.

I sat there a while before two vampires entered to fill the bath. They were playing with my head by dragging this out. They probably got some sick kick out of the psychological torture they were inflicting on me.

Next thing I knew, the door was being kicked in, and Michael was coming through it. Ava and My dad and Dylan followed him.

Oh no how did he find out? My heart surged in pleasure to see him but this is not what I wanted because they might kill him now.

He ripped the heads off the two vampires that were filling the bath and tore them apart before they even had a chance to alert others.

With one graceful move, he was beside me and he pulled me into his strong arms. My hero. Unfortunately, it would do neither of us much good now.

"Angel, why did you do this?" he asked frantically.

I clung to him. "I had to, Michael, they sent a messenger and told me they would kill you if I didn't take your place."

"They can't kill me, Angel, it is you they wanted to kill all along and I could have protected you if you had told me."

"I couldn't take that chance. I would rather die. How did you know I was here?"

"Your dad had a vision and they went to my house to ask me where it was but I was still away hunting and Ava had to find me because I had her on mute to concentrate. They couldn't have come here without me, nor would I have wanted them to so it was a frenzied dash to find you on time."

"What will happen now, Michael?" I asked worriedly.

"They will know we're here by now so we don't have a lot of time to get out, we must hurry, Angel, we can't transport from this room it is protected."

He was dragging me out the door and through the winding corridors.

We reached the outer room I had blown up earlier, before the immortal leaders arrived.

They had some of their guard with them and they were the most terrifying creatures I had ever seen. They had on long black cloaks and they floated eerily instead of walking. They wore stark white masks where all that could be seen was black soulless eyes and huge lethal fangs. They looked like what you would imagine the killer from the Halloween movies to look like if he was an evil vampire.

As they focused their attention on us, I felt myself weaken and become drained, unable to fight even if I wanted to. This must be what the guard's power is. I noticed Michael wasn't affected by it at all but Ava was lagging a bit.

Michael pushed me behind him roughly and used his body to shield me whilst keeping me from sliding to my knees as the guard's powers immobilised me.

"Ahh, Prince Michael, you grace us with your presence," Drake said lightly.

"Drake, you will not harm a hair on her head or I will kill all of you," Michael growled.

"You are rather outnumbered, your majesty."

Michael lifted his head slightly, his eyes were dark with danger. "Do I look worried, Drake?" he asked arrogantly.

Everything was so still you would be able to hear a pin drop as Michael and Drake faced off.

Michael's voice was loud and sure as he spoke to the guards, "In the name of Lumia Regius, I command you all to stand down now."

The guards hesitated unsurely but floated backwards away from us. I felt my strength returning as soon as they moved away.

"You cannot marry a witch, sire; our world will not allow it, unless you turn her," Adrianna said, all sweetness and light now.

"I am aware of that, Adrianna. I want assurances Angel and her family will not be harmed if I agree to end our relationship?"

"Wont it be simpler to turn her?" she asked puzzled.

"No." His voice invited no further comment.

He made all six of them swear an oath on my safety, and then suddenly, his arms moved faster than I could see, all I caught was a flash of silver as he pulled out a katana – the one from his bedroom wall I assumed – from his coat and sliced Drake's head clean off.

It went bouncing across the room to where the guards were standing.

"That is a warning to the rest of you as to what will happen if you betray me." His voice was icy calm.

The five of them looked horrified and swore they would uphold their oath to him.

"Sire, if you turn her, we will have a powerful ally," Adrianna tried again.

Michael turned slowly towards her. "I said no, Adrianna, do not make me say it again." His voice was cold with the veiled threat and Adrianna looked down in a gesture of subservience.

He turned to me and pulled me aside as the rest of the immortal leaders and their guard left the room in silence. His eyes had tears in them and his beautiful face was anguished.

"You must go, Angel. You are safe now."

"Go... what do you mean go? I won't leave without you, Michael." My desperate need for him knew no bounds and I didn't care.

"Angel, do you remember when I told you there would come a time when I would have to choose between being with you and saving you?"

I nodded, too afraid to speak.

"Well that time is now and I'm choosing to save you, my love." His face was contorted in pain as he slowly brushed the hair from my face.

Tears fell from my eyes. "You sending me away isn't saving me, Michael, it's condemning me to a slow, painful death. I would rather die quickly now than spend my life without you."

"The nice thing about being mortal, Angel, is the pain will ease in time and eventually you will move on and marry someone who is good for you."

"No, no, how can you... how can you... no... I... no." My voice was breaking. "How can you say that? I will never marry anyone else, Michael. I don't want anyone else. Why can't you just turn me and then we can be together. Please Michael don't do this... not this." I cried.

He gently stroked my cheek with his thumb, wiping my tears. "You have a magical destiny to fulfil and I am setting you free. Fly high and save the world, my Angel."

I was sobbing now, and as he turned away from me, I crumbled to my knees in a silent scream and put my head to the floor.

I watched him walk away in a blur through my thick tears.

The End